BY NORAH

LOVERS ALL UNTRUE

LOVERS

ALL

UNTRUE

❧ NORAH LOFTS ❧

Doubleday & Company, Inc., Garden City, New York

1970

LIBRARY OF CONGRESS CATALOG CARD NUMBER 74-116229
COPYRIGHT © 1970 BY NORAH LOFTS
ALL RIGHTS RESERVED
PRINTED IN THE UNITED STATES OF AMERICA
FIRST EDITION

LOVERS ALL UNTRUE

I IT WAS POSSIBLE TO say, "Yes, I understand, Papa," and to think I hate you. I wish you would drop dead, there on the hearth-rug!

"What I fail to see," Mr. Draper said, "is why you should bring up the subject again. I thought I had made it clear, in September, that I had no intention of allowing you and Ellen to go running about the streets after dark."

Running about the streets. What a way to describe a brief walk, out of Alma Avenue, into Honey Lane, across the Buttermarket, on to the Square and into the Guildhall.

"Mr. Marriot himself suggested that I should ask you again, Papa. The membership of the Musical Society has fallen below his expectations."

"As I warned him. Mr. Marriot is in many ways an admirable man but when a clergyman, who should know better, suggests forming a society, the only qualification for membership of which is a fondness for music, he cannot expect support from decent people."

Marion Draper felt her hands clench. Fortunately they were hidden by the voluminous folds of her skirt. She was aware that she was about to argue with Papa. She was careful to speak very meekly.

"Angela is a member, Papa. She has often urged . . ."

"That will do," Mr. Draper said in a crushing voice. It irked him not to be able to deny that the daughter of the town's leading solicitor and related, through her mother, to a county family, was to be reckoned amongst the decent elements of the town.

"How Mr. and Mrs. Taylor permit their daughter to behave is no affair of mine. I do not intend to imitate it. You will oblige me by not mentioning the matter again." He consulted his watch. "Ring the bell. Supper will be late by two minutes."

She pressed the white china handle inset in the crimson-papered wall, and the bell could be heard ringing at the bottom of the kitchen stairs. Betty, however, had been waiting in a state of palpitating agitation just outside the dining-room door, balancing a laden tray on her hip. As she entered she brought with her the good smell of roast beef. Mr. Draper took his midday meal at a little chop house near his Maltings, so the evening meal, called supper except when there were guests, was always of a substantial nature. Marion went to the sideboard and took from the drawer a highly starched white cloth and spread it over the fringed red velvet one on the big table. She placed the heavy silver cruet in the centre and the decanter of claret within reach of Papa's place at the top of the table.

Presently I shall perform these actions in reverse and that will complete my day's work! Oh God, how long? How long?

She went out, across the black and white tiled hall and upstairs to the room which she shared with Ellen. Ellen had chosen not to be present when Marion made her request, but she looked up eagerly. Marion's face gave nothing away; it never did; she had learned to control its expression and was the fortunate possessor of pale, rather thick skin not unlike the best kid gloves in texture; it never coloured from any emotion and was equally impervious to outside influences.

"Well?"

"A point-blank refusal. And the subject never to be mentioned again."

"Oh dear," Ellen said, but she spoke with a comfortable resignation. "I never had much hope. Poor Marion, it is worse for you. Angela is more your friend."

"It was not for the sake of seeing more of Angela . . . Nor for the music. It was the thought of one evening, just one evening a week, with something positive to do. Out of this house!"

"I know. It is a shame." For herself Ellen minded little. She had a placid nature, was practical minded and docile and fitted quite easily into the way of life which Papa considered suitable for his daughters. She was not, like Marion, clever, or restless, or rebellious; but she could sympathise. She now said, "Anyway, this evening we shall have something positive to do. The shells arrived and if we sort them beforehand it will save us time when the glue is hot." She had already begun her orderly little preparations; on a vast papier-mâché tray she had arranged a number of containers into which the shells were to be sorted according to size, and the white linen sack full of shells—exotic ones from places far away. An enterprising young man in London was importing them by the ton and making a good income by pandering to the latest craze—the making of shell-encrusted boxes.

Downstairs, Betty, having placed a tureen of soup and four well-heated plates at the lower end of the table, beat upon the gong, a copper half-drum slung in a framework of bamboo. The girls hurried down and took their places. Mamma had

3

appeared and as they sat down she lifted the tureen lid, dipped in the silver ladle and began to serve. Mamma had vanished as soon as Marion had announced her intention of speaking to Papa, once more, about the Musical Society. To use the words appear and vanish was completely apt where Mamma was concerned. No ghost could be more elusive. In a house which though spacious enough was not rambling or many-roomed, Mamma managed to perform astonishing vanishing tricks, especially if any trouble threatened. On her plump little feet she could move without noise; no door she ever opened creaked, or slammed and she was completely impervious to cold. In the dead of winter when other people, however unwillingly, centred about the dining-room fire, Mamma could be anywhere, in the drawing room where the frost had etched flowers and ferns on the windows, in the unheated conservatory where only the hardiest plants survived the cold season, in the seldom-used room known as Papa's study or up in the box room. The only time when her presence in any of these places was announced was when she played the grand piano in the drawing room. She did it about once a week, or once in ten days and then everyone knew; for Mamma played the piano with power, with authority, with something approaching violence; and never, at such times, any gentle, sentimental popular tunes, nothing in any way like the music she produced for the entertainment of guests after the rare dinner parties. Marion, in the last two years, since she had left school and come home and begun to observe and form judgements, had often thought that Mamma's private sessions with the piano—Liszt one of her favourite composers—offered a clue to a real personality, suppressed and lost. But it was a clue that could never be followed; the trail was too thoroughly concealed by the plump, completely subservient and seemingly contented woman who

4

was not only Papa's wife, but his willing slave; and who said things like, "You must ask Papa," and "Papa says," and who could do a vanishing trick and then reappear, calm and incurious, and dish up soup.

The soup this evening was one of Ada's best; a smooth blend of chicken stock, sieved leeks and cream. Ada, with all her skill, her bulging book of recipes and her unpredictable temper had been, as Mamma had once said, "One of my wedding presents." And Ada was rare. Most cooks, married or not, insisted upon being called "Mrs." Ada had no patience with such nonsense; many cooks refused to do anything that was not directly concerned with their culinary art, and some were oppressive to their underlings. Ada was unique, a treasure, and up and down Alma Avenue Mrs. Draper was much envied.

Only animals ate in silence. Papa spoke; he said, "Excellent soup, my dear." And to that Mamma said, "The leeks were especially fine. Ada bought them at the door. A young man named Smith is attempting to establish a market garden at Asham. He is prepared to deliver daily and to take orders. Ada thought favourably of him."

Papa remarked that enterprise should be encouraged. He then inquired how the girls had spent their day. His temporary displeasure with Marion had vanished and he had regained his usual paternal geniality.

"This morning we visited Nanny," Ellen said. "We took her a few things." A harmless, indeed creditable way to spend a morning, but over the last of his soup Mr. Draper looked disapproving.

"I hope you did not stay long. All the hovels on that side of the Common are very insanitary. They should be pulled down. The old woman—and most of her neighbours—would be better off in the workhouse."

5

It sounded ruthless, but Marion, rising to remove the soup plates and to ring the bell to summon the roast, felt obliged to be just. Papa's rule was rigid, heavy, galling; but he was concerned for the health and well-being of his family. And over a few things, the old woman whom they called Nanny, for example, he was of divided mind. It was right that she should be visited, taken a half pound of tea, a dozen eggs, as well as her regular allowance of five shillings a month; but it was wrong that his daughters should be exposed, even for a few minutes to the atmosphere in which the old woman, after a lifetime of faithful service, spent her last days.

"I thought Ada visited Nanny regularly."

"Ada," said Mamma gently, but sticking up for her own, "is becoming lame."

"I am sorry to hear it," Mr. Draper said. It was quite a long time since he had seen the woman who twice a day provided him with well-cooked meals.

"She finds the stairs increasingly trying," Mamma said. "I am seriously considering turning that little room under the stairs into a bedroom for her."

"An excellent idea," Papa said, looking appreciatively at the sirloin now before him. He took up the carving knife and gave it the few strokes on the steel without which the knife, however well-honed below stairs, would not be considered quite serviceable in the dining room. He carved swiftly and skilfully. Mamma, at the other end of the table, placed roast potatoes and Brussels sprouts on each plate. The cruet, the gravy, the dish of freshly made horseradish sauce went from hand to hand. After a few mouthfuls Papa made another contribution to the conversation. Clegg, his head clerk, was away, ill again; the second time this autumn.

No real business details were ever discussed at home but illnesses, marriages, deaths, and births amongst the workmen

were often given mention. Now, hearing of Clegg's indisposition, Marion's hands tightened again, for it called to mind
an occasion, almost a year and a half ago when another
clerk, named Tompson, had gone for a swim in the river and
been drowned . . . She had then been home from school for
six months and was finding the boredom unbearable and she
had said across this table, "Papa, could I be of assistance? I
am rather good at figures." Papa's reaction to that suggestion
had been one of shock and anger. "Have I ever allowed you
to set foot in the Maltings? When I cannot run my business
without aid from my womenfolk, I will burn the place down."
The rejection hurt, but oddly enough the scarcely warranted
violence of the second sentence had struck an echo from a
deeply buried streak of violence in her own nature. She was
also capable of strong feelings, preferences and prejudices,
and occasionally made—in the company of Ellen or Angela—
what were called sweeping statements.

"I shall have to think seriously about replacing him," Papa
said. "Fortunately clerks are easily come by."

Baked apples, done to a turn, fluffy within their neatly
scored skins, their cores replaced by chopped dates, completed—with a jug of yellow cream—yet another of the good
solid meals to which they were all so thoroughly accustomed
that no gratitude was involved.

"And what is the work this evening?" Papa asked. He
liked to see his daughters happily and busily employed. He
always considered that the things they contributed to the
Church Bazaar were superior to all others. On the actual day
he would take an hour off and walk around the stalls in the
Guildhall, saying, with shameless self-satisfaction, "Ah yes, I
seem to have seen that before!" He would buy the teapot
stand painted by Ellen, the crocheted antimacassars made
by Marion, the little shoulder shawl knitted by his wife. Then,

with a benevolent air he would give them away, the purely decorative articles to ladies of his acquaintance, the more utilitarian ones to the humbler sort.

"The shells have arrived, Papa," Ellen said. "This evening we are going to sort them, ready for sticking on."

"Good," he said. He seated himself in the large leather chair, went through the evening ritual of selecting a cigar from a box of identical ones and opened *The Times*. Mamma took the smaller, tightly buttoned little velvet chair and put her feet on the beaded footstool. She began to knit. Ellen fetched down the tray.

On the black marble mantelpiece the black marble clock, shaped like a Grecian temple, showed the time to be twenty minutes to eight. Another interminable evening had begun.

Marion wished that on this particular evening there had been some occupation of a more demanding kind; or no work at all, in which event she and Ellen could have played some paper game. Ellen was not very good at supplying the names of twenty given nouns all beginning with the same letter of the alphabet; once when the letter was S she had filled in the name of the river as *Sane* and she cheated over the book titles; unable to supply one when the letter was F she had written *Fanny's Birthday*. Marion said, "There is no such book!" "How can you know?" Ellen asked. "Can you prove that in all the world there is no book called that?" "No." "Then I get my mark." After that she would often slip in a bogus title, and mild as the joke was, it served.

It was possible to think a little about the places from which these pretty things, all pearly and glistening, came; to imagine them being gathered by brown, laughing, almost naked boys from white beaches against which blue seas broke. Possible also to think that each once held a living creature. Now, empty and cleansed, they awaited the moment when they

8

should be rendered immobile forever, stuck with glue on to boxes, large and small, around the edges of photograph frames. And all for the benefit of some unfortunate Indian ladies living in a state of purdah.

Who is in purdah, if we are not?

With her hands busy shell sorting, Marion looked at Papa, master of this harem. He was handsome, not unlike one of his own well-fed, well-groomed cart horses; the same glossy look, almost the same colouring, a dark chestnut—her own hair was the same shade, but plentiful, whereas Papa's was receding, a fact that gave his forehead a height, almost a nobility. He was fifty. He had deferred marriage until he was properly established. And by that she knew his age, putting together things he said when lesser men married early . . . "I was thirty before I thought of marrying." Mamma had once said, "I had begun to despair. Over two years." So, now seventeen herself, the first born, Marion, could tell Papa's age. Fifty. But he had kept his figure and only the faintest hint of jowls under his clean-shaven jaw indicated that he was a day over forty.

A father to be proud of, had the slightest touch of fondness been involved. But he had disliked her from the start. It had puzzled her for years and then she had understood. Papa had wanted a son and been given a daughter. That daughter's resemblance to him, in all but sex, had been the final affront. Such a near miss! Oddly enough, he was fond of Ellen. One would have thought that the second failure on Mamma's part would have been even more strongly resented, but Ellen was fair, blue-eyed and meek like Mamma.

It would have been far better had Ellen made the plea to join the flagging Musical Society but Ellen had backed away: "I never think of the right word."

Marion's critical eye looked upon Mamma who had long

9

since given up looking for the right word. Mamma never argued, or exercised persuasion, and if she made a comment it was always of an uncontroversial nature. After Ellen's birth Mamma had retreated into a vague semi-invalidism which excused her from even the mildest social duties—it was understood, for instance, that the Draper girls never had birthday or Christmas parties; Mrs. Draper was not "up" to any form of entertaining except the rare, staid dinner party; she was not even regular in Sunday morning church attendance. Mamma was, in fact, what Papa had made of her, a plump placid bird in a comfortable cage, and if, at the piano, she beat frenzied wings against the bars it was when Papa was out of hearing. Her very name was lost; when Papa addressed her he always said, "My dear," and when he spoke of her he said, "Your Mamma" or "Your mistress."

Mr. Draper was not unaware of the fact that since Marion had said something about Angela Taylor's membership of the Musical Society she had not said a word. Sulking! After downright defiance or giddy-mindedness, sulkiness was the worst trait a female could show and Marion had, from an early age, been sulky. Worse, not better, since he had withdrawn her from Miss Ruthven's Academy.

Sending her there had been one of his few mistakes—forced upon him by the fact that he could not find a suitable governess. He had tried. The capable ones were pert, if young; dictatorial, if old; the incapable—doddering old indigent gentlewomen—were a nuisance with their headaches, their backaches, their snuffling colds. So Marion, and presently Ellen, had been sent to Miss Ruthven's and too late Mr. Draper had learned that Miss Ruthven held and inculcated some extremely radical and modern views—that women were capable of earning a living for themselves, for instance.

Marion, at fifteen, had declared her intention of going to a place called St. Hilda's and training to be a teacher.

Abruptly he had withdrawn both his daughters from this poisonous influence. Ellen who had had only one year of exposure to contamination was happy to be freed from routine and lessons. Marion had argued; pleaded; and then sulked. In the intervening years she had argued less and less and cultivated a moderately meek demeanour, but she still fell into silences which Mr. Draper always resented, feeling them full of unspoken criticism and now and again those lowered eyelids would lift and reveal a look that Mr. Draper found distinctly unpleasant. However, she was still young and malleable, and in the end would conform.

Presently he lowered his paper and addressed her directly.

"Marion, have you written to Mr. Marriot informing him of my decision?"

"No, Papa. There has been no time . . ." And he knew that perfectly well since she had not been out of his sight since he made the decision. "I thought that Ellen and I could call at the Rectory in the morning and acquaint . . ."

"That would be to lay yourself open to further persuasion," Papa said. "Write a note now. I need hardly tell you how to phrase it, need I? Miss Ruthven thought highly of your powers of composition." Part of his power lay in his capacity for saying sarcastic, sardonic, hurtful things in a silky voice— the other part lay in his complete self-confidence: he was invariably right. It was not only his family and his business which he dominated. People who had no reason to be subservient to him, people completely independent of him, felt their self-confidence ooze when faced with his.

Marion wrote with slightly tremulous fingers because of the strain of trying to set down something acceptable to Mr. Marriot and to Papa, who was sure to ask to inspect the letter.

Impossible to tell the blunt truth—Papa will not allow; and
uncivil not to offer some excuse. "My sister and I have
thought again . . . Much as we should have liked to join . . .
The calendar always so crowded at this time of year."

"It will do," Papa said. It was just possible that if Ellen
had written it he would have said, "Quite well put." Since
he could not fault the wording of the letter he attacked at
a vulnerable point—the calligraphy which was distinctive,
absolutely upright and inclined to spikiness. "I still maintain,"
he said, "that Miss Ruthven is in error in abandoning the
copybook." Miss Ruthven held that girls could use their time
better than in copying *Honesty Is the Best Policy* six times
making the down strokes thicker than the up ones. Dear,
dear Miss Ruthven—the one person, except Mamma and
Ellen, whom Marion had ever loved; the only person she
had loved *and* admired. She had been silly enough, at the end
of her first term, to let this esteem be obvious, and thus
handed to Papa a weapon which he wielded with assiduity.

"Would you wish me to post the letter or deliver it by
hand, Papa?"

"The answer to that must be obvious. If you deliver it the
whole point in writing will be missed. You may take a stamp
from my study."

o   o   o

"OH. ARE YOU GOING TO READ?" ELLEN ASKED.

"I must. Just for a little while. I won't disturb you. I will
turn out the gas and manage with a candle." Marion had
taken, from under the neatly piled underclothes, the latest
example of what Papa called trashy novels—Miss Marie
Corelli's *Romance of Two Worlds*. All evening as the clock
lagged and her temper chafed, she had thought of this moment when, the dull day lived through, she could escape. She

guessed—correctly—that Miss Ruthven would share Papa's opinion of most of the books she devoured these days, but she often felt that without them she would go mad. To obtain a supply was difficult. There was a little lending library at the back of Blake's the tobacconist's, but Papa had forbidden her to use it. Without having read a word that Ouida had written, he condemned her out of hand, together with Miss Rhoda Broughton, Miss Braddon, and Miss Corelli. He never wanted to see a book by one of them, or by Mrs. Hungerford or Mrs. Henry Wood, in *his* house. Hopelessly addicted, Marion was dependent upon Angela, who—and this was irony—never wanted to read anything that was not connected with clothes, but who was free to go into Blake's three or four times a day should she wish. Angela, soul of good nature, would borrow the forbidden books and Marion would smuggle them in.

In return for this and other lesser favours, Marion had lately been able to reciprocate, for Angela's freedom, though comparatively vast, was not absolute and since September . . . At the thought of the risks which Angela had been taking, connived at, alibied for, Marion broke into perspiration and the page blurred before her eyes. I must get out! But how? She could think of only one way . . . Realising that for once even Miss Corelli had failed her, she put the book under her pillow, blew out the candle and lying in the dark said:

"Ellen, are you asleep?"

"Nearly."

"Could we go to Angela's to tea tomorrow? At least, arrange to and you go and make some excuse for me?"

"We can always go to tea with Angela. But suppose Mrs. Taylor should ask about you. What can I say?" Curiosity banished drowsiness. "Where will you be?"

"I want to see Miss Ruthven."

"Good grief! Whatever for?" A year of Miss Ruthven's governance had been enough for Ellen; she had left the school and its headmistress without a single regret. But she saw that it had been different for Marion, who had she stayed another year would have been Head Girl, and who had actually been already chosen to play Rosalind in the performance of *As You Like It* which was to mark the end of the summer term. "And anyway, you couldn't get there and back in the time," Ellen said. "It's three miles."

"Walking pace," said Marion, who had read this interesting fact somewhere, "is four miles an hour. I shall run, once I'm in the country. We could leave at half-past three. If I run all the way there, and all the way back. And if you would tell Mrs. Taylor—should you see her—that I have gone to hunt for that special blue silk . . . but most probably you won't even see her. Since Angela has a sitting room of her own . . ."

"Well, all right," Ellen said, not very willingly. "But you know that Papa said . . ."

"I know; that is why I have to go this roundabout way. Will you, Ellen?"

"Of course. But I hope I shall not encounter Mrs. Taylor."

"Thank you, darling. I'll do as much for you one day."

"Not over visiting Miss Ruthven," Ellen said with a chuckle. She flung herself over and went to sleep.

o o o

"BUT MY DEAR GIRL," MISS RUTHVEN SAID, THOROUGHLY discomposed for once in her life. "It is impossible. You must see that without your Papa's consent it is impossible. You are under age, he is your legal guardian, you could not even make a marriage, however suitable, without his consent. How much less this that you propose?" Miss Ruthven had tested

Mr. Draper's strength of mind at the time of Marion's removal; she had written urging, almost imploring, that a girl with so much mental ability and with an inclination to study—all too rare—should be allowed to remain at least another year. To that letter Mr. Draper had not replied directly, but he had chosen to regard her plea as arising from concern because he had not given a full term's notice; he had sent a cheque for both girls' fees for the term between Christmas and Easter. She had returned the cheque to him, saying that his daughters' places had already been filled, from her long waiting list.

"Besides," Miss Ruthven now said, "there are other considerations. It is two years since you ceased serious study; it would take a year's intensive work, probably more, before you could qualify for entry to St. Hilda's Training College. I'm sorry, Marion, the plan is simply not feasible."

"It was the only thing that occurred to me, Miss Ruthven. But I would do *anything*. Any work at all. Could I become an *unqualified* teacher? Or a governess?"

"Not without your father's consent."

"Need he know? If you could assist me to find some post, I could just walk out—as I have done this afternoon. As you know, we have never been allowed to come back, even when invited to functions. I could just walk away and never go back." She saw herself transferring a few absolute necessities, one at a time to Angela's house; borrowing her fare to wherever it was from Angela . . . She had no money of her own; Papa was very generous in his own fashion, bills for clothes were never queried, he liked his womenfolk to be the best-dressed at any gathering; he gave expensive gifts at Christmas and on birthdays, but he thought two shillings a week ample pocket money for girls whose real needs were provided for.

"That is wild talk," Miss Ruthven said rather sternly. "Your whereabouts would be discovered within a week. Your Papa would be fully justified in asking police aid in tracing you. And if I were known to have encouraged such a scheme there would be a scandal which would affect the school most unfavourably."

She looked critically at her visitor. Marion's street wear, a knee-length, well-fitting jacket with full matching skirt, was a buff-coloured cloth, so fine and good that it had a silky sheen; her small round hat was of matching velvet with a brown feather; her long tippet, now loosened and thrown back upon her shoulders, and the muff which lay on her lap were of sable. Good shoes and gloves. At least the man was not mean! And the girl was now seventeen and though not pretty by the standards of the day, remarkably good-looking. Perhaps there was some reason, not yet stated, for this wish to break away.

"So you cannot help me?" Marion said.

"Not along the lines you indicate, Marion. But to talk over a problem is always useful. Tell me, have you any reason, any *personal* reason, for wishing to escape from your father's control?"

"No. Only what I said at first, Miss Ruthven. The utter tedium, the emptiness, the complete futility of life as we are compelled to lead it."

"You have not formed a romantic attachment?" Miss Ruthven wore her inquisitorial face and she put the question bluntly. She had had much experience in probing out truths from those anxious to conceal them.

"None at all, Miss Ruthven. We never see a man who is not Papa's friend. All old, all married." There was something about the placid assumption that a romantic attachment

16

could only be formed between people who had met socially, that convinced Miss Ruthven that the girl was telling the truth. That and the straight, candid gaze of the almost amber-coloured eyes.

"Unfortunately such attachments can be formed outside the family circle," she observed—but more as a warning than as an accusation.

"I never think about it," Marion said. That was not quite true. In every one of the smuggled books there was at least one handsome hero with whom she was in love so long as the book lasted; but such men were not real people.

Miss Ruthven made another effort to be helpful.

"I freely admit," she said, "that the life you describe sounds extremely dull—particularly for a girl like you, with an active mind. Is there no voluntary work you could take up? Something in the charitable line?"

"Papa has such a horror of infection. Even our old Nanny . . ." She briefly explained this allusion. "And Mr. Marriot once suggested that we should help with the Sunday school. Papa would not even consider it. The children, he said, had perpetually running noses. And ringworm!"

There was a little pause. Then Miss Ruthven said:

"I am afraid, my dear Marion, that all you can do, for the moment, is to exercise patience and cultivate resignation. And bear in mind that your way of life offers certain compensations." A thought occurred to her. "Were you contemporary with Louise Hayward?"

"For one term. She was older."

"Now Louise did succeed in entering St. Hilda's, and did well. She obtained a post in a Church School—it was always clear that Louise would be obliged to support herself. She is bitterly unhappy. The village parson sounds to be a most unpleasant character—straight out of *Jane Eyre,* and his wife exploits Louise to the extent of making her dressmake for her, write her invitations, cut her sandwiches and wash her hair! An incredible situation in this day and age; but the Church Schools retained their independence when the Board was set up and a schoolmistress who refused to be a general amanuensis would be quickly replaced. I have Louise's letter here. She complains of too much to do; you complain of having too little. I sympathise with you both, but I think, perhaps . . . Probably Louise and many other young women would gladly change places with you, Marion."

She could, in fact, have named a dozen. Miss Ruthven, an ardent disciple of the redoubtable Miss Beale, a believer in the education and the equality of women, had within the past few years received some sharp shocks which made her see that in a world shaped and completely governed by men, the forward-pressing women if not actually martyrs, were misfits. She had her days of discouragement; days when she realised that it was only her grandfather's money which had enabled her to set up school and be independent enough to scorn—for example—Mr. Draper's cheque. As things stood, behind every woman who successfully broke away, there must be a man. Look at Elizabeth Garrett!

At the same time she was aware that Marion Draper who had come asking a crumb of bread was being sent away with a stone. And upon that thought, her spirit once ardent and lively, but now failing and dubious, sickened.

She said, "And doubtless your father has some martrimonial plans for you, Marion."

Marion gathered and fastened the sable tippet.

"I think not, Miss Ruthven. Papa's attitude towards us is *possessive* in the extreme."

○   ○   ○

A MAN'S WALKING PACE WAS FOUR MILES AN HOUR; A
girl, holding up her skirts and running, except when not
alone on the road, when decorum must be observed, could
cover the three miles in under an hour; and she did it. She
reached Angela's house just slightly late for tea, but not too
late for a girl who had been hunting that particularly elusive
brand and colour of embroidery silk. The coldness of her
reception astonished her. "Good afternoon, Marion," Mrs.
Taylor said, "so you have got here at last. I am afraid the
tea has cooled." She did not, as she would have done in
ordinary circumstances, ring for a fresh pot, nor did she
smile. From Mrs. Taylor, usually easygoing about time, this
was direct rebuke and Marion hastened to apologise. Her
breathlessness bore witness to her statement that she had
hurried. There was an unpleasant tension in the room. Neither
Angela nor Ellen spoke. They both looked pale and Angela
had been crying some time that day. She was one of those
girls whose eyes remained red-rimmed for hours after the
last tear had been shed.

Pouring and passing a cup of tea which was not only
tepid but stewed, Mrs. Taylor said, "You are in time to take
leave of Angela. She is going to her grandfather at Asham
tomorrow morning. For a protracted visit."

Marion's heart, already beating fast from running and swift
walking, gave a sickening thump. It could mean only one
thing. She glanced at Angela and their eyes communicated.
Fear confirmed! She tried to remember on how many occasions she and Ellen had covered up for Angela. She tried
not to think about how Papa would act when he knew.
Momentarily incapable of swallowing she held a gulp of the
bitter brew in her mouth and waited for Mrs. Taylor to ar-

19

raign her for treachery, lying and deceitfulness. *She* would be blamed, being the oldest of the three; she was two months older than Angela.

The attack never came. Angela said, "Mamma, I beg you not to inform Marion or Ellen as to the way in which I have disgraced myself." Oh blessed Angela, offering a pointer; brave, loyal Angela, under the frivolous manner. Marion swallowed the mouthful of tea.

"I have no intention of doing so," Mrs. Taylor said in a chilling voice, not looking at her daughter but at Marion. "I have no notion of the extent to which you and your sister have been in Angela's confidence and I do not propose to make inquiries. This I say, and I say it very forcibly: whatever you know, much or little, you are never to speak of it. Never. My faith in Angela's veracity has been severely shaken but she swears that nobody knows anything of this disgusting business. So, if a word of gossip is *ever* heard I shall naturally suspect you, her closest associates, of starting it. Is that understood?"

How, Marion wondered, would someone in complete ignorance reply to that speech. While she wondered and hesitated Ellen, who could not spell *Seine,* had the answer.

"Whatever Angela has done, Mrs. Taylor, we should be the last to talk about it—*even if we knew*. We are her *friends*." Ellen spoke with exactly the right touch of earnest innocence. In fact she made Mrs. Taylor wonder if she had not handled this whole thing clumsily. Perhaps there had really been no need to inform even the Draper girls that Angela *was* in disgrace. The truth was that the whole thing had been such a shock that all day she had hardly known what she was doing, or thinking.

"So long as you remember that," she said with a marked decline in aggressiveness. "Angela has been . . . rather

20

naughty." She should have used that word in the first place. And to end the awkward interview she said, "And now she must go and pack."

The parlourmaid came in and said, "Madam, there's the boy from the office; the master left some papers he needed . . ."

Poor Alan, Mrs. Taylor thought, rising from the tea table, he was upset, too, not knowing whether he was coming or going and not absolutely sure, from a legal point of view, whether he had been right, in giving the young man, found kissing Angela in the shade of the lime tree by the gate, "something to remember," in fact beating him over the head with a heavy walking stick.

"I will come," Mrs. Taylor said.

She had no sooner gone than Angela launched herself at Marion and, beginning to cry again, said, "Will you tell him? Please, Marion, please. It was all so sudden and so dreadful. Please tell him I am sorry he was hurt and that I may not write or ever see him again . . . He is so gentle and there was Papa, lashing away with his stick. I can't tell you how horrible. Tell him how sorry . . . He's in Freeman's . . . you know, the chemist's. . . ."

The parlourmaid came in to take away the tea things. Marion managed to say, "I hope you will enjoy your stay, Angela. The country is lovely just now."

"Promise me . . ."

Remembering gratefully that Angela, taken by surprise, shocked, made miserable, had not let one incautious word slip, Marion said, "Yes. I will tell him. I promise."

o   o   o

"A SHOP ASSISTANT," ELLEN SAID. "AFTER ALL THE MYSTERY about a well-connected Frenchman! Marion, honestly, when

I went in, and Mrs. Taylor seemed to have taken a dislike to me, and Angela, I could see, had been crying, I could hardly *breathe*. I was obliged to sit there—Angela and I had no opportunity to exchange a word—and explain why you were late. I was so afraid, I felt quite *sick*. I thought of the two Sundays when Angela was supposed to be spending the day with us, and all the other times . . . and until you appeared, I thought about you . . . I haven't felt so ill since I had measles."

"You managed to say exactly the right thing, darling. I am certain that the way you said *even if we knew* averted Mrs. Taylor's suspicion that we did know."

"Shall you keep your promise to Angela?"

"I shall try to. Not being allowed to use Freeman's makes it rather difficult."

Freeman's chemist's shop was under ban because its owner was a nonconformist and Papa suspected all nonconformists of being radical in their political views. He himself was such an extreme Tory that had he had the power he would have reimposed the Corn Laws. He never knowingly employed, or spent a penny with, anyone who was not prepared to claim, at least, to be Church of England.

"That can be got over," Ellen said, after a moment's thought. "I'll look up a few things in the advertisements, things Baxter's is unlikely to have yet, and that will be an excuse. When we made the potpourri, if you remember, Baxter's had no orris root."

They were obliged to walk briskly, for the Taylor home lay on the opposite side of the town; and even when the girls had been out on such a respectable errand as taking tea there, or other reputable places, Papa liked them to be home, washed, tidied, changed from their street wear by the time he himself arrived. But even the pace at which they walked and the fact that they held their muffs high against the cold, frost-threatening air, did not account for Marion's silence. It suddenly occurred to Ellen that Marion was a little put out because she had not inquired how Miss Ruthven was. She did so.

"I found her somewhat . . . changed."

Ellen would have liked to say: For the better? But that would give offence and the one thing which their manner of life had taught them was to maintain an amiable relationship with one another; so instead she asked, "In what way?"

"She seemed older." Neither of the words she had used to describe Miss Ruthven was exact, but they were the best she could find.

"Well, she is. It is two years since you saw her," Ellen said sensibly. "And she must be getting on." Marion thought, *patience, resignation, matrimonial plans;* words that had not been included in the vocabulary of the Miss Ruthven she remembered.

"She seemed worried about a girl—you wouldn't remember her, she was before your time—Louise Hayward." As they crossed the Market Square, hurried along the Buttermarket, turned into Honey Lane and then into Alma Avenue, Marion told Ellen about Louise's predicament, trying all the time to derive a little comfort from the comparison between their two lots, and failing dismally; better to have too much to do, better to be compelled to perform even menial tasks, than to have nothing, absolutely nothing to do.

Ellen, whom Miss Ruthven, disappointed at not having been presented with another Marion to instruct, had once called witless, said, "I expect she does all these things too well. I should blot the invitations or get the addresses wrong and cut horrible, thick sandwiches and pull the parson's wife's hair."

"Louise has her living to earn," Marion said. "She would be dismissed . . . Ellen, I've just thought of something. With Angela gone I shall never have another book from the library." With this simple statement, a recognition that life in future would be even more dreary and empty than it had been in the past, they were home.

Thirty years earlier a farsighted builder had gambled upon the chance that with the coming of the railway, the building of the gasworks, the expansion of Draper's Maltings and Frewer's Iron Foundry there would be a tendency for prosperous men of business to move from Fargate and other similar areas, into more salubrious and prestigious surroundings. He had planned and built for the strictly middle-class man, not of the carriage class, the man who wished to reside within walking distance of his office or his works. So he had bought land on either side of what was then known as Goose Lane; left enough of the ancient trees to justify the name of avenue, and reared some buildings of a kind never before seen in the little country town.

A row of railings separated the tall grey houses from the footpath. Each house had two gates, one leading to the eight steps up to the front door, one leading to the rear where more steps led down into an area, off which opened the kitchen door, a coal- and woodshed and a water closet. The water closets—there was a second one for family use—wedged in halfway up the main stairway, the piped gas and water, were the selling points. The multiplicity of stairs was no disadvantage; willing, labouring legs were easily and cheaply hired. And the uniformity of the frontages was a spur rather than a deterrent; in the narrow front gardens an unacknowledged competition was waged throughout the year. Number 10, into which, twenty years earlier, Mr. Draper with a feeling that he had arrived, had brought his bride, was distinguished by the four tubs of agapanthus lilies, two at the bottom, two at the top of the stairs that led to the door. All along Alma Avenue there were in due season displays of daffodils, tulips, geraniums, salvias, begonias, closely clipped bush roses; regular as the habits of those who had caused them to be planted.

The Draper girls sped up the stairs. Copper cans, shrouded in towels, awaited them. They washed. They put on their house dresses; Marion's brown velvet, Ellen's blue. As always they assisted one another in the twenty-four buttons down the back.

Ellen said, "Marion, I have thought of something. Papa forbade *you* to set foot in Blake's. Not *me*. I can take your book back and fetch another."

"Darling, that is splitting hairs. But if you only would, I should be everlastingly grateful."

Almost ready they went, as one person to the chest of drawers that they shared and took, Marion from the left-hand top drawer, Ellen from the one on the right, a clean handkerchief. Marion first and then Ellen, sprinkled, from the wicker-encased flask that stood on a crocheted mat in the centre of the chest's top, exactly four drops of eau de cologne. As they emerged on to the wide landing Mamma came out of the conjugal bedroom, smiled and said, "Good evening, my dears. Did you have a nice visit with Angela?" She took precedence of them down the stairs and Papa, entering by the front door, looked up and saw them, velvet-clad, dove-grey, brown and blue, their kid-slippered feet soft on the stairs, the sweet-scented aura meeting him. All present and correct! My family. He said, "Good evening, my dears."

The door at the top of the kitchen stairs was closed and would remain so until Betty came up to set the table; but the scent of roast pheasant, of braised celery was just discernible—Louise and many many other young women would gladly change places with you . . . And I would gladly change places with any one of them, I would change places even with Betty . . .

o   o   o

"PARSON'S TONIC PILLS," ELLEN SAID, "FOR COLDS, ASTHMA and all pulmonic afflictions. Advertised *this* month, but not *last,* so it must be *new* and safe to ask for at both shops. We can go to Baxter's together, then I'll go to Blake's and get you a Ouida if I can, you go to Freeman's and give Angela's message."

The threatened frost had fallen and Mamma had been apologetic about sending them out at all; but somewhere in the vast desert of the evening of yesterday she had come to the end of the wool she was using. "I had no idea," she said, "it seemed quite a big ball, but it must have been *hollow*. You should wear your fur coats." So, out of the muslin bags, smelling of lavender, thyme, rosemary and cloves —all moth repellents—they had taken the sealskin coats, the matching hats and the little ankle-high, sealskin lined boots that constituted their winter wear. Well-clad, well-fed, most enviable, they pattered along. They bought Mamma's wool, carefully matching the two-inch piece she had given them as a guide to colour and thickness; then they went into Baxter's where Parson's Tonic Pills had never been heard of. "We must buy something," Marion said, recognising in Mr. Baxter's demeanour almost the identical sense of failure as she had sensed in Miss Ruthven.

Ellen said, "Twopennyworth of liquorice, cut please and a packet of black-currant lozenges." Mr. Baxter took the thick black strap of liquorice, cut it, weighed it, reached

26

down the packet of lozenges and said, "I trust that no member of your family is suffering from the prevalent cold."

"Thank you. No," Ellen said. "We do a few errands for those who cannot get about." She put sixpence on the counter and took up the little packages. Outside in the cold that could make itself felt through the sealskin, the silk lining and all the good woollen stuff, Ellen said, "I don't suppose Freeman's have ever heard of it either. But it is an excuse . . . Be as quick as you can. It's too cold to wait about."

On Freeman's forbidden door the bell jangled and from the far end, out of a kind of loosebox of polished mahogany and ground glass, came the young man about whom Angela had been at once so reticent and so confiding. She had described him as handsome. This morning he was not looking his best, having a swollen nose, a black eye and above the eye a strip of sticking plaster; he also wore the slightly greenish pallor which a naturally swarthy skin takes on when its owner is not in the best of health or spirits. He wore a very clean, knee-length white coat.

"Good morning, Madam," he said, and moved to the angle of the L-shaped counter, ready to hand down from behind the shorter one soap, scent or any toilet preparation, from behind the longer one anything in the medical line.

Brusquely, because she was nervous, Marion said:

"Are you Mr. de Brissac?"

"That is my name."

"I have a message for you. From Miss Taylor. She asked me to tell you that she was very sorry, very sorry indeed. And that she has gone away and will not be able to see you, or to write. And that . . . that she was sorry . . ." It was difficult to look at only half a face. The young man seemed to sense the difficulty and before speaking lifted his hand so that it covered the bruised and swollen eye, the plaster and one side of the swollen nose. His hand was long and slender, an elegant hand. On his little finger he wore a heavy seal ring.

"I am most grateful," he said. "It was extremely kind of you to convey the message. Thank you." With the injured half of his face covered she saw him differently, could see what Angela meant. His hair, very dark and glossy, grew beautifully from his forehead and then dipped in a romantic, Byronic curve; the visible eye was a clear grey, lustrous and long-lashed. "May I ask you something, Miss . . . Miss . . . ?"

"My name is Draper."

"Thank you. Miss Draper. Will you be in communication with Miss Taylor?"

No order had been issued. Angela had not involved them in her disgrace; Papa and Mamma had received with mild interest the information that Angela was going to stay with her grandfather, Sir Miles. In the circumstances it would indeed seem strange *not* to write.

"I suppose so."

"Then would you please be again kind and tell her that I also am sorry, very sorry. And that my injuries were slight."

She saw then that his mouth was beautiful. As he said the word "slight" it both smiled and sneered, mocking the word. Mocking—absurd thought—everything.

"I will do that. When I write," she said. A feeling hitherto unknown to her, a warm weakening, a yielding, a yearning, ran through her. She said a little breathlessly, "Parson's Tonic Pills, have you any in stock?"

"They are on order. Friday, Saturday at latest."

"I will look in again," she said; and armoured in sealskin, in respectability, in virtue that had never been tested and in integrity only slightly tarnished, she was about to make for

28

the door. Then she thought of Angela's words about Papa lashing about with his stick. What use to hustle Angela away, to forbid her nearest friends to say a word, with this possible source of gossip wide open? Had the Taylors thought of that?

She said, awkward again, "Your poor eye . . . I have no wish to sound unkind; I hope it will soon be better . . . but it would be a kindness to *her,* to Miss Taylor, if you would avoid telling the truth about how you came by it."

" 'What is truth, asked jesting Pilate'," the chemist's assistant said. "Last evening I slipped on an icy patch and hit my face on a step." The good eye said—Trust me! It also said—Those who will believe that will believe anything!

Outside, in the plain, straightforward, ordinary world, Ellen waited, cuddling a book. "My trouble was I did not know what you had read and what you had not. *Under Two Flags* was the only Ouida there today. All right; then you owe me twopence. Did Parson's Tonic Pills work over there?"

"As an excuse, yes. But I am now more or less committed to buying some."

"Mamma will pay—if we tell her we wanted them for Nanny," Ellen said in her cheerful, practical way. "And what did you think of Angela's *beau?*"

Marion tried to speak judicially. "He is, in fact, more like Angela's mysterious French gentleman than a chemist's assistant. In looks, in speech . . . and in demeanour. Mr. Taylor must have hit him very hard; he had a black eye and a patch on his forehead. I had the sense to ask him not to reveal how he had come by his injury. He understood."

Ellen then voiced the doubt which Mr. Taylor was himself entertaining; "You know, Marion, I'm not absolutely sure that you are allowed to hit a person with a stick even if he is meeting your daughter secretly. Suppose the young man made a fuss."

"I don't think he would. He is not at all the type."

"He seems to have made a favourable impression on *you*, too."

"A shop assistant who uses one of Miss Ruthven's favourite quotations is something of a rarity. At least in this town."

○　○　○

MARION WROTE TO ANGELA—CAREFULLY, FOR NOW, DOUBT-less, Angela's correspondence would be subject to the strict scrutiny which had always applied in the Draper household. The writing was rather a delectable task, calling as it did for some little exercise of skill. "Old Nanny, whom Ellen and I visited on Tuesday has been advised to try a new remedy for her asthma, Parson's Tonic Pills. They *do* exist, but not in Bereham, yet. We tried Baxter's first but without success so we were obliged to go to that horrid Mr. Freeman's shop. Fortunately he was not there himself and we were waited upon by his assistant who had had a fall and blacked his eye which gave him a somewhat sinister appearance. In contrast his manner was agreeable and he seemed to be intelligent. At least he had heard of the new remedy and was obliging enough to offer to procure it for us within a few days. We had had no time to obtain Papa's permission to go to Freeman's; we must do so before we go there again, but I am sure it will be forthcoming since the errand is to benefit Nanny . . ." And that was sufficient. Angela would read between the lines and understand. Yet she found herself reluctant to quit the subject and paused for quite a while before relating how many shell boxes she and Ellen had assembled that afternoon. "We cannot work at the gluing in the evening as the glue has an unpleasant odour." She hoped that Angela was enjoying her stay with her grandfather. A letter that anyone could read . . .

On Friday, armed with Papa's permission—"Well, we will make an exception, for Nanny's sake, though none of these newfangled things work. She would do better with Friars' Balsam"—the girls entered the shop together. The young man's nose and eye were less swollen, but even more discoloured than they had been on Wednesday. The tonic pills, he said, had not yet arrived. There was no opportunity to say a private word because Mr. Freeman himself was behind the shorter counter, wearing the frock coat, green with age and much spilled upon, but a frock coat which marked him out as the owner of his business. He was surprised to see the Misses Draper in his establishment, and took it as a sign that a go-ahead business must, by God's law, outstrip its competitor. Parson's Tonic Pills, he said, interrupting, would almost certainly be in the shop by Monday; and could he send them as soon as they arrived? Marion said no, it was no trouble for them to look in again. He opened the flap in the counter and obsequiously bowed them to the door. All there had been time for was an exchange of glances. Above the young man's uninjured eye the narrow, clearly defined eyebrow had lifted in a question which she had answered by a nod of her head.

Monday brought, by the early post, a letter from Angela. All letters were placed by Papa's left hand, all were studied before being passed over. Marion, taking hers and recognising Angela's writing which had displeased Miss Ruthven so much that she had once called it a broken-down fence, felt her heart jerk. She hoped that Angela had been discreet. Papa was inclined, now and then, to ask whom letters were from and at unpredictable intervals demand to see them.

31

Angela wrote discreetly and meaningfully. "You may have thought that the country, in October, would be *dull*. The contrary is true; there was a shooting party—twelve guns—here on Friday; two more are planned for next week. My grandpapa says he has long missed the presence of a female, 'to do the honours' as he says in his old-fashioned way. He calls me a *minx* but when he says this I gather that he rather likes minxes; perhaps because, greatly daring, I made his *fearsome* old housekeeper bring out the proper dinner service. Why should he and his guests eat from plates oddly assorted and mostly cracked? He is too easygoing in *some* ways. Seventy-three years old, Marion, not at all Victorian, though he saw her Coronation." (That was the kind of sentence of which Miss Ruthven disapproved!) "I am sorry," the broken-fence writing ran on, "not to be with you at the stall at the Bazaar. One of the men who came to shoot and is staying on for the next is a kind of relative, cousin once removed. Army, on half pay. Quite gorgeous. A V.C. at Kandahar and one day a title." The broken-fence writing suffered a complete collapse and its meaning, patiently sorted out, became incoherent; then it righted itself. "I only wish my *dearest* friends to know this. Early days yet! But I think, perhaps by Christmas . . ." Then there was a line heavily crossed out and the words, "I wanted you and Ellen to be prepared, and to know what to say . . ."

"And from whom is your letter?" Papa asked.

"From Angela, Papa."

"Oh yes. She is staying with her grandfather."

"Yes. And she sounds very happy."

Mamma said disconcertingly, "She left very *suddenly*."

"It would seem that her grandfather rather wished for someone to play hostess, Mamma. Would you care to read

Angela's letter?" It was harmless, the term my *dearest* friends would mean nothing to the uninformed.

But, just as it was possible to feel hatred for Papa and wish him dead, so it was possible to feel a truly green-eyed envy of Angela. Discovered, disgraced, banished—to a doting old grandfather, to a new admirer, possibly to a husband; fortunate girl! While to me nothing happens, nothing ever will, and the only excitement, the only landmark in the stretch of dreary days, is the prospect of going again into Freeman's.

It then occurred to her that Angela had entrusted her with another commission—that of breaking the news of her new interest to Jean de Brissac. That was why Angela had underlined the word dearest.

A week ago she would have approached this business without any sympathy; the young man must have known that nothing could come of the clandestine meetings save disappointment. She might even have thought, Serve him right! But now that she had seen and spoken to him she felt differently; sorry for him. He was a foreigner, perhaps he did not understand the finer shades of class distinction in England; meeting Angela socially, at the Musical Society and being encouraged by her . . . The confident, jaunty tone of Angela's letter was evidence of the progress she could make with a man in very short time . . . and she had been seeing de Brissac regularly ever since September. Now, in addition to having been beaten over the head with a stick, he was to learn that he was virtually forgotten. Poor fellow.

It was a bright, invigorating morning and they had more shopping than usual to do. Mamma was again in need of wool and she also wanted hairpins, stockings and toilet soap; the girls needed velveteen with which to line the shell boxes and some stiff canvas from which to fashion another con-

33

tribution to the stalls—some of those little pouches in which gentlemen hung their watches at bedtime. Marion, at any time a quick reader, had become so engrossed in *Under Two Flags* that she had read each evening until the candle guttered out, and now wanted another book. "I'll go to the library while you fetch Nanny's pills," Ellen said.

The young man had discarded the plaster strip and so arranged his hair that the soft dark fall concealed all mark of the injury. His nose, aquiline and rather thin, was its normal size and the bruise about his eye almost invisible.

"Good morning, Miss Draper. Your order has arrived. I am sorry, I have not yet had time to wrap it. Mr. Freeman is confined to his bed with lumbago." She was relieved to hear it. Busying himself with the white paper and the little blobs of sealing wax, the young man said, without looking up, "Have you yet been able to convey my apologies to Miss Taylor?"

"I took the first opportunity to do so. I think . . . I think you had better read this." From the little pocket inside her muff she took Angela's letter and held it out. While he read it she turned away and studied some bottles of hair oil, each of which bore a picture of a hirsute gentleman who had obviously used the preparation with satisfactory results. Then the young man said, "I am very glad to know that Miss Taylor is enjoying her stay in the country." His voice was pleasantly conversational; his face bore no sign of emotion. She said awkwardly, "It was . . . the other part that I thought you should see."

He smiled, his sharply curved, rather flat-surfaced lips moving again into the expression she remembered, a sweet mockery.

"If I seem stupid, forgive me. I do not aspire to be one of the dear friends to whom Miss Taylor wished to hint at such

34

exciting news. Merely an acquaintance." For a second Marion said nothing, but she looked at the still faintly discoloured eye. And Jean de Brissac thought, This one is *not* stupid! He put his hand to the side of his face, repeating the gesture she remembered. "That," he said, "was the absurdity. I think that Mr. Taylor—shall we say—paid me an undeserved compliment? Suspected me of designs I had never once entertained. Miss Taylor extended to me, a stranger in a strange land, a friendliness as valuable as it is rare. I was grateful. But . . ."

The shop bell jangled, a heavy, shabbily clad woman came in. He said, "Excuse me, please . . ."

"I want," the woman said, "a box of Beecham's Pills." She was gratified to see that Mr. Freeman's new assistant, holding what looked like a long order, one item of which was already packed, white and red upon the counter, should break off to serve a chance customer; but why not? The other customer was obviously a lady, with time to spare, not like herself, with three children under four years old and a husband whose constipation made him bad-tempered and Beecham's Pills a necessity.

The little interruption had given Marion time to take from her purse the elevenpence and the halfpenny, the price of the Parson's Tonic Pills. It had also given her time to recover herself, to retreat. The shop bell jangled.

"You have been so kind," the young man said. "So kind in conveying my apologies to Miss Taylor for a situation neither foreseen nor justified, but I am glad to know, culminating happily, that I wonder whether you would resent it if I tried to make amends? It is nothing much." He reached down into the recesses of the counter and brought out a small parcel, wrapped in tissue paper. "It belonged to my mother . . ."

35

She said, "But I have done nothing . . ."

"Please. It is only a token." She took it, unwrapped the paper and saw a little scent bottle, not like those most fashionable in England at the moment, either white or ruby coloured glass with silver stoppers; this was of green glass, gilded, the gilding inside the glass, veins of gold.

"I couldn't possibly," she said.

"Smell it, please."

The stopper was not just a rounded knob of silver; it also was gilt, a daisy. Hardly knowing what she was about she unscrewed it and the potent, poignant concentrated scent of lily of the valley rose up, swamping the mixed odours of the shop. She thought idiotically, The very breath of life . . . And she must refuse it and turn away.

o   o   o

NO OTHER BREATH OF LIFE PENETRATED INTO THE STUFFY claustrophobic atmosphere of 10, Alma Avenue as the days darkened and grew colder. The Church Bazaar was at least something to vary the monotony and although its first hours pursued the routine course, at about half-past three something happened. The young man who had lived in her mind for some weeks, a curious double image, half Angela's mysterious French gentleman and half Freeman's shop assistant in a white coat, presented himself, alive and real, by the muslin-draped stall where Marion and Ellen were selling the things made by their own and other nimble fingers. In his top hat, dark coat, plaid trousers, silver grey cravat, silver grey gloves, he was indistinguishable from any other gentleman who was patronising the Bazaar. And he had—as Angela had once said—beautiful manners. He did not merely shift his hat; he removed it and bowed.

"Good afternoon, Miss Draper. Good afternoon . . ." he included Ellen in his greeting, but halted, on an inquiring note.

"Ellen, this is Mr. de Brissac. Mr. de Brissac, this is my sister, Miss Ellen Draper."

It was as much as she could do to effect the introduction; the same weakening, overwhelming feeling swept over her and she was grateful for Ellen's presence, brisk and business-like. Ellen was quite capable of thinking, Yes, Angela was not so far mistaken, and at the same time saying:

"I am sorry—no, I should say I am glad—we are almost sold out. There are some gloves . . ." But they had been knitted by somebody who had extraordinary ideas about the shape and size of the human hand. There was also—since everything must be enclosed and embroidered and elaborated —some cases designed to hold thimbles, little cones to place upon boiled eggs, and a few other articles whose purpose was less definable.

"I am late," Jean de Brissac said. "But I came to contribute, too." By some sleight of hand he produced the green, gold-veined scent bottle which had made Marion turn dizzy, able only to repudiate.

"We," Ellen said, "are handiwork. Mrs. Marriot, over there, is Treasure Trove."

"I see," he said, and replaced the hat which must be removed anew in the greeting to Mrs. Marriot.

The hubbub of the morning had died down and Mrs. Marriot had a good, carrying voice. She said, "Oh, Mr. Brisket, what a delightful little treasure! What a pity that Lady Mingay has gone. It would have been just the thing for her. But I am sure it will sell for at least ten shillings. Thank you very much."

37

Ellen said, "Yes, I see what you meant, Marion. And what Angela saw. Who would have thought that he was a shop assistant? But did not a number of most respectable people have to flee from France, very lately. He could be . . . Marion, are you all right? Is your back hurting? Do sit down. We have nothing left to sell—except gloves for elephants."

"I must just," Marion said, and deserting Ellen she went over to Mrs. Marriot's Treasure Trove. The young man had moved away, accepting the coy invitation over a white-clothed table. It read, *"Come to Tea."*

"Mrs. Marriot, would you reserve that for me? I have so far spent nothing with you . . . but Papa will be along presently. He will buy it for me."

Mrs. Marriot did not wholeheartedly welcome this suggestion. She was reasonably sure that if she took the pretty little object out to Lady Mingay and said, "I was so sure that you would like it," she would obtain not only the pound she meant to ask, but some measure of goodwill. On the other hand, the Draper girls worked faithfully and well, year after year; so did their mother; and Mr. Draper had made his usual morning round, spending freely. So she compromised, saying, "It is a very pretty thing and rather unusual. Fifteen shillings?"

Papa arrived, as was his custom on such occasions, to collect and then distribute his morning's purchases. Also to accept the coy invitation and to treat the various poor women who had drifted in hoping to buy left-over buns or to pick up articles from the various stalls whose holders preferred to sell them very cheaply rather than carry them home, store them for a year and bring them out next December. As Mrs. Marriot had said in a caustic moment, "What isn't sold by twelve o'clock is simply unsaleable."

So now Papa, his purchases made well before twelve o'clock,

stood under the awning with its playful invitation; and he had seven poor sycophantic women around him, stirring in the sugar, slopping up the tea, gobbling the buns—though Marion noticed, as she had done before, that every now and again one of the women would slip something into her canvas bag. She felt a little ashamed to attack Papa in a most vulnerable moment, but it had to be done.

"Papa," Marion said, "Mrs. Marriot has such a *pretty* thing left on her stall. I long to possess it and she agreed to reserve it for me. Until you arrived. I am afraid it will cost you fifteen shillings."

"Good gracious!" Mr. Draper exclaimed in mock dismay. "Fifteen shillings! What can it be? A diamond tiara?"

"Oh no, I do not know, Papa, what it is exactly. But it is pretty and I would like to own it."

Mr. Draper wore a thick gold watch chain from which hung a cylinder, also of gold, a sovereign case. It worked on a spring; a pressure, a tilting and out into the palm of the waiting hand fell the coin—the most sought-after coin in the world, the English sovereign, the pound sterling.

The women who had accepted Mr. Draper's invitation to take tea with him under the awning that said *"Come to Tea,"* watched while he performed the manoeuvre. Most of them on less than fifteen shillings a week fed hungry husbands, growing children, paid rent, had boots mended.

"You girls will be the ruin of me," Mr. Draper said jocosely. "Buy whatever it is. And you may keep the change. And now, Mrs. Beeton, Mrs. Mison, Mrs. Plume, another cup of tea? Another bun? A sandwich?"

Marion took and held in her hand the pretty little thing which had been offered her as a gift, which she had refused, and which was now hers. And there was Jean de Brissac. He said, "It would seem that you were meant to have it."

After that there was Christmas; two deadly dull dinner parties at 10, Alma Avenue, three, equally dull elsewhere. And then January. "A happy New Year," everybody said to everybody else.

In the rectory the new year brought Mr. Marriot face to face with the question of whether it would be worth while to continue the dwindling Musical Society.

"I think not," his wife said positively. She was far more worldly than her husband and, like Mr. Draper, could see the basic weakness of that experiment. "The truth is that what is open to all is valued by none. To get anything really going you must have support from the middle class." She thought with complacency of her Bazaar which had been a great success.

"I had hoped," Mr. Marriot said wistfully, "to bring a little pleasure and a touch of culture within the reach of all. But with only six regular attendants . . ."

Mrs. Marriot, after years of marriage, was still fond of her husband and hated to see him discouraged.

"It must be done *gradually*," she said. "We must form some Society which it will be regarded as privilege to join, and then we can admit working class people by degrees. And there is another thing to consider; seven o'clock in the evening is a most inconvenient time, it disrupts the evening meal. I am practically certain that when Mr. Draper refused to allow the girls to join it was that which he had in mind." She herself had had almost a quarter of a century of disrupted meals, meals put forward, meals delayed, with cooks and maids smoulderingly resentful. "Now, let me think . . . A Literary Society, perhaps. Held here, in our drawing room. Not open to all. By invitation and commencing at a quarter past eight. I think it very possible that Lady Mingay would join."

"The enlightenment of Lady Mingay's leisure was not my object."

"I know. But one must start somewhere. If we could make a small, thriving Society then we could launch out, hire the Guildhall again and have Penny Readings such as dear Mr. Dickens used to give. And then we could interest the poorer people by running a competition for original poems or bits of folklore. That would make their inclusion seem natural. I am not trying to be a snob."

"My dear, you have no need to *try*," Mr. Marriot said, but he said it mildly, with a smile, and she took it with a hearty laugh.

"Just to show you," she said, "and to salve your conscience, I shall invite to the first meeting, that nice Mr. Brisket—he never missed a Musical, and Mr. Clegg and Miss Sharp. I will also," she said bravely shouldering the burden, "serve tea at a quarter past nine."

Mr. Marriot saw that another compromise was necessary. And so the Literary Society was born and Lady Mingay consented to join and even suggested what she thought was a more attractive name, A Literary Salon. Mr. Clegg and Miss Sharp realised that they were specially favoured beings and showed their gratitude by doing little helpful things like moving the dining-room chairs into the drawing room and trotting about with tea trays. Jean de Brissac was less conscious of being honoured, but he offered to give a little talk about French novelists. Mr. Draper, unable to find any adequate reason why Marion and Ellen should refuse what amounted to a personal invitation to spend an evening in the Rectory drawing room in most respectable company, gave his grudging consent.

The Salon opened on the second Thursday in January. Nice Mr. Brisket arrived in good time and took upon himself the duties of usher, inquiring whether people wished to sit near to or away from the fire, sometimes shifting chairs about. In the midst of shaking hands and speaking greetings designed to make this seem to be a gay social occasion, Mrs. Marriot found time to note his activities and approve them; he was behaving almost like a son of the house, she thought quite fondly. She had no son.

Jean de Brissac's interest in people's comfort and seating arrangements ceased abruptly when Marion and Ellen arrived. He led them to three chairs which occupied a space beside the china cabinet, and when they sat down, sat down himself.

His proximity prevented Marion from benefitting from what Lady Mingay assured her hearers was in no sense a lecture, simply a little informal talk about Her Majesty's genius as a writer. Mrs. Marriot had insisted that Lady Mingay, as the most important lady present, must be asked to give the first talk. It went a little wrong because Lady Mingay, herself a writer of some trite verse, seemed to suffer some confusion between her own work and that of her sovereign. The applause when she finished and sat down was partly sycophantic, partly polite, but in even larger measure due to relief.

Jean de Brissac said, "I am able to see a resemblance between the ladies." He spoke solemnly and only Marion, catching just a flicker of malicious amusement in his eyes, realised that a joke was here, simply waiting for acknowledgement. She decided to acknowledge it and gave him her sudden, flashing smile. Ellen said, "The resemblance has been much remarked," in rather a crushing tone.

Mr. Marriot rose to thank Lady Mingay and to offer foretastes of delights to come. He realised as he faced his audience that it was, almost to a man, the same as he faced twice a day every Sunday. But it would be wrong to resent this; these were the faithful. His efforts to obey the Biblical order to go into the highways and byways and *compel* them to come in had met with another defeat. Mrs. Marriot faced her own problem. Her budget simply did not run to providing *good* tea for some unspecified number, but Lady Mingay and a few other ladies would recognise what was called "kitchen tea" and might take it amiss. "The little blue lustre teapot, please, Mr. Brisket," she said to that helpful young man, again active and handy. Jean de Brissac, having obtained two cups of tea from the little blue lustre teapot, carried them to Marion and Ellen and said, in a low, conspiratorial voice, "It is the *best* tea!" Ellen missed the allusion but Marion caught it and smiled again and said, "I always loved the Mad Hatter."

Encouraged, he asked, "Are you to be called for, Miss Draper?"

"Oh no. It is so short a distance."

"May I then have the honour of escorting you home?"

Taking control of the situation again because Marion, ordinarily so handy with words, seemed at a loss, Ellen said:

"It is very kind of you, Mr. de Brissac, but quite unnecessary. There are two of us; the road is well-lighted and other people are going our way. Indeed Alma Avenue is well represented here."

"I think it was a bit cheeky," Ellen said as they pattered along the lime avenue which led from the Rectory to St. Mary's Church and then debouched into Honey Lane which after about a hundred yards branched off into Alma Avenue. "After all, we only know him through Angela. And we have never been properly introduced."

"I know."

"And Papa would be very much annoyed. Mr. Freeman's shop assistant . . ."

"I know."

"If everybody from whom we ever bought anything walked us home," Ellen said, "it would look decidedly odd."

"I know."

"Why do you keep saying 'I know,' in that gloomy voice, Marion? Of course, I know you know. I saw, at the Bazaar, why Angela had become infatuated and you thought him unusual. But he should not presume on his looks or his manners or," Ellen said shrewdly, "on being the only mysterious Frenchman in a place like Bereham."

"He did not presume. He merely offered to walk home with us."

Ellen took some steps before she spoke again; then she said, "And you wanted to accept the offer. You've fallen in love with him, too."

"Yes. From the first moment I saw him. I realised that this evening."

"Marion! Think! Mr. Taylor hit him over the head with a stick and sent Angela away. What would Papa do? Darling, this is all nonsense. He is good-looking, he has nice manners, he is well-dressed; and he seems to have ingratiated himself with the Marriots. But you cannot, you must not . . . In any case, I am going to have *nothing* to do with it. Angela taught me a lesson . . . And now for you to go and do the very same thing. It is entirely ridiculous."

"You are too young to understand, Ellen. Nobody in her senses would choose such a thing to happen, but when it does . . . It happens and there is absolutely nothing one can do about it."

After that they walked in silence until they were home. The front gate creaked and once they were within it, mount-

44

ing the steps both were conscious of being again within Papa's orbit and of the necessity for unity.

"I am sorry if I sounded sharp," Ellen said.

"I am sorry if I sounded silly."

They went in and reported that there had been between forty and fifty people present and that Lady Mingay had given a most *interesting* talk, all about Queen Victoria.

Mr. Draper looked at the black marble clock and checked it against his watch. Mrs. Marriot, tackling him personally, pleading that any venture, to be successful, must appeal to the young, had mentioned tea at nine fifteen. The serving of tea to a considerable number, and the drinking, the taking leave; yes, at least half an hour. They were back in good time and he was able to say, with sincerity, "I am glad that you have had an entertaining evening."

The next Thursday evening, potentially entertaining, found Ellen dreadfully torn between common sense and sisterly loyalty.

"Really, Marion, you put me in an impossible position. You know what would happen if Papa ever knew."

"Darling, I know. But to whom else can I look for help. I'd do as much for you."

"But, Marion, no good can come of it. And harm could. I shudder to think . . ."

"Ellen, *please*. I know how you feel. You are too young to understand; but one day you will. And you know that I would always stand by you."

Ellen stood by; on that and several other Thursday evenings. Her role was passive. On leaving the Rectory she and Marion hurried along and at the end of the lime avenue did not proceed into Honey Lane but turned instead into what was known as the Old Cloister, part of the ruined Abbey

45

out of which St. Mary's, once a mere Lady Chapel, had been preserved as a parish church. It was a place generally avoided because, though it was four hundred years and more since any living monk had walked there, phantom ones were said to be seen. Indeed the sexton, a hardy old man, swore that he had seen a cowled figure glide through the ruins and go into the church at a point where there was a built-up doorway. Into this eerie place, all ruins and nettles and elderberry bushes, Ellen and Marion turned and presently the young man, whom Marion now called Johnny, joined them. He and Marion then walked off and Ellen sat on a stump and waited, all her nerves on edge. She disliked the trysting place and threatened Marion that if she and Johnny went out of earshot, leaving her with the ghosts she would never wait again, she would go straight home, she would tell Papa . . . In fact she was more frightened of Papa finding out than she was of the ghosts and was terrified that he would notice that they were ten minutes later on every subsequent Thursday than they had been on the first. So the lovers' time for the exchanging of kisses and embraces was limited by Ellen's impatience and the last clutching clasp was usually interrupted by her reminder that it was time to go. "Marion, we must *run*. Marion, unless you come now I shall never wait for you again."

It was all hurried and unsatisfactory, and at the same time so wonderful that for Marion life became enchanted, the hours that had dragged so tediously now spent in happy memories of last Thursday, joyful anticipations of next.

Ellen's manner became astringent. "Really Marion, you must pull yourself together; anyone with half an eye could see that you were in love. I wonder Papa has not observed already." In fact Mr. Draper had observed a change, but a change for the better. It did not surprise him, he had always known that Marion would outgrow her childish sulkishness. He could just imagine, for instance, how only a few months ago she would have behaved over the reassignment of bedrooms. Now she took her banishment to inferior accommodation in the right spirit, meek, cheerful, making the best of things.

For Mamma's scheme to make the little half-basement room under the stairs into a bedroom for Ada—thus saving her from all climbing—had come to nothing. "I should be nervous, down there all by myself and everybody else so far away. I know I can't manage the top stairs any more, they're the steepest. So maybe my time has come."

"Ada, you must not say such things," Mamma said. "How could we manage without you? I shall think of something."

The solution was obvious; move Betty and Ada down, Marion and Ellen up. But there were difficulties. The young ladies of a family naturally owned more clothes than the maids; they had a wardrobe, they had a chest of drawers.

"And even if they could be got up those steep stairs," said Ellen, the practical one, "there would be no room to move about. Our bed, for one thing, is bigger than theirs."

Mamma played put and take in her mind, hampered by the fact that Papa's dressing room was sacrosanct, and that the guest room, though seldom used, was a necessity to any decent establishment. In her secret mind she had always hated the prim, grey, tight-lipped house with its basement kitchen, its many stairs. She had spent her happy girlhood in a great sprawling farmhouse where anything up to twenty people could sleep in moderate comfort and no matter how noisily she played the piano, it disturbed nobody. But she faced the present problem sensibly. Ada and Betty could move down into the room now occupied by Marion and Ellen. Their room, with its cupboard for clothes would suffice for

47

Ellen. Given a single bed it would even accommodate a chest of drawers. *If* Marion would not mind the semi-basement room under the steps that led up to the front door.

"It would be only for a time, Marion dear. I know that Ada cannot last forever, but I do wish her last years to be as comfortable as possible. Would you object?"

"Of course not, Mamma. I should not be in the least nervous in the basement."

Gratefully Mamma spoke of hanging better curtains in the little room and the possibility that the wardrobe could be moved down.

Ellen was secretly rather pleased at the prospect of having her own room where she would not be disturbed by Marion's habit of reading in bed.

And when Marion thought of the little basement room she thought of Johnny. As she now thought of him in every connection; the first snowdrops and crocuses, the first green buds, the promise of spring in an apple-green sky and in the first, premature bird cry. She had already counted the weeks, the Thursdays until Easter when the Literary Salon would close down for the summer and it was like a foretaste of death. Now, with a room of her own, she could look forward to living, not from Thursday to Thursday, but from evening to evening.

Her first move was to oil the hinges on the screeching gate. Her second to absolve Ellen from further complicity. The new plan, though it promised great happiness, also threatened enormous risk and Ellen must not even be aware of it. Therefore on the Thursday evening after the move was made, at the end of the lime avenue, Marion instead of swerving off into the Old Cloister walked ahead and turned into Honey Lane. Ellen was greatly relieved, but surprised, too, and curious.

"Have you quarrelled?" she asked, almost timidly.

"No; there was no quarrel," Marion said, managing to inject the implication that although there had not been a quarrel there had been something equally final.

"Oh, I am so glad and happy, Marion. I knew all along that you would get over it, just as Angela did. And I kept thinking all the time how horrid it would be if Papa should find out and there was a terrible row over a mere infatuation."

Now that it was over, and Marion had returned to her senses, Ellen was prepared to give her own opinion of Johnny and indeed of the whole affair.

"I would not deny that he has charm," she said. Johnny had always gone out of his way to flatter and cajole her. "But there is nothing behind it. I could see, of course, because I was not in love with him. I never felt that he was sincere. And I must confess that his style of dressing seems pretentious and not altogether suitable."

"There have been no sumptuary laws in England for a long time," Marion said rather coldly.

"What are sumptuary laws?"

"Laws ordering that one must dress according to one's station in life."

After a few more steps Ellen said, "Are you sad about it?"

"Not in the least. But I do think I would prefer not to talk about it."

"Then we won't," Ellen said happily. "I will never mention the subject again." She squeezed Marion's arm. "I am so glad it is all over and done with and you are yourself again."

On this as on every other ordinary evening the household at 10, Alma Avenue retired at ten o'clock. Papa made his round, locking all three doors, the front, the kitchen and the

49

one in the conservatory, too. He looked to the window fastenings and then went upstairs, taking the keys with him. All those for whom he was responsible were now safe in their beds, well-fed, well-housed, well-guarded.

At eleven o'clock, obeying the instructions in a long letter from Marion—a letter beginning, *"Johnny Darling, a wonderful thing has happened . . ."*— Jean de Brissac walked along Alma Avenue, let himself in by the now-silent gate, took the few steps over the little sloping garden and into the shadow cast by the eight steps up to the front door. The better curtains which Mamma had provided were not quite closed and a streak of light was visible as a guide. He tapped very gently on the window, a sound inaudible to any but a waiting ear. Marion then blew out the candle, parted the curtains and opened the window, which unlike the others in the house was a casement. The little room had been designed as a sleeping place for servants, unpredictable creatures, so the window was stoutly barred. It was just possible for Johnny standing at the lowest level of the little garden and straining upwards, and Marion, kneeling on the floor and craning outwards, to exchange kisses; it was possible for hand to reach for hand, it was possible to talk. There was no longer the time limit of ten minutes, or the sense of Ellen waiting; but in other ways it was less satisfactory as a meeting place than the Old Cloister and very soon Johnny whispered, "Darling, you must let me in." He had been quite certain that that was what Marion intended to do when she wrote of wonderful news and a room of her own down in the basement.

"I cannot. The doors are locked and the keys are on Papa's dressing table."

"There must be other windows."

There were. One in the kitchen, also barred. All the

others, due to the design of the house, were high above ground level. To clean them Betty needed the taller step ladder. Also they were sash windows, and they rumbled. Equally important was that she dared not move about on the next floor with only a ceiling between her and Papa.

She relayed all this in a muted voice.

"There must be *some* way," Johnny said. "This is worse. I want to hold you in my arms." She wanted to be held. She realised that she had been mistaken in thinking that this was a wonderful thing and that lovers whose bodies had known close, if inconclusive embraces, could be content with kisses and hand clasps between bars, and with talk.

"I will find a way," she promised recklessly, her mind veering wildly between plans for stealing the back-door key and replacing it before morning when Betty, taking up Papa's hot water, retrieved the keys and unlocked doors, and plans for filing through the iron bars. Prisoners were said to have managed such performances.

"Tomorrow?"

"If possible, by tomorrow."

They kissed again and he said, "Until tomorrow, Chérie." She was always pleased when he used that term, so entirely his own. But after he had gone softly away she lay for a long time wondering whether, and how, she would be able to keep her promise. A forged key? Reading romantic novels had made her aware of their existence and she had some idea that wax was involved, but exactly how? She thought of stealing the key to the kitchen door; it stuck out, never used, from the moment when Betty unlocked the door to the moment when Papa locked it. Take it to Rancy's, ironmongers, and ask for a duplicate? Very dangerous; she was known in that shop. Mr. Rancy did a lot of work for Papa; he might casually, innocently mention the matter. Could the door be wedged in some way so that when Papa locked it it did not lock?

Betty was upstairs; Ada was making a beefsteak pudding which to be up to standard must boil, very gently, for at least six hours.

"It's that door, Miss Marion. I knew you'd notice it, sleeping down here. Rattling. I've said to Betty sometimes it's enough to drive a body mad."

"I can see no cure for it," Marion said. She had seen all that she needed to see. In this door, when the key turned and the tongue of the lock shot out it did not enter a socket in the door post, it entered and was held by a kind of case of brass, properly polished, attached to the door post by two screws, one at the top, one at the bottom. Remove one screw and swing the case upwards or downwards . . . All one needed was a screwdriver.

"Darling, go very softly round to the back. Get on to the other path. Go round and wait. There are more steps down. I will bring a candle." She had already used the screwdriver and by the time Johnny had stolen around the house and reached the area, she had the door open.

She was ignorant of the mechanics of love; partly because at school she had never formed a friendship intimate enough to permit of the handing on of information, some wildly distorted, some speculative and superstitious, some very practical. The books she read had stopped short with a passionate kiss and the avowal of everlasting love. But the body had a knowledge of its own and in the Old Cloister, armoured in whalebone, linen, broadcloth, it *knew;* and so did Johnny's; and now in a secret place, time no longer to be considered, the night was their own.

What she had not counted upon was the effect. The shattering, the uplift, the sensual pleasure beyond the reach of the imagination. The very breath of life, hinted at in the scent of lily of the valley caught, fleetingly in a chemist's shop, now expanded, filled the whole universe. For this and to this she had been born. Every sunset, every book, every line of poetry, every flower, now all one in the merging, the entry into another dimension.

When it was over she was sorry that it should have taken place in this small bedroom with the faint, pervading kitchen odour. It should have happened in some vast pink marble palace or in a green glade where wild hyacinths grew, or on one of those palm-shaded beaches where brown boys gathered shells. But there it was, it had happened here, with Papa and Mamma and Ellen, and Ada and Betty sleeping, all innocent, above stairs. And there was Johnny to be let out; the lock to be readjusted.

It was partly to fight off the sense of anticlimax that she sat down immediately and began to write to him. She wrote that she hoped that her easy yielding would not lead to any lessening of his esteem for her; she wrote that she now regarded herself as his wife; she wrote that she was the happiest woman in the world and pitied all others; she wrote that she was already longing for tomorrow evening. As thoughts occurred to her she set them down, writing quickly, eagerly and lovingly.

She was without any sense of wrongdoing. Nothing in her upbringing had led towards the Puritan conscience which would have accused her of sin. Mr. Draper was not one of those weak disciplinarians who must always make references to God. Within his own sphere he *was* God and his will was sufficient. Churchgoing was as perfunctory a social duty as being correctly dressed on any occasion. Mr.

53

Marriot's sermons were strings of gentle platitudes. Miss Ruthven had been agnostically inclined and her moral teaching had largely concerned itself with doing unto others as one would be done by and being true to oneself. So in Marion's joy there was no feeling of having sinned in a manner likely to invite punishment. She knew that the letter must be smuggled out and posted without Ellen's knowledge; but she had managed to post one earlier in the week, she could manage it again. And if it were slipped into the pillar box by eleven o'clock it would be delivered to Johnny's lodgings at about five and await him when he returned from work.

While Marion wrote Johnny walked swiftly home. He was jubilant; a not-inexperienced seducer he was able to measure the force of her response and felt that he was now sure of her. He had her now. He judged from the way in which the Draper girls were clad and guarded that Mr. Draper was a doting father; a few casual inquiries had informed him that there was no son in the family, nor even a nephew being schooled to take over the business. He did not delude himself so far as to think that a prosperous maltster would welcome a penniless shop assistant as a son-in-law; there would be protests; but if Marion stood firm and said, This is the man I love, the only man I wish to marry, the doting father would give in and very soon see the difference between Jean de Brissac and the ordinary employed man. Other people—Mrs. Marriot was one—had seen it. Jean de Brissac had great confidence in his charm, in his looks, his manners, even in his clothes.

He had known from an early age that his one hope was to make an advantageous marriage; family circumstances had taught him that. His claim to be connected with the noble family of de Brissac was not without foundation, but the branch to which he belonged had for three generations been

54

penurious, mere peasant farmers. His grandfather and his father had both married serving-girls with no dowries save physical strength and fertile wombs; but an uncle had married well and then, from the new sphere of prosperity, found a husband for one of his sisters. The old French sense of family was still active, however, and the young Jean was frequently confronted by the sight of his cousins, well-clad, well-fed, gently spoken, possessors of many enviable things. Manners and speech could be copied, clothes were occasionally handed down, on visits some of the possessions would be momentarily shared, but the real things—enough money to live without worry, a solid *bourgeois* position in life—one must attain for oneself. His immediate family thought that young Jean had done very well for himself when, after a long, gruelling, unpaid apprenticeship—*un apprentissage*—he became a chemist; but he was dissatisfied, seeing clearly that without money to buy or hire a shop of his own, he was doomed to life as a hireling. He had come to London because he believed, like many untravelled Frenchmen, that England was practically class-less, a place where the old system of arranged weddings had been abandoned. This, he quickly discovered, was far from true; and since in London his looks, his charm, his clothes went virtually unnoticed, he had thought that he might do better in a smaller community. So here he was in Bereham, with three failures as an adventurer behind him. One affair in London with his employer's daughter had led to his dismissal without that essential thing, a reference; from another angry father he had only just escaped by slipping out of his jacket; in Bereham Mr. Taylor had cracked his head with a stick. So far he had had no luck at all, but he now sensed that things would be different. For one thing Marion was different; she was serious, in the French sense of the word. She had dignity, intelligence and, he thought, strength of mind. He now knew that she had a sexually passionate nature.

He read her letter over one of those sustaining but often rather indigestible "teas" which Mrs. Fenner served up to her four young men lodgers. He was delighted to see that the letter contained nothing missish, no mawkish regrets over what had happened, none of the "it must never happen again" stuff. She was eagerly looking forward to this evening; she looked upon herself as his wife. A few more such evenings and he would begin to move towards the next stage, a meeting with Mr. Draper so that the maltster could see for himself that Jean de Brissac was no ordinary shop assistant.

When he first mentioned this idea to Marion he was astounded by her reaction.

"It would be fatal," she said. "If Papa ever knew that I had spoken to you, he would be so angry. I should never see you again. And life without you now, Johnny, would be quite insupportable."

"You think he would object to me because I am poor, and work in a shop?"

"No," she said truthfully. "Because you are a man. Papa does not intend either Ellen or me to marry."

"How can you know that?"

"Partly from what he has said when other girls become engaged or married. When Angela's engagement was announced, for instance. And on other occasions. Also, apart from that . . . After all, darling, I have lived with him for almost eighteen years. I *know* him."

"But unless I meet him and gain his approval we shall never make any progress, Chérie."

"Does that matter? We have so much, darling. We must not endanger what we have."

She was completely content with what she had. To her

56

romantic nature even the secrecy of it all lent an added enchantment. Each time in the day when she came down to her bedroom she would glance across the kitchen and see the door to the area, looking so ordinary and somewhere inside her something would turn over at the thought that it was not an ordinary door at all, it was the entrance through which love had come, and would come again. She had not felt a pang of envy for Angela, home again, everything forgiven and forgotten, a dark blue sapphire shining on her finger, preparations for a large fashionable wedding in June already going forward. How could Marion, with Johnny for a lover, envy anyone?

Jean de Brissac perceived that he had not been wrong in thinking that Marion had strength of mind—though he now called it stubbornness. He also perceived that if he were ever to make Mr. Draper's acquaintance it must be done without Marion's connivance. He underestimated her stated fear of and understanding of her father. Every now and again he had a dark suspicion that her reluctance to bring the whole issue to a head stemmed from her reluctance to make public the fact that she had fallen in love with a man of no estate. That she loved him, he could not possibly doubt; on the rather narrow bed installed so that the wardrobe could be accommodated in the small room, and in letter after letter he had adequate proof of her love, but in her repeated assertion, "Papa must not know," he saw equal proof of her reluctance to take the next, the necessary step. He decided that she must be forced to it.

On the last Thursday in May there came another of the annual landmarks in Bereham's social life, the Rectory Garden Party. Years ago Mrs. Marriot had observed that late May

57

usually brought better weather than June. Also June was crowded with other functions, particularly weddings.

This year she was right again; it was a beautiful day; there was a crowd of people, all in gay mood. The Rectory Garden Party was a bit of a hybrid combining a social occasion with the perpetual need to raise funds for the church. There were side shows, a competitive croquet match, a Hoop-La stall, another stall upon which some of the left-over articles from the Bazaar were exposed for sale; and in a ruinous summerhouse, draped with two old curtains and a rather handsome Paisley shawl, a fortune teller, an innovation this year. Mr. Marriot had been against it; fortune-telling smacked of black magic, of a belief in predestination, things not easily acceptable to a middle-of-the road clergyman. But Mrs. Marriot had overridden him, saying, "Alfred, what does it matter if it turns in an honest penny, or pound. I *know* it is all nonsense—so does everybody else. Whatever she says will be forgotten by next morning."

Ellen and Marion took their turn in manning the Hoop-La stall. Jean de Brissac patronised it—two shillings' worth—and won nothing. Marion, keeping up the pretence in front of Ellen that the whole thing was over and done with, turned aside in the little hot, canvas-enclosed space and busied herself with the mending of a toy, a model windmill which one of the hoops had injured. It was left to Ellen to say, "Good afternoon, Mr. de Brissac," and presently, "Oh, bad luck!" and "So near."

Papa seemed to know exactly when their turn of duty was done and was there, ready to conduct them, as soon as they were relieved, to the refreshment stall, a long white-clothed table set out in the shade of the cedar tree. Here again the ambivalent nature of the Garden Party was evident. Refreshments were not sold, but between the urn and

58

the teacups at one end the great bowl of fruit cup at the other there was a box labelled *"Repair Fund."*

Mr. Draper had seen to it that before his daughters took up their Hoop-La duties they had had a sustaining cup of tea, so he now guided them to the fruit cup end of the table where he was forestalled by a handsome, well-dressed young man who took the silver ladle and filled a glass and handed it to Ellen who said "Thank you," in a muted voice. The young man filled a glass for Marion. Mr. Draper looked at him closely. A stranger! On these occasions Mrs. Marriot called upon all available relatives and acquaintances, but they were always introduced. This young man had not been. So Mr. Draper said, "Thank you, I will help myself," and, in the deep shade of the cedar tree, he and Marion and Ellen stood and sipped. Only Marion knew that Johnny had manoeuvred an opportunity for the chance, casual meeting upon which he was set; and she had failed him. Ellen suspected that Johnny Brisket was dogging Marion. She said brightly, "Papa, let us have our fortunes told, please."

Papa said, "So long as you understand that it is a lot of nonsense, my dear, I have no objection. Suppose I go first. Mrs. Marriot said something about the woman being a gypsy. Let me see if she is clean and civil."

For a gypsy she was exceptionally clean and very civil. She asked, "By cards, by palm or by crystal, sir?" He chose cards and she shuffled them, asked him to cut, to choose. She said, "You are, sir, a very lucky man. Very lucky. You have had troubles which you have overcome. There are other troubles ahead, but you will overcome them in the same way." She then told him that he had excellent health and would see his eightieth birthday.

"Your next two customers are my daughters," he said. "I should be obliged if you would refrain from telling them anything of a sentimental nature. Or, of course, anything unpleasant."

"You are entitled to a third cut of the cards, sir," the woman said.

"I will not waste more of your time," Mr. Draper said in his most gracious way. She had been warned. He went out into the sunshine and said, "You may try her."

"You go first, Ellen, because you are due to help with the croquet. I have nothing else to do except help Mrs. Taylor and Angela to pack up the oddments."

Ellen chose to have her fortune told by crystal and the gypsy predicted for her a happy life. "You'll never want," she said. "You'll always get your own way—in the end. There's a little sorrow, but you'll get over it and live to a ripe old age." With that Ellen seemed quite content, somewhat to the gypsy's surprise; most young ladies wished to hear about handsome young men coming into their lives.

"For a shilling," Ellen said, emerging from under the Paisley shawl, "it really is very little. But all good."

"By palm," Marion said, offered her choice. She held out her hands and the woman, who had some skill in palmistry—the cards and the crystal were garden party trimmings—said, "Oh," and then hesitated. Nothing of a sentimental nature, nothing unpleasant. It left so little so say, particularly of hands such as these. "You're a very clever young lady," she said at last. "Yes, you have a good head on you. Health. Now there I must give you a word of warning. You must look to your health and be very careful not to overdo things. In any way." She was, within limits, a conscientious palmist and there were other warnings which she could have given, but she had been warned herself. She looked up, met Marion's grave stare in the shrouded light, and said, "You understand me? You need to be careful *over everything*."

"Thank you," Marion said.

Three shillings earned in little over as many minutes; sixpence of each for the fortune teller, sixpence for the repair fund; that was the arrangement, satisfactory to both sides. As Marion ducked under the shawl the gypsy muttered a charm, a few meaningless words, their origin lost in antiquity, something you said when you heard bad news or tried to sell linen pegs to somebody with a cold or a cough.

"It was the perfect opportunity," Johnny said quite angrily. "I timed it exactly and all you had to do was to greet me and effect an introduction with your Papa. You behaved as though I had been a waiter."

"Darling, please, please, do not be cross. It really was as much as I could do to take the glass and say 'thank you.' You looked so handsome and I thought how perfect it would be, how happy I should have been, could I have taken your arm and spent the remainder of the afternoon in your company. Johnny, please. Perhaps it was cowardly of me, perhaps I should be ashamed, but I know Papa. Compared with him Mr. Taylor has an angelic temper."

Not a very clever thing to say. She hastened to amend it.

"Truly, Johnny, my caution is not entirely selfish. If Papa thought I was sufficiently interested in you to make an introduction, he might do *you* some damage."

"How could he damage me?"

"He would find a way. He is ruthless. And jealous. Nobody understands. Look at this." She reached out and took from her bedside table a copy of *Adam Bede,* leather-bound, gilt-edged, a very handsome book. "I won, not this book, a cheaper copy, as a prize at school. I was very proud of it and *stupid* enough to say that I should always value it because Miss Ruthven had thought me worthy of it and had written my name in it. Do you know what Papa did? He said he had never read the book, so he borrowed it and spilt a cup of coffee over it. He then bought me this copy, better in every way, except for the inscription. Look, *From her loving Papa*. It should read, *From her possessive Papa*. And Johnny that is true. Nothing must come to us but by his gift."

"Then what future have we? If you are so much afraid of him, or ashamed of me, to what can we look forward?"

"To the time when I am twenty-one and may marry whom I wish without asking his permission."

Much good that would do! Four valuable years wasted. She could see that he was hurt, diminished in his own opinion. She cast about in her mind for some restorative.

"Darling, do you like brandy?"

"Cognac? Of all the things I miss in England, cognac is foremost. In France even a working man"—he used the term in self-derision, with that eloquent twist of the mouth—"can drink cognac occasionally."

"This may not be very *good* brandy," she said humbly. "It is what Ada uses . . . but it is on this floor. Tomorrow I will take some from the sideboard . . ." That would not be difficult. From shopkeepers and workpeople Papa demanded value for money but he was not one of those men who marked the level in the decanter or counted bottles.

She fetched, from the kitchen cupboard, and Johnny accepted, the peace offering. It even made him change the subject.

"This," he said, "may settle my stomach. It was again today the fat-and-lean pork which does not agree with me."

He was inclined to talk about his stomach. Perhaps because he was French.

She watched him sipping.

"Is it all right?"

"It is not good. Nor is it bad," he said. Inside herself, in her heart, in her head a more intoxicating brew fermented and presently she said:

"Johnny, I know that my behaviour this afternoon has made you doubt the sincerity of my love. There you are mistaken. Listen, I love you so very much that I am prepared to run away and go with you anywhere, somewhere where Papa could not find us, and marry you. Once we were married he could do nothing."

Of all the dim-witted ideas!

"Chérie, it is unthinkable. It would be to condemn you to a life of poverty."

"I would not mind being poor, darling. If we were together I should enjoy it."

"You have never been poor. Never in your life have you spent a day not knowing where your next meal would be or where, in the night, you would sleep. I have had that experience and I assure you it is nothing to enjoy. On what I earn—even if I found another job immediately—the two of us would be very poor."

"But *I* could work, Johnny. And I would. In London I should be free to work. I would do anything. I would scrub steps." Her face was alight with eagerness.

"London is a place where for every job, even the scrubbing of steps, there are four people ready to cut each other's throats. And for one bed there are four people willing to do the same."

"Some other place then, darling."

He said sombrely, "For the poor all places are alike. No, no, my Marion, for us the only hope is to act as you should have acted this afternoon. Allow your father to know me and let him see that you love me. Unless you are ashamed of loving a chemist's assistant."

"Johnny, you know that that is not true. How can I convince you? I swear that if this afternoon I could have said, Papa, this is the Marquis de Brissac, it would have made no difference. No difference at all. If we wait for his consent we shall never be married."

She and Ellen had compared notes on their fortunes and it was significant that marriage was mentioned in neither.

Unappeased, Johnny left without any love-making. In fact, for her it should not have been possible tonight. But she was two days late this month. Not that two days was anything to worry about.

o　o　o

AMONGST THE JUNE WEDDINGS WAS ANGELA'S. MARION and Ellen had seen little of her lately. Her fiancé's family was large and scattered about the west of England from Westmorland to Wiltshire; she had made visits to them all. She had also stayed with her rich godmother who lived in London and was providing her with a lavish trousseau.

Ellen was to be one of the six bridesmaids. It was her second time to serve in that capacity. Marion, just an inch too tall, had never been a bridesmaid. Mamma and Marion were both to have new dresses, very fine, Mamma's dove-grey satin, Marion's garnet-coloured silk, banded with velvet. And for her eighteenth birthday Papa gave her a pair of garnet earrings. "I know," he said complacently, "that it is said that most men are colour blind. I am not. I carried the colour in my eye pretty well, I think."

"They are very beautiful, Papa. And a perfect match. Thank you very much."

He then wished her many happy returns of the day.

64

Wearing the splendid dress and the matching earrings Marion stood and sat and knelt and heard Mr. Marriot's gentle parsonic voice say "for the procreation of children" in such a way that it could not offend any lady in the congregation who affected to dissociate cause and result. Now envy was there, not of the paraphernalia of marriage, of marriage itself; envy of the giving and taking of the simple gold ring which meant all the difference in the world; for it was now over a month. Behind and within the seams which tapered into the elegant waistline of the new dress a process had started, a process which, short of a miracle, could not be halted and must culminate in such shame that just to think about it made her tremble and sweat. Several mornings lately as she was dressing and the scent of the breakfast bacon reached her she had been overcome by nausea and been obliged to scurry through the kitchen to the water closet in the area—the other one being a flight and a half of stairs away. She wondered if Ada and Betty had noticed, thought it strange. Then there was the washing. The Draper laundry was collected each Monday by a gnarled old woman with a little cart drawn by a gnarled old donkey. It was returned on Thursday. The old woman was hardly likely to fret about certain omissions, but Betty who unpacked the clean clothes and put them to air might well have noticed.

Kneeling for the last time she prayed. *God help me. Let me come on or let Johnny marry me. Please God, I could not face the disgrace.* She prayed with great earnestness but without much faith. She had never been pious and it seemed a little dishonourable to turn to God simply because one was in trouble. In trouble! That was the phrase used for girls in her state. In trouble. The organ boomed and Mamma gave a little shiver. Then they trooped out into the sunshine.

65

That night she gave Johnny the brandy which was now a regular offering. She kept it in a bottle plainly labelled DR. MARTIN'S HAIR TONIC. The label also mentioned the long list of things the stuff was good for; dry hair, greasy hair, falling hair, fading hair, dandruff, alopecia. The bottle was replenished from the cooking brandy—"I reckon we need a new bottle," Ada would say—or from the cellarette in the sideboard. "Getting low," Mr. Draper would think. She watched while Johnny drank, hoping the liquor would provoke an acceptive mood. He asked a few questions about the wedding and she answered him rather absent-mindedly, thinking about what she must presently say.

"Darling, I know I have said this several times and that the idea finds no favour with you. But now . . . Johnny, it is urgent. We must get married. You see . . . I am going to have a baby."

He asked the ritual, banal question, "Are you *sure?*"

"Quite sure. I'm more than a month overdue. I'm sick in the morning. I'm sure. And, oh Johnny, the relief of being able to speak of it . . ." She began to cry, leaning against his shoulder, and he made some perfunctory gestures of comfort while his mind span.

Any respectable man, and Mr. Draper was nothing if not respectable, confronted with a pregnant daughter would prefer marriage to scandal. Any man in his right senses would prefer a shop assistant son-in-law to a grandchild born illegitimately.

"This needs thinking about," he said.

"I have thought. Day and night. Since I was sure I have thought of little else. Darling, in just over three weeks time we go on holiday to Yarmouth. Now that opens the way for us. Banns must be called on three Sundays and one of those about to be married must live in the parish." She had obtained this information from a book called *An Encyclopaedia of Knowledge* which had also been terse and lucid on the subject of pregnancy. "If you went to Yarmouth on your next half day and found a little church and gave some boardinghouse as your address . . . Do you see? At Yarmouth Ellen and I are allowed to bathe. Papa also bathes, but from a different part of the beach. It would be quite easy for me to make the usual excuse not to bathe. Then I could slip away and we should be married and nobody, not even Papa, could do anything."

Except disown and disinherit you, you foolish girl.

A pregnant, penniless wife, presently a baby. A bleak prospect.

"I do not think that this is the right way to go about things."

"Can you think of a better?"

"I can think of nothing worse. There is now, or soon will be, the child to think of. Three of us, Marion, to live on a guinea a week. Decent places take only single men—and in London charge fifteen shillings a week. We should end in a slum, probably sharing a bedroom, crawling with bugs with another couple. In the yard there would be one tap or one pump, one privy serving anything up to thirty people. I know, Marion, I *know*. I have experience. Would you wish your child—our child—to be born in such conditions."

"There is no alternative."

"There is. Your father must be faced with the truth. You say he is a very possessive man. It is possible that he would feel possessive towards his grandchild; wish it to be legitimate, to be properly brought up. With you, Chérie, he may be angry, with me very angry indeed. But not with the child. There will be some unpleasantness and then all will be well."

"You say that because you do not *know* him. I do. Sooner

than tell him the truth I would kill myself. I would sooner die than face Papa in such a situation. Johnny, unless you go to Yarmouth and make arrangements for us to be married, I will drown myself."

"Darling, that is wild talk. But wait . . . Something has occurred to me. I also have a plan. Listen . . ." It was positive inspiration and he outlined it in detail. He was angry when Marion said, "It would not work. Papa would give you ten shillings, perhaps."

The last words were typical of something in her that he deplored. A harsh realism suddenly cropping up through the romantic unworldliness, disconcerting as a pebble in mashed potato. It jarred.

"Well," he said, "will you try it?"

"If I must, I suppose I must. But, darling, I know my way would be better. I know. Please, Johnny, try my way." She said, "Please Johnny," much as she had earlier said, "Please God," without much hope. Men were not open to reason, or persuasion.

Jean de Brissac's vanity persuaded him that before the testing moment came Mr. Draper should know that he was not the fellow to be dismissed with ten shillings.

So on the next Sunday morning, impeccably dressed, he took up his position outside the church door. It was a fine morning, so Mamma had come to church and had suffered from the organ. She and Ellen walked out ahead of Marion and Papa. Johnny did not greet Ellen, but as Marion came level with him he swept off his hat and said, "Good morning, Miss Draper." It was a shock; he had not warned her of this plan and the session of nausea had been very severe that morning. She just managed to say in a low, stilted voice, "Good morning, Mr. de Brissac." Papa raised his hat the

68

stipulated half inch and then said, in an audible, rather truculent voice, "Who *is* that young man?"

Ellen was alert; she was now certain that Johnny was dogging poor Marion and since Marion gave no answer to the question Ellen looked back over her shoulder and said with a disarming lightness, "Someone with whom we became acquainted at the Literary Salon, Papa. Mrs. Marriot could never get his name right. She called him Mr. Brisket."

Mr. Draper received this information with a silence that might or might not be ominous. When, halfway along Honey Lane, Ellen said, "Oh, that purple clematis is in flower. I always associate it with the holiday," and received no reply both girls knew that the silence *was* ominous. So did Mamma who, as soon as home was reached, did her vanishing trick, so quickly and quietly that no one could say whether she had made for the stairs or the drawing room. The girls were prepared to vanish too, but Mr. Draper, hanging his hat upon the stand, said, "Wait," and turned into the dining room. The table was set and Betty, coming and going, had not always closed the door at the head of the kitchen stairs. There was a faint but definite odour of roast chicken and green peas with mint. Let me not be sick! Please God!

"You may pour my sherry, Ellen." Ellen removed her gloves and performed this service. "Now," Papa said, taking the glass, "who is that very forward young man? I noticed and disapproved of his manner at the Garden Party last month."

He is my love; my husband in all but name; the father of my child. My *stupid* love who must always know best.

"As Ellen said, Papa; he attended Mrs. Marriot's Literary Salon."

"And does that justify his familiarity?"

"Papa, he merely wished us good morning."

Ellen could see that Marion looked pale. She always looked *pale*, but there was a difference; the same difference as there was between ordinary full-cream milk and skim. Bravely she moved to the defence.

"You must not take exception to his manner, Papa. He is French. They have different ways."

"And what else do you know about him?" Mr. Draper said, turning his penetrating stare upon his younger daughter.

"Only that he assists Mr. Freeman in his shop, Papa."

Typical, typical. Like master, like man. That rabid, non-conformist liberal would employ a foreigner, a dressed-up jackanapes. It was, in fact, worse, far worse than he had thought. At the Garden Party Mr. Draper had half-recognised the enemy—young, personable . . . And it was true that had Ellen said that the potential enemy were a well-connected young man he would still have been annoyed. But a shop assistant!

"A shop assistant!" he said in a voice of infinite scorn. "And since when, I wonder, have shop assistants, impersonating gentlemen, been accustomed to greeting young ladies *by name?*"

I must not be like Judas; I must not betray my lord; at least not wholly.

"Papa, he is a rather unusual shop assistant. He is a gentleman and a man of education," Marion said.

Ellen said loyally, "Yes indeed, Papa. His talk to us about the French novelists was generally agreed to be the best we had heard. I did not understand a word, of course, but those who did had nothing but praise."

"Arrant nonsense," Mr. Draper said. "A dressed-up popinjay. Encouraged by Mrs. Marriot with all her Jack's-as-good-as-his-master-if-not-better notions. This is what comes . . . What is the world coming to? If he ever accosts either

70

of you by name in future you are not to reply. Say nothing, look straight ahead. Well-mannered men of that class know their place. They remove their caps and they should be acknowledged. But upstarts . . . 'Good morning, Miss Draper!' indeed, they must be firmly kept in their place. And there is another thing. Whatever idiocy the Marriots intend to perpetrate next autumn, you will have no part in."

I shall not. I shall be married to Johnny and far away; or I shall be dead.

The curious thing was that Mr. Draper had what he called "a nose." He was a practical man and not given to fancies. But more than once, ten, a dozen times he had refused to give credit to firms which seemed sound enough, firms with nothing wrong with them upon which one could put a finger. Then, when the crash came, he was not one of the creditors who must take a shilling in the pound. Even over so small a thing as a faulty horse, dosed and tortured into giving a good performance, his nose served him. "No, it's not what I want," he would say. And it was the same with samples of barley. And now, as his daughters went off to remove their hats and he drank his sherry, while his mind informed him that the situation might easily have been more embarrassing—a young man backed by Lady Mingay even, some offshoot of the Taylor-Everett family, Mrs. Marriot's nephew—his nose now recognised in its blind, instinctive way some threat from the chemist's assistant. It was vague, it was undefined, but it said quite clearly, Watch out for that young man.

"Darling, that was a foolish thing to do."
"Because once again you failed me, Marion. If you had only said my name, introduced us, I had the words ready. I

71

watched him all through the sermon. It bored him. I had a suitable comment, something that would have arrested his attention and made an appeal."

"Johnny, could you have heard him. Merely because you *greeted* us. Ellen and I had *such* a scolding! Darling, you do not understand . . . But there is time yet. We could be married in the *second* week of the holiday . . . If you would only do as I say. Darling, I know that your plan . . . It might work with *some* fathers. With Papa it will not. Please, Johnny, please, if we are ever going to be married, if this child is to be born in wedlock, there is only one way. *My* way. I do not mind being poor. Somehow we could manage. I have a few things, of no great value but they would fetch something. Johnny, if it came to the worst we could buy a barrow, sell flowers or fruit or fish . . . Darling, if you would only realise that there is nothing to hope for from Papa and if your plan fails, as it will, as it must . . . Johnny I cannot bear it . . . I simply cannot bear it." They were sitting side by side on the bed and she turned away, towards the pillow end and wept violently, her sobs muffled, her clenched hands beating on the bed rails.

She knew that he was wrong.

He knew that she was wrong.

She was frantic.

He was adamant.

o o o

THE ANNUAL HOLIDAY AT YARMOUTH WAS, LIKE EVERY-thing else in the Draper household, a matter of routine. The Drapers never stayed in a hotel—open to all and sundry —but in a boardinghouse kept by a Mrs. Radley who had a house, Sea Vista, overlooking the South Beach. Her best apartments, two bedrooms and a dining-room-parlour, facing the sea, were booked from year to year for exactly the same fortnight, chosen so that Mr. Draper might be fortified for his busiest season when the barley was harvested.

It would have been foolish to pretend that Mrs. Radley's beds were as comfortable as those at home or that her food was in any way comparable to that served by Ada, but the holiday was the only real interruption in the year's routine and it was valued accordingly. Preparation for it began well in advance. Trunks and valises were brought down from the box room and set to yawn in the sunshine. The word holiday found its way into almost every conversation. A new hat, a new dress, new shoes, a new parasol for the holiday; this to be done before the holiday, this to be deferred until after the holiday; this not to be contemplated even, because of the holiday. Had the Draper family been planning to emigrate there could not have been more stir and bustle. On one dreadful occasion there had been so much stir and bustle that nobody had remembered to cancel Papa's papers. He had thought of it as soon as he was in the train and had grumbled all the way to Norwich, where, changing trains, he had been able to send a telegram. Such an oversight was unlikely to happen again.

Nothing else was likely to happen and everyone knew it. Life at 10, Alma Avenue was simply lifted up and set down in Sea Vista; but there would be the sea, the sea air, the sea sky stretching infinite towards the east; a change of scene. For Mamma no piano and nothing to take its place; though there was always the hope, shared by Ellen and Marion, that Mrs. Radley's apartments which did not face the sea might be taken by a family of whom Papa could bring himself to approve. It had happened; admittedly only twice within Marion's memory, but it might happen again.

Ellen and Mamma talked about and prepared for the

73

holiday in the usual way; Marion, feeling slightly unwell, but terrified of seeming different, pretended.

o o o

LADIES WHO WISHED TO BATHE USED WHAT WERE CALLED bathing machines, conveyances not unlike caravans but set lower, on smaller wheels. Each had a door at either end, and a pair of shafts. A lady entered from the landward side, fully dressed. The old woman who owned the machine cried "Hup" to the horse, hitched to the seaward end, and it advanced into the sea, knowing exactly where to halt— when the water was a shade more than belly deep. The lady then emerged through the front door and slipped modestly into the sea, wearing her bathing costume. This was made of thick navy-blue serge and consisted of a pair of drawers reaching halfway down the shin and a kind of tunic extending from collarbone to knee, and of elbow length. One could have little white frills at neck and elbow and at the ends of the drawer-legs, but to do so was considered to be very dashing and daring; to abandon the regulation navy blue and choose instead grey, or buff or even cream, was to be almost abandoned.

In the water the ladies enjoyed, for the only time in their lives, freedom of movement; no corsets, no clinging skirts. Elderly ladies, advised to bathe for their health, remained staid, bobbing and plunging conscientiously; younger ones, made lively by the informality of the circumstances, frisked like porpoises, splashed one another, laughed and emitted screams of mock terror. While they enjoyed themselves the old woman unhitched her horse and harnessed it again at the other end, ready for the short return journey that would convert a sea nymph into a sedate lady, fit for the public eye.

74

The Drapers had arrived on Saturday, too late to bathe; there was no bathing on Sunday. Mr. Draper had taken stock of the family on the other side of the house and decided that they were not to be known. Very common indeed; the sort of people to whom one might say good day if one came face to face with them in the doorway, but certainly would not offer any encouragement, such as a remark about the weather.

This was disappointing, but on Monday at the bathing place, Ellen quickly found a friend, a girl named Florence, very gay and dashing; her bathing costume was cream-coloured and her manner what Papa, should ever he meet her, would call "pert." They were mutually attracted and frolicked and laughed together, leaving Marion to her thoughts. Marion seemed not to mind; indeed on the first day she said, "I am taller than you. I must go out farther to submerge my shoulders."

She was still undecided. Go Johnny's way which had perhaps one chance in a thousand of being successful; or take her own?

"You're a bit venturesome, young lady," said the old woman who owned the machine they patronised. "It's a sandy beach and sand can shift. You could find yourself out of your depth in no time at all."

Undecided on Monday: on Tuesday: on Wednesday. It was fine weather; the holiday atmosphere, with, in their case, nothing but the holiday atmosphere to sustain it, was infective. She was eighteen. Life was—or at least could be—so good. Trust Johnny and take the one in a thousand chance? Go your own way?

No decision could be forever deferred. Thursday came. Another beautiful day.

The actual area where the bathing machines operated and

the ladies went in and out was roped off, but the bit of rough pathway, ambitiously called the Promenade, was free to all. A few louts, residents or day trippers who could not afford to patronise the offered entertainments or the places of refreshment at the other end of the beach, would gather and stare, hoping for some revelation, a momentary glance of a female figure, clad in wet, clinging serge. At a time when a female ankle, exposed by the lifting of a skirt to avoid a puddle, was something upon which lascivious eyes could feast, the ladies' bathing place was an attraction. Real ladies ignored the watchers, and their calls and their whistles. Florence counted them. "Six today," she would say.

Florence was fortunate. When she came to bathe, a carriage, two sleek horses, and man in a cockaded hat brought her, deposited her, and waited. Ellen and Marion were fortunate too. Mrs. Radley's house overlooked the South Beach and they had only to cross the stretch of sand and marram grass, the path that pretended to be a promenade and they were home. Others were less lucky; fully dressed they had to walk past the louts who chanted, "I sawyer; I sawyer in your drawerser. Your drawers dropped, your belly flopped. I sawyer."

"Oh, look," Florence said on this Thursday morning. "A different-looking vulture!" Ellen looked and recognised Johnny Brisket. She was surprised to see him there, amongst those rude, ill-dressed, ill-behaved louts. He looked completely out of place. He wore a natty summer suit, light tan in colour, trimmed with braid of a darker shade and a white straw boater hat with a bicoloured ribbon.

She waded and splashed her way to Marion and said, "Look! Fancy Johnny Brisket with those louts!"

"Fancy," Marion said, not even looking. "Ellen, dear, your chin is practically awash. Go back."

Now, now was the moment; the decision no longer to be deferred. Johnny's plan could never work. She had known it from the first and been a fool to agree. In a sharp, self-revealing moment she saw that to the natural instinct of self-preservation, in her case had been added that something more, the intent of the gravid female to protect . . . She had allowed herself to be talked round, but she had never been certain of anything but her own power to avoid the issue. And that was still hers.

She turned and walked deliberately into the glittering sea. She lost her footing, was lifted, buoyed up, rolled over, smacked down. I am going to die; I have done with it all . . . She had thought of water as a soft thing, something to be yielded to, a blessed, obliterating embrace. In fact it was hard . . .

The old woman, having taken the horse to the rear of the machine, had come back to sit on the front shaft and smoke her little black pipe. The place where Marion had gone down was too far out to be under the casual supervision which she exercised over her bathing ladies. Johnny stood by the barrier, waiting for the waving arms, the screams for help that had been prearranged.

It was Ellen who screamed. She would have gone out to where Marion was rolling over and over, now visible, now submerged, but Florence caught and held her and joined in the screaming.

Johnny jumped the barrier and ran into the sea. He had said to Marion, "Never for a moment will you be in danger. I swim like a fish." He could swim, after a fashion, but in effecting the life-saving exercise which was to bring Papa to his knees from gratitude Johnny had counted upon a living, conscious collaborator, not a limp inert corpse.

The old woman, moving without haste, but with every

movement certain and economic, unhitched her horse, clambered astride and turned him into the sea. "Hup," she said, and when he halted at the usual level, just over belly deep, she said "Hup" again. She snatched Marion up and laid her across the horse. "Catch hold of his tail, if you can," she said to Johnny. She allowed no time for this act, nor did she look back to see if it had been performed. She owed a certain duty to her bathing ladies; none to a stranger.

"She's dead! Oh Marion, Marion," Ellen said.

"Give us a chance," the old woman said. Marion lay face downwards across the horse's withers and the old woman beat her across the back. Anger as well as a desire to resuscitate weighted the blows. I warned you. Headstrong. Getting bathing a bad name. Thump. Thump. Thump! The seawater was expelled in spurts, like vomiting.

"She'll do," the old woman said, hearing the gasping intake of air. Marion's hair hung straight and limp, reaching almost to the ground. Water streamed from it, and this water was reddened.

"Oh, but she's hurt," Ellen wailed.

"You're up at Sea Vista, ain't you. Run on ahead. Tell them to get a bed ready. And send for the doctor." Ellen sped away. The old woman said "Hup" again and the horse moved forward. Some people followed. "There's nothing to stare at," the old woman said sourly, but they still came on.

Mr. Draper had already bathed, and invigorated by it and a brisk rub down, he took his *Times* onto the verandah outside the sitting room and was about to settle down when some slight commotion drew his attention. He looked out and saw Ellen, in her bathing costume, soaked and clinging—as bad as naked, not even a towel, as he said afterwards—running towards the house. Behind her came the plodding old horse, two other shameless females, one in a pale costume looking even more naked than Ellen, and a group of the Peeping Toms. In the one immediately alongside the horse Mr. Draper, even in that moment of shock, recognized a fellow townsman. That impertinent shop assistant.

Mr. Draper remained in control of himself and of the situation.

"It's Marion," Ellen gasped. "She's hurt. Doctor!"

"Find yourself a wrap," Papa said, before snapping out his orders. The maid to run for the nearest doctor; the odd-job man to help him in getting Marion upstairs. "On the sofa, no need to soak the bed," he said with great presence of mind. To Mamma who had come, white-faced out of one of her mysterious retreats, and to Ellen, now decently covered by a dressing gown, he said, "Dry her off and get her into a nightdress." This, he thought angrily, was the result of Dr. Barlow's drivelling talk about the value of sea bathing as a restorative of health in the summer when Ellen had suffered a series of sore throats and showed signs of being delicate. He'd actually spoken of "Dr. Yarmouth." Well, there'd be no more of that!

He went down prepared to deal sternly with the riffraff. Mrs. Radley had forestalled him and there remained only the old woman, anxious to exonerate herself, and Johnny waiting for the fructification of his plan. "Stay on the verandah, then," Mrs. Radley said. "One body dripping about is one too many. And get that horse off the flowerbed." The old woman's skirts were soaked, but they were seldom completely dry and she suffered no discomfort. Johnny was beginning to shiver and his face wore the dirty look of a naturally dark complexion turned pale.

"Now," Mr. Draper said, "I understand you wish to see me."

"Yes sir," the old woman said. "I don't want you to go thinking it was my fault or giving bathing a bad name. I always warn my ladies. Twice this week I warned that young lady, but she's a bit headstrong. And I keep a sharp look out. I'd have had her safe sooner but for interference." She gave Johnny a scathing look of contempt. "People think they can swim. Interfering!"

"I had the privilege of rescuing the young lady," Johnny said.

"Rescue. All you did was screech 'Marion,' waste of breath. And get in the way. Had to be rescued yourself. Drag on the horse you were."

"But for me she would again have hit her head on the groyn." That was true. Under the gently rippling surface there had been a strong drift towards the groyn and half his efforts had been directed to keeping himself and Marion clear of the stone. Neither of his hearers was prepared to give him any credit.

"You'd both be drowned now, but for me and old Trot here."

Johnny had now attained his wish, a face to face encounter with Mr. Draper, in circumstances favourable to himself. But the plan which had begun to go wrong when Marion failed to give the signal, continued to misfire. Not a word or look of gratitude, no handshake, no slap on the shoulder. Apart from one flicking glance which took in everything, Mr. Draper had paid him no attention at all.

"Well, so long as you know," the old woman said. With amazing agility she scrambled astride her horse again and turned him beachwards. In her job time was money.

"Wait," Mr. Draper said. The whole episode had angered him extremely, but the old woman, turning against the young jackanapes against whom his nose had warned him, had ingratiated herself. He worked his sovereign case. Click, click, click! Three gleaming gold sovereigns lay in his palm and were transferred to her horny, salt-encrusted hand.

"Well, sir," she said. "Thank you indeed. There was no call . . . I wasn't looking to be paid . . ."

Even to her he had expressed no obligation but she noticed the omission only in a roundabout way. There were a lot of gentleman who'd have been more lavish in thanks and less generous with their money.

"And now," Mr. Draper said, before Johnny could speak, "we must be fair, must we not? Whatever you did or did not do, you appear to have ruined a very fine suit." His glance, his tone showed exactly what he thought of summer suits trimmed with braid. "You come from Bereham, do you not. Then I suggest you go to Ager's in the Buttermarket and tell him to supply you with another suit and charge it to me. Up to three pounds." It was a calculated insult. Ager's did not make suits for gentlemen; it was the place from which Johnny's fellow-lodgers, all working men, bought their horrible best suits.

Johnny told himself, and fully believed, that he could have said something then which would have done something to convince Mr. Draper of his difference, but he was unlucky again, for the doctor, who lived close by, came up, all in a flurry, carrying his bag.

Johnny lay on the firm warm sand and allowed his clothes to dry on him. The ridiculous rules that governed the issue of a cheap day return ticket compelled him to wait in Yarmouth till six o'clock. He lay and drank the cup of humiliation to the dregs. He had failed entirely; he had made a very poor showing; he had been dead unlucky. He could see now why Marion, poor darling, held her father in such awe. A horrible, inhuman man, a veritable ogre. And she had been right in predicting the outcome of the exploit—he will give you half a sovereign. Absolutely right, for the most expensive suit Ager could supply would cost fifty shillings at the very outside.

Though the sun and the sand were warm and his clothes were drying, he shivered again. He had suffered a shock as well as a humiliation. He had, like Ellen, believed that Marion was dead. In his hands she had felt like a corpse, across the horse she had lain like a corpse. And thinking her dead he had realised not only that all his chance of an advantageous marriage had vanished, but that he had lost someone who had loved him and whom he, as nearly as his nature would allow, had loved. He lay and remembered how she had offered to marry him and be poor; and then how she had begged and beseeched him to marry her because of the baby. He saw, as clearly as he would ever do, that he had treated her badly and that even in her most desperate moments—terrified, and rightly so, of that dreadful father —she had never once reproached him; never once said, You got me into this, you must get me out!

By three o'clock he was thoroughly dry; he had break-fasted at half-past seven and on the six o'clock train he would be back in Bereham long after the meal that Mrs. Fenner called tea would be over and cleared away. A man must eat. So he got up, brushed the sand from his clothes and tried to smooth out the worst of the creases. He had no hat and no man with the slightest claim to respectability went about hatless. He went back to the bathing area, deserted now, with the tide at its lowest and there was his hat. It had been cast up, sodden, but it also had dried in the sun, and apart from the fact that in the ribbon the colours had run, it was undamaged. He put it on his head, not knowing that it was at a less jaunty angle than usual and went in search of something to stay his stomach which, left empty for too long, or fed the wrong things, was always a trouble, with a pain as though a rat were trapped there and trying to gnaw its way out.

As he approached the more frequented area of the town he came upon the various places where honest pennies were turned by services to such day trippers as himself. Some were stalls, some were merely stands on a corner. All were manned by old women, sisters of the old woman, of all the old women who ran the bathing machines. Yarmouth herring, cockles and mussels, cups of tea, pigs' trotters, shrimps, jellied eels, sandwiches. He stopped by a corner stand where one of the old woman's sisters—but wearing a big white apron —sold tea and sandwiches. And flowers. In a bucket below the rickety little table that held the provender, there were bunches of sweet william, red, white, pink, and striped. Johnny paused there, bought himself a cup of tea and a sandwich which purported to be ham but was in fact the fat-and-lean pork which his stomach rebelled against. Even the mustard could not conceal that fact, plentifully as it had been applied. Johnny removed the meat and dropped it on the ground. A lean, watchful cat, with six kittens to support, pounced upon this unusual offering—most people only dropped crusts, and all too few of those. Johnny ate the thick, sparsely buttered bread which made the rest of the sandwich and sipped, cautiously, at the stewed dark tea. The rat in his stomach turned its attention to this provender and Johnny began to feel better. "And I'll have a bunch of these," he said, pointing to the flowers.

While the old woman lifted them from the bucket and shook off the slime which announced that the flowers were no longer fresh, Johnny tore the corner from the sheet of paper that served as a tablecloth. On it, using a well-painted gate as desk, he wrote, *"Get well soon. J."* At Sea Vista he went to the back door, hating it, but not wishing to risk another encounter with Mr. Draper. Not yet! The day would come when the score would be made even. But not today.

The little maid who had run for the doctor answered the door.

"How is Miss Draper?" Johnny asked.

"She's got the concussion." She said the word proudly.

"She is still unconscious?"

"She's alseep like. But they expect her to wake up any minute now."

"If you'll give her these . . . when she wakes."

"All right. That's the potatoes boiling over."

Over the whole of Sea Vista a thunderous atmosphere brooded. It was not merely that there was, under a shared roof, someone who had almost drowned and now, snatched from Death's jaws, lay unconscious in the second best bedroom. Mr. Draper's displeasure was making itself felt. The common, not-to-be-known little honeymoon couple felt it. They had gone straight out and bought a bunch of hothouse grapes.

"Much too kind," Mr. Draper said, not even putting out a hand to receive the offering. "I am afraid that it will be some time before my daughter will be in a state to appreciate your kindness. I really think it would be better if you enjoyed them yourselves."

Enjoying them the bride said, "But it was rude."

The groom said, "I'd say sensible. I mean after all . . ."

Mrs. Radley came in for her share of condemnation. "I am so sorry about Miss Marion, sir."

"If I remember rightly, Mrs. Radley, you recommended that particular bathing place. I suspect that it shelves sharply. I see no other way to account for the accident. I am of the opinion that bathing should be restricted to the farther end."

And she had been planning to expand, to build on, to have not two but four sets of apartments, all occupied by people who liked to be within such easy reach of the bathing machines.

But these little snubs and rebukes were merely froth. The real target of his rage lay elsewhere, protected for the moment by unconsciousness.

Ellen and Mamma took turns at watching by the bedside. Mamma was admirable, but Ellen, silly child, cried and cried. On the one occasion when Mr. Draper tried to get to grips with Ellen, she had sobbed so loudly that the couple across the hall had come out, "Is she dead? Is she dead?"

o   o   o

THE WATER WAS HARD, NOT SOFT, BUT AFTERWARDS IT washed up into enchanted lands, full of things that she had never seen, but had imagined, waterfalls, glassily smooth and musical, palm-fringed beaches, forests full of flowers and forests hushed with snow. Usually her progress from scene to scene was unimpeded but sometimes there was need for effort and a voice urging her, "Marion, please! Marion, try!" The voice sounded like Ellen's, but Ellen was not there. She was completely alone, yet not in the least lonely.

Then she was in the dark and someone was crying. Dark because her eyes were closed. She opened them. The light was not bright, but painful, so she closed them again and then in a series of brief squints saw Mrs. Radley's second best bedroom; and by the window Ellen crying. But I had done with all this. This is not where I should be. Desperately she willed herself back to the place where she had been alone and untroubled; but that was useless and something must be done about Ellen's weeping.

"What is the matter, dear?"

"Oh! Oh, Marion. My dearest, dearest sister . . ." Ellen ran to the bed, checked herself in the very act of throwing her arms around Marion and instead took her hands, very gently, and very gently put her warm wet face down to administer a butterfly kiss. For a moment she was quite incoherent, saying what a long time, saying how worried, saying how shocking. Then she said, "How do you feel?"

"My head hurts." There was another pain, too; the kind one learned never to complain about.

"You hit it on one of those horrid groyns." She quickly added what, in Marion's place, she would have wished to hear. "The mark will not show. It is under your hair. Dearest, perhaps you should not talk. I must tell them, too." Mamma would be relieved; about Papa she was not certain, he had shown no anxiety, nothing but anger, as though Marion had done something more than usually annoying.

"Where are they?"

"Having dinner. It is Friday now. You have been unconscious for a day and a half."

"Ellen, what happened?" She meant what happened *after*.

"I think you fainted. I think you should not have bathed yesterday."

What did that mean? Exposure? Disgrace?

"You came on. As we brought you back to the house." Again she said what she would have wished to hear. "Nobody noticed."

Oh! Out of that trap! Free. Her own woman again. The terror lifted.

"And then? Ellen, sit on the bed. Tell me everything."

86

"I think we should not talk too much . . ." But Ellen, rarely for long out of favour, had suffered in the last day and a half, and welcomed a chance to talk. "Well, I went back to Florence, then I turned and you had vanished and I saw you going over and over in the water, so I screamed and then . . ." She gave an exact account of the happenings.

"Did Papa see Johnny?"

"Truly, dear, all that can wait. I must tell them. And you must have something to eat, or at least to drink."

"I will not take a sip until you have told me everything." Whatever it was, she could bear it. Even if Papa had struck Johnny it would only serve him right for being so stupid and stubborn.

"Yes. Johnny and the old woman stood on the verandah quarrelling about who had saved you. Johnny Brisket said he had, and as I told you, he did try, but he muffed it. Papa gave the old woman three pounds and told Johnny to go to Ager's and get himself a new suit, to that value."

Marion startled Ellen by laughing, not very loudly, but for quite a long time.

"Well," Ellen said a bit dubiously, "now that you no longer like him, I suppose . . ." A few thoughts about love flitted through her innocent mind. Look at Angela, crazy about Johnny Brisket, engaged the next day almost to another man; Marion, crazy about Johnny Brisket and then all at once not caring at all, and laughing to hear how he had been insulted. Sent to Ager's! "What is less amusing is the way Papa has taken it all. And Johnny made it worse. He brought a bunch of flowers early last evening. That girl, Rosie, didn't give a very good description, but there was a scrap of paper in the middle of the bunch. It said 'Get well soon. J.'. and Papa wanted to know who knew you were ill. Marion, on the spur of the moment I couldn't think of anyone except that other woman we bathe with—she did come, with Florence, up to the house; or the old woman who keeps the bathing machine. Papa said neither one would have written in such familiar terms, or sent flowers so nearly dead. They were almost dead. Sweet williams."

"They would be," Marion said.

Every single thing he had ever given her had been dead; killed by greed, selfishness, pigheadedness. Even the baby was dead. When she thought how she had begged and besought him to marry her and give the baby a name . . . No, he must know best.

"Papa," Ellen said, using Papa's own phrase, "is very displeased."

Marion lay and contemplated Papa's displeasure without a tremor.

"He'll get over it," she said.

"I am in disgrace for not wrapping myself in a towel. I'm never to bathe again. He saw Florence in her cream costume and said she was fast and I am never to speak to her again. But," Ellen said bravely and with truth, "I do not mind, now that you are back with me. Until I thought you were dead, dearest, I did not . . . at least not fully . . . know how much I loved you."

"Dear Ellen. I love you too." She had done with them all, except Ellen, innocent, loyal Ellen.

Once Miss Ruthven had quoted Dr. Johnson's remark that the prospect of being hanged concentrated a man's mind. "I wish I could threaten this whole class with hanging," she had said. The prospect of death might concentrate the mind; facing death, taking the steps necessary to drown oneself did more than concentrate, it *changed*. Sir, the sage might have said, suicide gives a man a sense of proportion.

88

"Florence called this morning—luckily while Papa was bathing," Ellen said. "She wished to know how you were. I was obliged to tell her that I was not allowed to bathe again. And she gave me this, as a keepsake." She showed Marion a small gold locket, shaped like a heart, set with seed pearls and turquoises, slung on a thin gold chain. "I can never wear it, can I? And I feel I should give her something, but Papa might notice."

"Give her my garnet earrings."

"But he would certainly notice them—I mean that you were not wearing them."

"Whether Florence has them or not I shall never wear them again." Nor the garnet dress that she had worn for Angela's wedding. Nor the street wear in which she had entered Freeman's chemist's shop and worn to the Literary Salon. There were a dozen things she would never wear again; never do again; never think again; never feel again.

"Well, if you are quite sure. Do you not like them? But how should I get them to her?"

"You could post them."

"It sounds absurd," Ellen said, "but I do not even know her surname, or her address."

It was, in fact, what Papa had called it, a silly girlish fancy of which Ellen should be ashamed.

"The doctor said I might take a short walk tomorrow. It is a short walk to the bathing beach. And it is like the library, Ellen, Papa has not forbidden me to speak to Florence . . ."

He had, in fact, not addressed her directly since the accident. While she lay abed he had never paid her a visit, sent a message or made an inquiry. And when, shakily, she had ventured down to the family table, he had ignored her entirely except to say, "Pass your sister the salt," or "Marion has no bread."

Back home it was different. They returned, on Saturday, to a house which had been thoroughly cleaned and scoured during their absence and to a supper which put Mrs. Radley's dinners to shame. Immediately afterwards Mamma had fled to her piano. Through every holiday she had suffered the deprivation and this holiday had been exceptionally trying.

"You stay here. I want to talk to you," Mr. Draper said, when the girls, murmuring about unpacking, would have made their escape. "Now, I intend to get to the bottom of this and I will not be put off with evasions. A young man, of whose conduct I have already had cause to complain, was among the oafs at that bathing place. Was that by pre-arrangement?"

"I was never more surprised in my life," Ellen said. "I told you, Papa."

"I heard your account, Ellen. I wish to know what Marion has to say."

"I can offer no explanation, Papa. Except that it was Thursday when day trips are available and a few people who cannot afford to watch the puppet and Pierrot shows do tend to congregate."

"That is not a satisfactory answer. As he made his ineffectual attempt at rescue he screeched—that was the old machine attendant's word—'Marion,' Can you account for this use of your Christian name?"

"In a moment of panic, perhaps. He knew my name. Mrs. Marriot used it often enough; her Salon was very informal. And I was, by all accounts, about to drown. I think it would have seemed more extraordinary if he at that moment had said, 'Miss Draper'."

"Are you attempting to start an argument?" That was one of his tricks. He reasoned; other people argued.

"No, Papa. I am trying to explain."

"Actually, it might not have been him," Ellen said. "I was screaming all the time and I may have used Marion's name. In fact I am sure I did. There was so . . ."

"That will do, Ellen. Unless you wish to confess that you also sent the flowers, with an intimate-sounding message, signed '*J.*'."

Sarcastic facetiousness was another weapon, and against Ellen it served. She changed colour.

"Well?" Papa asked, looking at Marion.

"I never even saw the flowers, Papa."

He had said that he wanted no evasions, and evasion was all he was getting.

"There is altogether too much coincidence about this affair," he said. "First"—he laid the forefinger of his right hand in the palm of his left—"the Garden Fête. That young man did all he could to draw your attention. I observed his manner though I said nothing then. Second"—he laid another finger alongside the first—"the incident outside the church door. And now this. He was not merely in Yarmouth but at the bathing station which you patronised—incidentally the least accessible—at a time when you were bathing, waiting, I suspect, for you to emerge. A rendezvous? Was it?"

"No, Papa."

Ellen had an uncomfortable feeling that Papa knew more than he had yet revealed. Guilty memories of those spring evenings in the Cloister made her insides quiver. If they had once been seen and a whisper started, it would go the rounds, slowly perhaps but with deadly certainty.

"When did you last see the fellow?"

"Outside the church when his manner gave you such offence. He may have been at church on subsequent Sundays. If so I did not notice him."

"Then how do you account for a bunch of wilting flowers? And the message?"

"Is there any evidence to connect them with him?"

What had got into the girl. To answer a question with another question was perilously like answering back.

"Ellen saw him," Mr. Draper said, knowing that this was untrue, but he knew the worth of shock tactics.

"Excuse me, Papa, I did not. Rosie handed me the flowers. I did not see them delivered."

"Then I was mistaken. I am still far from satisfied." His look of disapproval included them both. "I need hardly point out that this has been a disastrous holiday. Ellen takes up with a thoroughly fast, immodest female and behaves hysterically over what was, after all, a simple mishap. You, Marion, brought about the accident by ignoring instructions. Your Mamma was too much worried to benefit by the change. And as for me . . ." He did not describe his own pitiable state.

"I am sorry, Papa," Ellen said.

"And I was punished for my rashness." Marion put her hand to her head where the wound, healing nicely and bristly with the regrowth over the shaven patch, still throbbed.

Papa saw that he was making no headway at all. The thought, They are united against me, formed in his mind.

"I am displeased with you both. Go and unpack," he said.

He saw that he had been far too lenient. Allowing them to have any part in Mrs. Marriot's runagate schemes—where all this had started. Allowing them to bathe. He tried to think of any other liberty which had been allowed and could now be curtailed, but he could think of none at the moment. Nor could he bring himself to believe that his infallible nose had misled him. Discontentedly he settled down to his cigar and a perusal of the weekly journals which awaited him.

At the point where one flight of stairs went up and one down, Ellen said softly, "At one point I was really afraid . . . Marion, you look quite exhausted. I will come and unpack for you."

"I should be grateful. My head still thumps when I stoop."

In the dining room Mr. Draper brooded. He knew what he would do about the chemist's assistant. He wished he could see an equally simple way of driving a wedge between Ellen and Marion. Ellen was fundamentally docile, yielding, dutiful. Marion had never been wholly satisfactory and this evening he sensed a change for the worse, difficult to define, but there, like a bad odour.

Presently he rose, went into the hall and opened the drawing-room door. In the unlighted room Mamma was playing passionately. He said, "My dear, that is enough of that infernal din." She lifted her hands instantly and in the sudden silence he could hear, drifting up the stairs, the sound of girlish laughter, some words, more laughter.

He was bound to go downstairs to lock the kitchen door. This evening he went more quietly than usual, intent, indeed, upon eavesdropping. The door of Marion's little room stood open; it was like looking at a stage. Marion lolled on the bed. The trunk yawned. Ellen had one of Marion's hats on her head. "But it is true," she said. "What suits you never suits me. I look like Mrs. Andrews." Mrs. Andrews had a face like a horse and a tongue like a viper. Ellen said, and it was a creditable imitation, "I wouldn't say this to just anyone, but I heard it on the best authority. That elder Miss Draper fell in the sea because she was inebriated at the time. Like Father, like daughter, I always say."

They both laughed. Giggled. Had he hoped, or feared to overhear something relevant to what he still thought of as a mystery; had he wanted, or dreaded to learn that the laughter arose from the fact that they had fooled him? He went to the door of the room and said, "Ellen. I thought I told you to go and unpack." It was rebuke, but genial.

"Mine won't take me five minutes, Papa. I came to help Marion, because of her head."

"To help is one thing; to do it all quite another. Unless you exercise care, my dear, you will end as your sister's serving girl. A common fate with younger sisters, I believe. You must not allow Marion to impose upon you and turn you into a Cinderella."

Mrs. Andrews at her most venomous could not compete with Mr. Draper.

"I have just finished, Papa. And I did *offer*."

"Marion has always been thought clever. Come along."

That he thought, turning away, was the line to take— until he thought of something better.

Ellen followed him out. As she did so she put her hand behind her back and waggled her fingers in a gesture that was both conspiratorial and derisive. Papa was not to know it, but by his behaviour towards poor Marion who had almost died and then, miraculously come back, he had lost ground with Ellen.

o   o   o

MARION UNDRESSED, PUT ON HER NIGHTGOWN AND ROBE and lay on the bed, awaiting Johnny's tap. It was sure to come; the holiday lasted exactly a fortnight.

She had made no plans at all, how she would act, what she would say depended upon so many things, most of all the effect of his physical presence. She had chosen to die rather than play his silly futile game and her mind was capable of regarding him as a fool who would not listen to

94

reason, and as a weakling who had failed her in her hour of greatest need. About her mind she knew; about her body she was less sure. It would be an interesting test. She was too young and inexperienced to realise that the test had already been made.

He tapped.

She said, "Hullo, Johnny."

"Darling," he said. "Darling. It has been a lifetime. Marion, I knew nothing, heard nothing, I have been in purgatory."

It was all right. His voice had lost the power to stir the marrow of her bones.

"Chérie, let me in. There is so much to say."

"Something has been done to the door while we were away."

"Kiss me, then. Kiss me through the bars. As in old times."

He stretched up, she crouched. Their lips met; the old raging hunger was less than a summer thunderstorm remembered in midwinter and even so only remembered for the damage it did.

"I cannot stay in this position," she said, withdrawing. "To stoop hurts my head."

"Ah, yes; your poor head. How is it, darling?"

"Better, but not yet well."

"When I saw . . ." He spoke at some length of his feelings on that calamitous day, recapturing as he spoke some of the genuine emotion that he had felt and which in some way he had enjoyed, proof that he was not simply mercenary, a fortune hunter. "And then your father," he said. "He is a monster, a man of no feeling. I did not know. I did not believe . . . Darling, I have done so much thinking. The plan failed . . ."

Yes, because it was idiotic and I was an idiot ever to consider it for an instant.

"I told you how it would be."

"Chérie, I know. You were right. I was wrong. I see now that he will never consent. We must marry as you planned."

It would happen like this! When I begged and implored, when I was half crazy with fear . . . When you and only you could help me, would you lift a finger? No, all you could do was mount a masquerade, and even that you mismanaged. Swim like a fish, and once your feet left land, glad to clutch at an old horse's tail. You wanted some of Papa's money; and you got it. Three pounds' worth of credit with the cheapest tailor in the town.

"Darling, are you angry with me?"

Not angry; finished.

"You have no need to marry me now. What with being knocked on the head, or nearly drowned—I lost the baby."

He said, "Oh," not knowing quite how to take this piece of news. To express the relief he felt might offend her; women were curious creatures; the prospect of having a baby might be appalling, the loss of it nevertheless a grief. Perhaps that accounted for her strange, off-hand manner. She was usually lavish with endearments. "And you are sad about it?"

"If you had done as I asked, Johnny. If you had made the arrangements. If we had been married, I should have felt the loss very much. In the circumstances it would be idle to pretend."

No doubt about it, she was angry with him. But he knew he had only to get his hands on her, be able to kiss her properly and all would be as before.

"There will be another—after we are married." He managed to inject a good deal of sexuality into that sentence. She remained unresponsive. "Because we are going to be married, my darling. In *your* way. I wish to talk to you about it. But not like this. Will you have mastered the new door by tomorrow?"

"No. I shall have no opportunity. Papa will be home all day. Besides it would not be safe. I am still regarded as an invalid, looked in upon from time to time. Papa and Ellen had just gone when you knocked."

"Then when shall I be able to see you—properly?" There was that note again.

"Perhaps in a week."

"But we have already been apart for a fortnight." She knew that she should have told him the truth, but she knew he would argue and after the journey, the scene with Papa and the discovery that her body was now as indifferent to Johnny as her mind had been for a week, she lacked the physical strength. She would write to him. Tell him not to come again. A letter could not be argued with. "I have so much to tell you. I have investigated a thing called a Special Licence. And the joke is that your Papa will pay for it."

"Another plan?" The weariness in her voice was unaffected. "I really am too tired even to talk any more."

"Poor darling, of course."

It was probably exhaustion which made her seem so different. She seemed unlike herself because, as people said, she was not herself. People were always coming into the shop seeking some remedy because they did not feel like themselves. Very considerately he said, "Do not stoop again. Give me your hand." He kissed it very lingeringly, back, front, on the wrist.

Going home he thought again, with complacency, of his deal with Ager. First he had explained the situation, setting five, not three pounds as the limit. This did not astound Mr.

Ager, a gentleman like Mr. Draper would naturally think in such terms. Then Johnny said that the summer now more than half over, he did not need a suit this year; so would Mr. Ager oblige him by letting him have the five pounds and charging Mr. Draper with that amount. The tailor minded very much indeed. It was the equivalent of lending five pounds with no interest; and think of the book work involved. Humiliating himself—for Marion's sake—Johnny suggested that he would be willing to take four. That made more sense and three-pounds-ten made even better. So the deal was made. And the buff and tan suit was as good as new after Mrs. Fenner had worked on it with a damp cloth and a flat iron. Not that three-pounds-ten was much of a nest egg; but it would pay for the Special Licence, and the fares to London.

o   o   o

THE BELL ON THE DOOR JANGLED. MR. DRAPER STEPPED INTO Mr. Freeman's shop, noted the mahogany and ground glass enclosure behind which the dispensing was done, the shining orderliness of the shelves, the absence of muddle.

It was just after nine o'clock on Monday morning, and the owner of the chemist's shop, not the assistant, was on duty.

"Good morning, Freeman. I want a shaving brush. The best you have."

Mr. Freeman was not exactly surprised to see Mr. Draper in his shop. The mills of God ground slowly, but they ground exceeding small. Industry and enterprise were, in the long run, rewarded, and Baxter was definitely on the decline.

Mr. Freeman busied himself. "All pure badger bristles," he said, laying one brush after another on the counter. "Only the handles vary; wood ten shillings, bone fifteen, solid ivory twenty-five."

"I think this will do," Mr. Draper said, indicating the ivory-handled one.

"And you couldn't find a better brush wherever you looked," Mr. Freeman said, faintly resenting the implication that his best was hardly good enough. "You could have a silver-plated handle, but no better brush."

"I'll take it."

He put a sovereign and two half crowns on the counter. Mr. Freeman busied himself making the neat little parcel, white paper, red sealing wax. "I can have it delivered if you wish."

"By that impertinent young man of yours?"

Mr. Freeman's errand boy was twelve, employed because his mother cleaned the Baptist chapel. He was stupid, humble, and afflicted with a cleft palate. How could he ever have been, how could even Mr. Draper say that he had ever been impertinent.

"Bobby?" Mr. Freeman said, taken aback. "You can't mean Bobby."

"I do not know how many people you employ, Mr. Freeman. But this I do know. Baxter's business is on the decline and quite a number of people would transfer their custom to you, but for the fact that one of your assistants is, as I said, inclined to be impertinent."

"I have only one assistant . . . French by origin. Is it possible that French politeness could have been misunderstood? In what way has he offended? I would call him to give an account of himself, but he is not well. Something that his landlady provides on Sunday upsets his stomach . . . this is not the first time he has been late on Monday. He makes up the time, of course. Did he offend you in any way, Mr. Draper?"

"Only indirectly. But enough to make me think again over

99

a move I was contemplating—the transference of my custom to you, Mr. Freeman." He paused to allow time for Mr. Freeman to do some mental arithmetic. "One hesitates to expose one's womenfolk to insult. Tales get around you know."

"If you'll excuse me asking, Have you got the right tale, Mr. Draper? I can hardly see de Brissac acting insultingly, to a lady. There must be some mistake. What did he do? Or say?"

"I do not propose to go into detail. What I can say is that if you want to catch Baxter's slipping trade, you'd do well to get rid of the fellow."

In almost any other shop in Bereham this would have been sufficient; and even Mr. Freeman was tempted. He knew about the ban and would have been glad to see it lifted. But his nonconformity reared up, he was not going to be bullied. He also remembered that lately even Mrs. Marriot, the rector's wife, had begun to use his shop.

"I am very sorry, very sorry indeed that my assistant should, in some way, have given you offence. I have never had any other complaint; I'd say he was popular rather than otherwise. And I could hardly dismiss a man, satisfactory in every way, on such flimsy grounds."

Mr. Draper picked up his little parcel.

Flimsy?

Flimsy! The custom of about fifty families, besides his own. But nothing was ever gained by allowing temper to show. He said "Good day" civilly enough, and stepped out into the sunshine, making for Baxter's, halting to study its dismal façade. It needed paint. The pleasant bowed window displayed no single item of merchandise; just the flagons of coloured water, very dusty; Freeman's shone like jewels. The rest of Baxter's window was covered with dingy, dusty, fine wire mesh on which the words, once written in gold, *P. Baxter. Chymist,* were still faintly discernible. Dating back to the time, Mr. Draper reflected, when some ancestor of the present John Baxter had not been able to spell the name of his own trade. He went in and to the young man behind the counter said:

"I want a shaving brush. A good one. Badger bristles."

The boy made some show of willingness to search; but the best shaving brush in this shop was a hog bristle. "The best hog though, sir. Russian." Mr. Draper then said, "Is your master about?"

"He's in the back, sir. Just finishing his breakfast. I'll call him. But that, sir, really, is the best brush we have."

"I don't doubt it," Mr. Draper said, almost genially. "Don't bother. I'll go through." He was not, naturally, on social terms with a shopkeeper, but he was an old and valued customer, and both of them worshipped at St. Mary's.

The interview was not prolonged. Mr. Draper went straight to the point, ignoring any hurt he might cause by his criticism, his use of phrases like "slipping downhill," "lagging behind." Mr. Baxter said simply that financial straits were responsible and that family responsibilities were responsible for the financial straits. His eldest, a daughter, was a widow with two children. "Her husband's folks give them a home, but she has no spending money except what I send her." His eldest boy—very clever—was at Cambridge, his second in Edinburgh, his youngest at the Grammar School. "It all takes money, Mr. Draper. I'm often hard put to it to pay my bills, leave alone go in for renovations and such."

Mr. Draper did not criticise or deplore this paternal concern and ambition. His own father had made sacrifices in order to give him a good education. He said, "It was a good business once, and could be again. And it stands on one of the best sites in the town. Have you ever thought of raising a mortgage?"

"Often enough—and I may be driven to it. And then I shall have the interest to meet, as well as the bills."

"Not if no interest were charged."

"And who'd take a mortgage without asking interest?"

"I might," Mr. Draper said. "On certain conditions, of course."

(This act of spite, decided upon in the course of a short walk, was eventually to prove one of his most profitable investments. Four years later a firm of wholesale chemists sent out their spies who, like Mr. Draper, knew a good site when they saw one and reported that for so thriving a business, for premises so recently brought up to date, the price would be high. And although Mr. Draper had received no penny of interest, he had a document, carefully drawn up by Angela Taylor's father, which established him as the virtual owner of the place.)

o o o

MR. DRAPER WENT HOME IN A GLUM MOOD THAT MONDAY. All through the day when his mind had not been occupied by other concerns, he had brooded over Freeman's lack of co-operation—he looked on it now as defiance. True, he had set revenge on the trail, but it would be some time before the results were seen. Moreover, ruining Freeman, as he hoped to do, would not get rid of that young man.

Ill humour did not spoil his appetite. He ate a plateful of one of Ada's "summer" soups, a crystal clear consommé, and then carved the cold joint, giving himself the pinkest, juiciest slices because he knew that women, always contrary, preferred their meat overdone. Then he looked about and said, "Where is the chutney?"

Chutney and mustard pickle were usually served with cold beef, brought to table in heavy cut-glass jars.

"I'll fetch it, Papa," Ellen said, pushing her chair back.

"You will ring the bell and then sit down."

Betty came in, a little breathless and flustered.

"You rang, sir?"

"If you will look about the table you may see *why*."

Betty looked, clapped her hand to her mouth and said:

"Oh. The chutney. Sorry, sir." She vanished.

"That girl is becoming slap-dash," the master of the house said, gladly seizing upon this trivial excuse to exercise his sense of grievance.

Mamma emerged with—in the circumstances—some degree of heroism and said, "It was my fault. I should have noticed when I looked over the table."

"We do keep a maid," Papa said.

"I know. But she has rather much to do these days. Ada is so incapacitated."

Papa, still awaiting the arrival of the chutney, refusing to start without it, pounced upon this chance to be unpleasant.

"If Ada can no longer pull her weight, she must go."

Mamma blanched and shrivelled. She regretted saying anything. Really, only silence was safe. But Ada and her piano were the two things that had never failed her. She felt bound to protest.

"Ada still cooks well. It is just that she is no longer very active and so all the running about falls on Betty. And Ada has no home. Where could she go?"

"To the Poor House. What do you think we pay rates for?"

Mamma made a little whimpering sound.

Marion said, "To send Ada to the Poor House would be like sending a faithful old horse to the knacker's yard."

Betty panted in, "I'm sorry I was so long, sir. I had to open a fresh jar."

"And now that it has arrived am I supposed to dig it out with my fingers?"

Betty, in her flurry, had forgotten the spoon.

Marion said, "That is all right, Betty. There are spoons here." She rose and went to the sideboard and opened the drawer where, nested and shrouded in baize, the "best silver" lay. It was fashionably heavy and ornate, used only when they entertained.

Papa looked at the spoon, brought into service on an ordinary day and felt an impulse to repudiate it. But Betty, sly creature, had scuttled away. To ring the bell, recall her and send her for one of the plain, very old, worn-thin-by-long-use-and-polishing spoons, would further delay his meal. So he dug into the chutney, Ada's own special concoction; Ada would give a recipe to anyone who asked for it, but she always seemed to withhold some vital thing. Having helped himself he passed the jar along and proceeded to eat in silence. His hunger was presently assuaged; his sense of injury was not and presently he turned to Marion and said, very smoothly, "Did my ears deceive me, or did I hear you say to that careless girl, 'That is all right, Betty'?"

"Yes, Papa. That is what I said. I meant that there was no need for you to wait any longer. A spoon was here."

"About Ada, also, you made a remark?"

"Yes, Papa. I remarked that to send Ada . . ."

"I heard. What has come over you, Marion, I am at a loss to say. I have borne a great deal one way and another, but disruption of my household I cannot and will not tolerate. I am of the opinion that the blow on your head had more serious results than were evident. I feel that you are not fully responsible and that a stay at Heatherton would be advisable."

The horrible word "Heatherton" exploded in the quiet room.

Ellen said, "Oh, no, Papa, please. Not there!" and even Mamma looked distressed.

"And what, may I ask, do you know about Heatherton?"

"A lot," Ellen said incautiously. "Mr. Taylor had something to do with that case. A great many things were said then that couldn't be put in the papers because of libel."

Mr. Draper remembered the case. An old man, a medical, not mental patient, had changed his will and left three thousand pounds to the woman who owned and ran the place —a Miss Rose. The family had contested the will. There had been talk of undue influence, of coercion, of downright intimidation. Miss Rose had emerged triumphant and in possession of her legacy, but with a curiously particoloured reputation. There was no lack of ex-patients ready to vouch that Miss Rose had been consistently kind to them or other patients confided to her care. Other people had said other things and Miss Rose herself, asked if she had ever struck a patient, replied, "Of course I have. And shall again I am afraid. It is the most effective way of dealing with incipient hysteria in the mentally unstable. But Mr. Woodhouse was not in that category at all. He was in the terminal stage of carcinoma and in need of nursing."

Locally, after that, Heatherton had come to be regarded as a place to be avoided and nowadays those under Miss Rose's roof tended to come from distant parts of the country.

"If a statement is likely to be libellous when printed, it can hardly be accepted as Gospel," Mr. Draper said. "If Marion goes to Heatherton determined to behave herself, and to get better, she will have nothing to fear. Ring the bell, Ellen, we are ready for the pudding." Ellen, beginning to cry, did as she was told. "And if you propose to make an exhibition of yourself, go to your room. Enough tears were shed at Yarmouth to suffice for a year."

With Ellen gone and the pudding served, Mr. Draper looked at Marion who had sat throughout as though the talk concerned some other person. At that moment a really abject apology, a promise of better behaviour in future, might have saved her. Mr. Draper might, between accepting the apology and the promise, have had a few cogent things to say about playing upon Ellen's emotions and allowing her to become too dependent. But Marion for a time said nothing and when she did speak what she said confirmed his self-inculcated suspicion that she was not in her right mind.

"It will be further expense for you, Papa. It would be cheaper to let me go back to school and then on to St. Hilda's."

"Back to school, at eighteen! How absurd. You appear to have taken leave of your senses—and to have lost your memory. I must remind you that I positively forbade you ever to broach that subject again. As for expense, you can hardly have failed to observe that I never consider expense when it comes to providing the best for you all." As he said this he looked from his sullen, unresponsive daughter to his wife who managed a nod of the head and a rearrangement of her features, too slight to be called a smile. It was true; disapproving as he did of the kind of music that appealed to her, Jonathan had provided her with the very best grand piano.

At the end of that dismal meal Mr. Draper went to his study and hesitated between a forthright, "Dear Miss Rose," and "Dear Matron." It was the salutation to which Miss Rose was entitled, for before an eccentric old uncle had left her his large country house, with contents, but not a penny for its upkeep, Miss Rose had been matron at St. James's, one of London's famous hospitals. Finally he compromised with "Dear Madam." That letter completed, he wrote another, beginning, "Dear Dr. Barlow . . ." He wrote that one in the comfortable assurance that had he been about to suggest that Marion was suffering from rabies, Dr. Barlow was unlikely to contradict. He was not only the Drapers' family doctor, he was the pivot of a very progressive insurance scheme, devised by Mr. Draper himself. For years all but the feckless few of the Maltings' employees had contributed twopence a week to the scheme; to each twopence Mr. Draper added a halfpenny. The scheme was of benefit to all; to the workmen who received medical attention that they could not otherwise have afforded; to Mr. Draper because men properly treated and not left to homemade remedies based largely on super- stition, recovered more quickly and more thoroughly; to the doctor who received a small but certain income, and who had by his manner and rather drastic treatments taught the Malt- ings men—and their wives—not to come running to him with trivial ailments; not to disturb him at mealtimes, not to wake him from sleep. Dr. Barlow would readily agree that in a house with so many stairs, and only one maid active, with a vaguely ailing mother, a sister so easily provoked to tears, there was no place for a young woman who, though the wound on her head was healing well, "was not herself." Was in need of care and attention.

Yet, in his own fashion, the old man had integrity. Having examined Marion, he said:

"I would suggest the medical, not the other side, where sorry sights and sounds might retard rather than aid re- covery."

"I propose to leave that to Miss Rose." Mr. Draper poured

sherry. "The truth is, Marion's condition is variable. This evening you saw little wrong with her. Is that not so?"

"The wound is healing well. Her manner seemed composed."

"Yet last evening, believe it or not, she was pleading with me to send her back to school! She has had her eighteenth birthday!"

"I see," Dr. Barlow said, sipping his sherry.

o   o   o

"IT IS VERY SHORT NOTICE," MAMMA SAID, "BUT I HAVE NO doubt that Ada will rise to the occasion."

A dinner party, arranged with almost dizzying haste, for Friday, and this was Wednesday, would surely show Ada at her best. Mamma was anxious to rehabilitate Ada, infirm as she was becoming. Artichoke soup, lobster mousse. Grouse; no, too early; duck; Ada's special tipsy cake.

"It is rather short notice," Mr. Draper agreed. "It so happened that Mr. Taylor—who has just done a useful job for me—expressed a wish to meet Mr. Horridge. Hoping for a new client, of course. Not that it will come to anything. Horridge, I have no doubt, has his own man of business, probably in London. But I made the gesture, hurriedly, because the Taylors start their holiday next week. And we owe the Andrewses hospitality."

"Ada will manage."

There was altogether too much emphasis upon Ada. It smacked of reproof. As though Ada, whom he regarded as expendable, was in fact indispensable.

He said, quite affably, "Ada's efforts will be adequate, I do not doubt. But there is more to entertaining than the food. Betty needs stricter supervision. You know, my dear, you are inclined, when at the piano, to lose all thought of time and mundane things. I think that, as a precaution, I shall lock it until after the party."

Mamma accepted loss of her piano as stoically as Marion accepted banishment to Heatherton. Ellen wept enough for all. She wept as she said, "Dearest, I am sure you have only to apologise and it would not be too late even now." Miss Rose had written to say that she could accommodate Miss Draper on Monday. "I cannot bear to think of you in that horrid place. Promise me you won't let it drive you crazy. Angela said lots of people, not a bit mad to start with, did go mad through being locked up with people who were, and treated like them. And Miss Rose is so bad-tempered they say."

"I am not exactly unaccustomed to ill humour."

"It has been bad lately," Ellen admitted. "You won't be away long, will you? I honestly don't think I could bear this house without you. It was bad enough when I was young." She remembered the two years when Marion was at school and she was not. "I just hope and pray that Papa will forget that silly idea that a young lady should not go out alone. Without you, without Angela and Mamma so inactive . . ." She drooped at the prospect. Then she mopped her eyes and her soft little face took on an obstinate expression. "Anyway, of one thing I am determined. You are going to have dinner with us tomorrow."

"Ellen, please. I do not mind in the least. If you speak of it you'll get into trouble, too. It will in any case be a very dull party."

"There will be a new face. Mr. Horridge sounds exciting. Imagine just walking about in Africa and picking up gold."

"Who said he did?"

"Angela. Mr. Taylor said he is very rich indeed. He made himself into a company or something."

Ellen went about persuading Papa to change his mind about allowing Marion to be present at the party with a certain amount of subtlety. A sidelong attack.

"I wish," she said, "that Marion felt well enough to face company for just a little while."

"In her present state Marion is not fit for company," Mr. Draper said.

"But the Andrewses are invited." *A non sequitur* if ever there was one.

"And what," he asked testily, "has that got to do with it?"

"*You* have no idea, Papa, what Mrs. Andrews' tongue is like. She restrains herself in front of gentlemen. But I *know* that if she does not see Marion tomorrow and then hears that she is going to . . . that place, by Saturday, she will be saying that Marion was chained to the bedpost. Or something worse."

"Ridiculous! People go to Heatherton to be nursed after breaking a leg."

"Anyone Mrs. Andrews knew who did that she would say he broke it kicking his wife."

Mr. Draper gave one of his rare laughs.

"Then perhaps Marion should be present. On the strict understanding that she is not to be surly or jump about doing Betty's work. And something must be done about that bald patch. She is convalescent but there is no need to be unsightly."

"I will see to it, Papa."

o   o   o

THE BEST DINNER SERVICE HAD BEEN TAKEN OUT AND washed, not merely dusted; the best silver had been rubbed with a chamois leather, the best glasses repolished. Two extra leaves in the dining table, now spread with the best damask cloth which bore within its starched white-and-silver surface a design of pheasants; napkins of the same damask had been made into water lilies. In the centre of the table an epergne sprouted, at various layers, white roses, white carnations and trails of asparagus fern. Exercising an unusually severe supervision, Mrs. Draper was sure that all was in order.

And also in the drawing room. The door to the little conservatory was open and that lent a feeling of space, the pot plants on the slatted shelves gave colour. On the table at the other end, sherry and Madeira, suitable glasses to the forefront of the vast silver tray, and to the rear of it the blue-hued syphon, the whisky, the tumblers from which the gentlemen would drink later in the evening. On the closed piano was what was beginning to be called an arrangement of flowers. Against the black, polished surface the flowers, mainly white, in a white bowl looked well, but Mrs. Draper looked at them with disapproval. Nothing should stand upon a piano. But the piano, locked, used as a stand for flowers, shared her mental withdrawal. Impossible, this evening to play those stupid, sickly, sentimental little tinkling tunes. And thank God for that! She went upstairs to dress.

In the basement kitchen Ada pulled the soup aside and stooped down, painfully, to look into the oven to see how the ducks were doing. The lobster mousse, her own special secret, lobster being a tough thing and few people knowing how to reduce it to a creamy smoothness without loss of flavour, and the tipsy cake, there again her own, stood ready on the dresser.

The ducks were doing nicely; but straightening up from the oven Ada said, "I don't know, Betty girl. I somehow feel that this'll be the last party I shall see to. I'm getting past it, and it comes hard on you."

"When you go, I go," Betty said. "And there's that blasted bell."

"Heavens, that'll be the Andrewses," Ellen said. "Darling, it is the best I can do—and though I say so, not bad."

She had pulled Marion's hair—so plentiful on one side, mere bristles on the other—up to a kind of coronet on top of her head, the end of the tail brought over to conceal the shaven spot and the scar. A little action with the curling tongs assured that the falling tail curved inwards. "I think it is rather becoming," Ellen said. She was aware that she was not very clever—but her hands were.

Betty said, "Mr. and Mrs. Andrews," and thought, what a lot of rot. They know each other. It was a kind of game, designed to keep idle footmen employed. "Mr. Horridge. Mr. and Mrs. Taylor."

Inside the drawing room Mr. Draper took over. He named his daughters in a peculiarly casual way. "Mr. Horridge," he said, "my daughter Marion, my daughter Ellen."

Later he would have something to say to them both. A fringe, a Piccadilly fringe! The very badge of a prostitute, except that the Princess of Wales . . . Not that that was any recommendation. Mr. Draper had nothing against Alexandra but he disapproved strongly of the Prince of Wales's goings on . . .

But, as usual, he controlled himself. "Sherry or Madeira?" He was at his best when dispensing hospitality.

Mr. Horridge, subject of this hospitality, found himself slightly confused. In the year and a half that he had spent in Norfolk, he had gone through a peculiar social mill, the upper grindstone plain avarice, the lower simple snobbery. He had denied that he was related to Sir Charles Horridge of Swaffham, or to Dean Horridge of Hadleigh. "No. Never heard of them in my life. Nor them of me." Disappointing, but at least the man was honest. And presentable. And rich.

Mr. Horridge knew the drill. But in this comparatively modest house—no stables, he had been obliged to leave his horse and gig at the livery place, in Honey Lane—there was a difference; Mr. Draper was certainly not trotting out his fillies. He introduced them by name, rather as a dog owner might say "This is Rover. This is Fluff." And the girls, after giving him the briefest acknowledgement, had gone off to join the older women at the far end of the room. Probably both spoken for. They were a good-looking pair; one very pretty in the ordinary way; the other one most unusual. A beauty!

It took Mr. Horridge several minutes, several peeps, to learn that neither Ellen nor Marion wore the outward tokens of betrothal. He found himself hoping that in Marion's case this was true evidence. The more he looked, the more he liked. He was not a romantic man and he was past his fortieth birthday, but he found himself thinking, There is a face I could live with; something secret, mysterious about it.

Mr. Draper intercepted one of Mr. Horridge's looks and for once his instinct failed him entirely. No wonder the man stared. The hair style was deplorable; and why on earth was she wearing that shabby old green frock? Heaven knew she had a wardrobe crammed with newer, more sumptuous ones.

Mr. Horridge would have liked to step over and speak, first to all the ladies and then to Marion in particular; but he had lived in Norfolk long enough to know that, except with parents who had designs on him, this was the usual predinner form, men in a clump pretending not to be talking business, but actually doing so, women in another clump discussing whatever it was women talked about. He hoped that he would find himself beside Marion at table.

He did not; he was seated between his hostess and Mrs.

Andrews; he wasn't even directly opposite the face he wished to study. He could, however, hear her voice which pleased him as much as her appearance. It was soft and she did not, as most young women did, try to lend animation by over-emphasis. Nor did she laugh. Once or twice she smiled. When she did so it made more change than on a more generally lively face and Mr. Horridge found himself wishing that he had been the one to bring about this transformation.

None of the old tricks were played at this table. Nobody drew attention to how beautifully Marion—or Ellen—had done the flowers, folded the table napkins, supervised the preparation of the excellent meal. No mention was made of the girls' interests, good works, talents, or foibles.

Mr. Horridge found his hostess difficult to talk to. To each of his remarks she murmured some sterile agreement upon which the subject died; and she offered no comment of her own. Occasionally, especially when the maid was changing plates, she looked a little anxious and preoccupied. Fortunately his other neighbour was garrulous and inquisitive. She asked again the question he had answered so many times about his relationship to the eminent Horridge. "Yet it is not a common name," she said. "It's common enough where I come from," he said. He did not say where that was. His reticence was not—as Mrs. Andrews suspected—due to desire to conceal his origins, it was simply that the Cumberland village which he had left at the age of fourteen held no interest for him and he could not imagine it being of interest to anyone else.

At one point Mrs. Andrews addressed Marion directly, leaning across the flowers. "Marion, dear, remember I am counting upon your help next Thursday with my croquet party."

The fascinating, inscrutable face turned; the low clear voice said:

"I am sorry, Mrs. Andrews, I should have let you know. I shall not be here. On Monday I am going to Heatherton."

The word evoked a curious silence, broken by Mr. Draper.

"Marion is still far from fully recovered. Dr. Barlow advised a convalescent period in the Nursing Home."

"I am sorry," Mrs. Andrews said. She then turned to Mr. Horridge and said, "Marion had a terrible accident." She gave him what details she knew, adding in a lower voice, "I should hardly have thought Heatherton . . . but I suppose Mr. Draper knows best."

Mr. Horridge would hardly have thought Heatherton, either. It adjoined his own estate, Sorley Park, and most of his staff was related, either directly or by some involved process of intermarriage, with most of Miss Rose's. Still servants' gossip was not to be trusted.

He remembered that the Drapers kept no carriage; so he addressed himself to Mrs. Draper, offering, should she wish to visit her daughter, the use of his carriage and pair.

Mrs. Draper applied one of her conversation stoppers. "How very kind," she remarked, neither accepting nor refusing the offer.

The ladies withdrew; the gentlemen remained to drink Mr. Draper's first-class port and to resume the business-tinged conversation. Back in the drawing room Mr. Horridge was disappointed to see Marion seated on a sofa between Mrs. Taylor and Mrs. Andrews. The sofa was so placed that it was impossible for him to go behind it and lean over its back. Nor could he approach it from the front because exactly opposite her daughter Mrs. Draper sat in a low chair, with a table and the coffee tray before her. Mr. Horridge must content himself with staring; and although through the rather boring evening he did not manage to exchange a word with the girl he admired so much, he knew by the end of it that he was in love. He had always avoided matrimony because of its threatened tedium; the same face, the same voice three hundred and sixty-five days in a year; but here was a face, he was certain, that one could look at forever, and still not know it all. He thought, rather naïvely, that just as his physical wanderings had ended and he had settled down, so his emotional journeyings were over.

A sign of encroaching old age? He thought dolefully, Of course I'm almost twice her age. He reckoned that she was over twenty; twenty-two perhaps.

The evening was enlivened by one curious small incident. Mr. Andrews said gallantly, "I hope you are going to give us some music, Mrs. Draper. Of all the delights that hospitality under this roof offers, your playing is the greatest."

Taking her assent for granted, he went to throw open the piano. It was locked. There was nothing extraordinary about that. What was unusual was that Marion and Ellen exchanged a long eloquent look, while Mrs. Draper behaved as though the piano had nothing to do with her. She sat staring down at her hands.

"Ellen, my dear. The key. It is on my dressing chest."

Ellen sped from the room as though she had been propelled. Mr. Andrews assured Mr. Horridge that Mrs. Draper's playing was positively of concert standard; a piece of information that was received with indifference since music to him was noise, varying only in loudness. However, when the piano was opened and the flowers removed and Mrs. Draper began to play her competence and dedication were obvious. She played without printed music and with her eyes half closed. She played the kind of music popular in drawing rooms, not very loud, drifting from one tune to another. And then suddenly she changed her style and seemed almost to attack the piano. It was very loud music indeed, with something about it of passion and power. Mr. Draper rose, crossed to where she sat and spoke into her ear. She struck three crashing chords and stopped. "I dislike loud music," Mr. Draper said.

The guests hastened to congratulate Mrs. Draper upon her performance. Mr. Horridge hoped that either Mrs. Taylor or Mrs. Andrews would now be asked to play, or to sing. Then he thought that with so gifted a mother one of the girls would sing. But when Mrs. Draper resumed her seat the room became static again and presently, with the arrival of the Taylors' carriage, the party began to disperse.

"One would have thought," Papa said in his most cutting voice, "that one of you could have remembered the key. Three of you about here all day long with absolutely nothing to do; yet what I happen to overlook is neglected."

Mamma and Ellen said the only thing there was to say, "I am sorry." Mr. Draper noticed that Marion did not speak. "You, I suppose, take no blame for the oversight?"

"I never considered it necessary to lock the piano."

A daft answer if ever there was one.

"I have seldom known a more unsatisfactory evening. I told you, Ellen, to do something about your sister's hair. I meant an improvement, not a vulgar imitation of your chance-come-by friend. And why are you"—his attention shifted —"wearing that old dress? If your object was to shame me, you succeeded admirably. You have earrings, bracelets, a locket and chain, and you look like a pauper. As for you, my dear"—he could use the term like a smack in the face— "you know how much I detest that kind of noise. One would have thought you had gone mad."

"I am very sorry. I momentarily forgot that company was present."

"And the meal was not what it should have been. Roast potatoes with duck, in itself a greasy dish. Is Ada now too infirm to mash a potato? And the girl breathing so hard. I was mortified. And not helped, Ellen, by hearing you give to Mr. Taylor a quite unnecessarily detailed account of Marion's accident. Blood is not a subject for dinner table talk—especially when eating tipsy cake."

Marion felt an almost overwhelming desire to laugh, thinking of the strawberry jam oozing out between the layers of sherry-soaked sponge cake.

"But he asked me, Papa," Ellen said. She began to cry. She had done her best with Marion's hair; had urged unavailingly, the wearing of some ornaments. And it could have been such a lovely party. Ellen's standards were not high; to look pretty, to have a nice meal—and despite what Papa said it had been a nice meal—fully appreciated—and to have everybody happy and amiable, was enough for her. So she wept because what should have been pleasant was not. And because of the music . . . Whenever Mamma played in that particular way something in Ellen responded. She had herself wished to learn to play the piano and was sure she could have done—not so well as Mamma, but with pleasure. Papa, however, had decided otherwise, "One pianist in a family is enough," and Mamma had given no support. But when Mamma played real music, Ellen often stopped and listened; tonight the sudden breaking off had jerked her nerves.

"Go to bed. You are overtired. Go along, Marion can manage to unhook herself for once. She will have no maid at Heatherton."

Over Marion, ever since Monday, Heatherton had cast

its shadow. But she had lived through the time of terror and felt that she was hardened to anything, even the company of drooling lunatics. Going to Heatherton would rid her of Johnny and it might offer her a chance of escape, since the precautions taken would be such as were effective for those infirm of mind or body. Which I am not!

But there was Ellen, sent away, crying, and there a minute after was Papa locking the piano again, saying, "When you wish to play, agreeably . . ."

Marion remembered that twice, monumentally selfish, she had tried to escape. Once through marriage to Johnny; once through death in the water. Oh, no, another time too, through Miss Ruthven.

I thought only of myself.

I did not think of them.

I have been as selfish, as self-centred as *he* is.

Different now. I will save us all.

Ellen shall have parties so different from this.

Mamma shall play the piano, as she likes, all day, all night; go to concerts . . .

If it works.

She had written to Johnny, telling him that it was over, that her feelings had changed and she no longer loved him. She had added that arguing about it would be useless, and in fact impossible, since she was going away, probably for a long time. She intended the letter to be posted on Saturday morning so that it would reach him by the late post. He would imagine that she had already gone. Or if, hopefully, he came along after all, she would not reply to his tapping.

She had planned to ask Ellen to post it, telling her that it was merely a civil note to thank him for the flowers.

Now she tore the letter into shreds and dropped them

into the kitchen fire where a few red embers still glowed. Let Johnny come tomorrow, as arranged, and be made use of.

She was half undressed when Johnny tapped at the window. Coming so unexpectedly the sound made her jump, but she hurried to the window and greeted him with a good imitation of her old warmth.

"Why, Johnny, what a surprise. I did not expect you until tomorrow." She sounded as though the surprise pleased her.

"I could wait no longer. Can you let me in?"

"Soon. Papa may be moving about. We are late tonight. We have had a party."

"I know. I saw the lights. I have been walking up and down."

His coming on Friday seemed providential, if one could use the word in such a connection. Silence fell on the house and presently she used the screwdriver which she had thought never to use again.

Tonight her behaviour confirmed his belief that her odd manner on the previous Saturday was due to fatigue. Except for the fact that there was no actual love-making, they seemed now to be back on the terms which had existed before she was pregnant and had begun to nag about marriage.

She gave him some brandy. He told her about his arrangement with Ager; what he had discovered about Special Licences. It was he who now urged a run-away marriage, the sooner the better.

"It cannot be next week, Johnny. I have to go to Heatherton."

The word had its usual effect. "What? Oh, no. Not that abominable place. This I will not permit." He looked wildly round the little room. "You must dress, darling, get a few things together and come away with me. Now."

"Johnny, the last train has gone. What about all your belongings?"

"Tomorrow, then. You must not go to that place. In a shop one hears things and if you knew as much about it as I do . . ."

She pretended to hesitate. "No. I think that would be unwise. For one thing Papa has convinced himself, and Dr. Barlow, that I am not quite right in the head. I should not merely be a runaway daughter, I should be a lunatic at large. He would be justified in asking police aid in finding us."

"We could cover our tracks." He was now as eager as he had been reluctant.

"There is another thing, too. I want to find out about my money." How easily the lies came nowadays!

"What money?"

"A legacy my grandmother left me. It might come to me when I am twenty-one, or on marriage. I do not know, but I mean to find out."

"How much?"

"About five thousand pounds."

"And you never even *told* me."

She said with just the right touch of lightness, "I had no wish to be married for my money! Now that you *have* asked me, I felt I could mention it. Have a little more brandy."

He sat and sipped happily. This put a completely different face upon things. Even if they had to wait until Marion was of age, the poverty would be bearable, since there would be a limit to it. In fact it might be possible to borrow money immediately on the strength of such expectations.

"You are a strange girl," he said, giving her a hug with his free arm. "Perhaps that is why I love you so much."

Now.

She studied the backs of her hands and said, "It is a curious thing; my face never tans, but my hands are like a gypsy's." Then, as though the thought had just occurred, "Johnny, you could get me some pure white arsenic, could you not?"

The theory that arsenic was the best whitener for skin was a popular one, and the request for it in its pure form was not remarkable if it were to be used as a cosmetic. In order that the dangerous stuff should not be confused with salt or fine sugar it was often adulterated with soot or indigo or other colouring matter.

"I suppose I could," he said cautiously. "It would not be easy. Mr. Freeman is fussy about checking the contents of the poison cupboard against the poison book."

"Is arsenic a poison? We never knew that. We used it at school, regularly. It never hurt anyone."

"How did you obtain it?"

"We soaked flypaper. But that is so messy. The sticky stuff soaked off, too. And it could not be done secretly, so then we were teased about being vain. I thought that if you would get some for me I could sit and soak my hands at Heatherton. It would be something to do. But of course, if you cannot . . ."

"I can. I will. If you promise to be very careful. It will not be like soaking flypaper. You could soak a dozen and not get a very lethal solution. Pure arsenic is deadly. You must promise me that after soaking you will wash your hands thoroughly before touching your eyes or your mouth, or any food. And another thing, darling, if your hands should develop a rash, or even a redness, you will stop using it at once."

"Such a fuss! Very well, I promise."

When on the following evening he handed her the little white-wrapped, red-sealed packet, she said, "Oh, Johnny, you did not manage much!"

"I am not sure that you are to be trusted with it, darling. There is enough there to kill a regiment."

"You exaggerate, surely."

"Well, perhaps not a regiment. But several men."

His feeling that she did not know what she was dealing with was confirmed by the way she handled it, laying it carelessly on the dressing table as though it were a box of matches. "Darling, it must be kept in a *safe* place. Under lock and key." He told her some cautionary tales of cases of arsenic poisonings in France. She said, "The safest place I know is my jewel case," and she laid it there alongside all the things which Papa had given her.

She had led him to believe that she was going to Heatherton on Sunday. He now reverted to this.

"Whatever you do, darling, do not cross Miss . . . Miss Rose. She has a villainous temper, I understand."

"I hope not to provoke it. I shall be careful."

"How long shall you be there?"

"Not more than a week. It is really a token stay." It would be less than a week.

"And you will write to me?" Some of her later letters, insistent and nagging, had not helped his faulty digestion to deal with some of the substantial dishes which Mrs. Fenner provided; it had sometimes seemed boring to read the same pleas and arguments as he had fended off on the previous evening. But now that all was well again he would welcome a letter in the old style.

"If I possibly can, Johnny."

"And I will write to you. At Heatherton your father will not be there to read your letters."

"Johnny, I must spy out the land first. I know it sounds absurd, but I am supposed to be in need of care and attention. I am not sure yet how much care or what sort of attention. It would be better if you waited until I wrote to you."

"It will be another week in the desert."

And who is to blame for that? There was an oasis, I tried to steer you towards it, but you would pull away! It was quite overwhelming to think that had Johnny only listened and heeded, they would by now be in London, the baby moving towards quickening and she so grateful . . .

Well, things shaped as they would. One day, quite soon, Johnny would get a letter from her. And it would surprise him very much!

Ellen cried so much at the prospect of parting from Marion that Papa was justified in thinking the bond between them too close and sentimental; almost morbid. "Ellen," he said, "it is time you learned some self-control. For every time you cry—whether I see you or not, I shall know by your eyes—Marion will remain at Heatherton an extra day." This drastic threat was effective and Ellen managed not to cry even when the moment came to say goodbye. "I shall soon be back, dearest," Marion said. "I shall behave impeccably and convince Miss Rose that there is nothing wrong with me at all."

With luck I shall be home on Tuesday.

o   o   o

"HERE WE ARE," MR. DRAPER SAID AS THE CAB DREW UP outside a flat-faced house with nothing but a strip of well-raked, weedless gravel between it and the road. On either side of the house high red walls extended, the one to the left broken by the carriage entrance, but with the gates closed.

Mr. Draper rang the bell and the door was opened by a man with a hard-bitten face, a jockey's face, who wore a garment that Mr. Draper had never seen before on a male servitor; a waistcoat with sleeves, the body of it striped yellow and black, like a wasp, the sleeves all black. The man's attitude was defensive rather than welcoming.

"I am Mr. Draper. Miss Rose is expecting me." Mr. Draper turned and said, "Coker, bring in the trunk." He then said to the waistcoated man, "Give him a hand." The trunk was heavy and Coker, who had been driving Jarvey's hired vehicles for as long as Mr. Draper could remember, and pretty old even then, needed some assistance.

Miss Rose, coming down into the hall, did not see it that way; what she saw was a man ordering her servant about.

She said, "Very well, Stubbs, help Mr. Draper's driver, *if he cannot manage.*" It was the kind of sidelong blow that Mr. Draper himself was adept at administering. The choice of the one word, "driver" was designed to put Mr. Draper in his place. Gentlemen had coachmen.

She then said, "Good afternoon, Mr. Draper," and held out her hand, thin, dry, and hard. "And this is Miss Draper?"

"My daughter, Marion." Miss Rose ran her experienced eye over her new patient.

"If you will come this way . . ." she said and opened a door upon a room the like of which neither Mr. Draper nor Marion had ever seen before. A stripped stark room in which there was not one of the fashionable colours, no brown, no crimson, and none of the usual trappings, no drapings, no fringes, no antimacassars, no ornaments. The walls were white, painted, not papered, and the floor, bare except for a few rich-toned rugs, was of highly polished, honey-coloured boards. There were two sofas and three armchairs, dressed like orphan children in starched calico patterned leaf green and brown. On one side there was a naked marble fireplace—little boys with some sheep—and on the other side shelves, from floor to ceiling, full of books.

Mr. Draper had never been into a hospital but he thought the room had a clinical, sterilised look, quite comfortless. Exactly right. And Miss Rose, standing herself, not inviting him to take a seat, was right enough too in her stark blue and white, taut, brisk, businesslike. But she was a challenge and he accepted it.

"Perhaps my daughter could be taken to her room, Miss Rose."

"But that is the point, Mr. Draper. Your letter told me so little. I could not decide whether to allot her a room on the medical or on the other side."

That one knowledgeable glance had informed her that Miss Draper was neither very ill nor mad. Her nose, as alert as Mr. Draper's, scented something peculiar. She addressed Marion directly.

"Miss Draper, would you like to go into the garden? There is a seat . . . And some of my lilies are interesting—some rather rare varieties sent to me by a patient who had spent some time in the East . . ."

"And now," Miss Rose said, having seen Marion through the French window into the garden, "perhaps you would care to tell me, Mr. Draper, exactly what is wrong."

"That, as you may have judged from my letter, is rather difficult, Miss Rose. My daughter had a fall—in the sea at Yarmouth—and suffered injury to her head. The wound has healed, but she is not herself. A change in personality is difficult to describe. But what I am bound to bear in mind is that my wife is not strong and that my younger daughter is very easily distressed by what I can only call domestic scenes. Our family doctor, Dr. Barlow, advised a convalescent period here."

That was, in itself, astonishing. Since the legal case no local doctor had sent a patient to Heatherton.

"This is all somewhat vague, Mr. Draper. Is she forgetful? Melancholy? Hysterical?"

"Not precisely. Prone to moods of irritability—though of course she is less likely to give way to them here than in the bosom of her family. We have had some rather trying scenes . . ." He gave a little sigh, an appeal for sympathy, a request to be excused from further questioning. It missed its mark entirely. Miss Rose had taken against him on sight; pompous, self-assured, archetype of the dominant male.

"I can see," she said crisply, "that I shall be obliged to form my own judgement." She sensed that he was not being frank with her. The sooner she had the girl to herself the sooner she would get to the bottom of this little mystery. She did not offer him tea, though it was just on four o'clock. Instead she rose and said, "We must not keep your driver waiting, must we? You may depend upon me, Mr. Draper, to take the best possible care of your daughter." Mr. Draper rose and turned towards the outer door. Miss Rose, who missed little, said, "You will wish to say goodbye to her?"

There was, she observed, a marked lack of warmth in their leave-taking.

When Mr. Draper had gone Miss Rose said, "We will have tea now," and rang the bell. She was still in the dark as to Marion's real condition and she was cautious; sometimes people who were quite severely deranged could put up a show of normal behaviour for a short period. And that might be what lay behind the father's caginess—an unwillingness to admit that his daughter was prone to anything worse than moods of irritability.

"What a beautiful room you have," Marion said looking around and thinking that when she was free to make decisions and choices she would furnish somewhat in this fashion.

"Many people regard it as too bare, but I dislike clutter," Miss Rose said. Across the tea table they took stock of each other. Marion thought that Miss Rose looked completely unlike the ogre of the rumours. She had a plain face, sallow, with a flattish, wide-nostrilled nose, a large mouth and eyes that were like . . . that were like those of the organ-grinder's monkey, lively, wary, sad. Miss Rose thought that Marion had a touch of melancholy in her face, something, not easily definable, that was at odds with her youth, and her beauty.

"Your Papa," she said, "mentioned an accident. He told me very little about it. What happened?"

"There is so little to tell." I chose death and death rejected me. "I fell, in the sea, and hit my head on a groyne. I was unconscious for some time. My head has healed, but still pains me on occasion—when I stooped to smell your lilies. How very beautiful they are! I have never seen anything like them."

Her glance and her manner were candid but she was evasive too.

"It gives you pain when you hold your head down?"

"Yes. But much less than it did."

"Are you under medication, Miss Draper?"

"Under? Oh no. There was no need. The scar is nothing. I am in good health. I am here because Dr. Barlow thought that Mamma and my sister worried unduly. But I assure you, there is nothing to worry about and I shall not be a trouble to you, Miss Rose. If I may just sit in your beautiful garden . . . And perhaps borrow a book."

"You are fond of reading?"

"It is my chief joy. And you seem to have a wonderful collection."

"You may take what you like. The bottom shelf contains mainly medical works—very dull reading. Some of the others are the remains of my uncle's library. I was obliged to utilise the room that was his library for other purposes and I could not retain all his books. The novels are my own. Who is your favourite writer, Miss Draper?"

"Oh, that is impossible to say—except, well, I think the author of the book I happen to be reading." Marion smiled as she said this and Miss Rose noticed what a vast difference a smile made.

"Once," she said, "whenever things went wrong with me —in the real world—I took refuge in Ouida."

That was bait, and Marion avoided it. Nothing must seem to be wrong; for the next, how long? twenty-four hours? the game must be Happy Families.

She said, smiling again, "Yes, that is understandable. I have indeed been so absorbed in one of her books that I forgot a dress-fitting. And then there is Mrs. Hungerford and so many others."

"Oh yes," Miss Rose said. They had found common ground and explored it happily; but Miss Rose kept her professional eye open and within an hour had decided that Marion was not ill, either in mind or body. There was just the remote possibility that the moods of irritability of which Mr. Draper had spoken might be fits. A severe blow on the head could result in fits, easily distinguishable from epilepsy, but distressing to watch. Furious anger over nothing . . . But somehow, she thought not. This very lovely, intelligent, agreeable and apparently healthy girl had been sent to Heatherton for some peculiar reason which in due time Miss Rose would fathom.

She said, "If it is agreeable to you, Miss Draper, it would be a convenience if you took your meals with me. All my other patients, on this side, are bedridden and there are trays to carry . . ."

"I should like that very much," Marion said. Breakfast tomorrow; luncheon perhaps . . . "And if, while I am here, being so able-bodied, I could do anything to help, I should be happy to, Miss Rose."

A perfectly safe thing to offer. She smiled, Miss Rose smiled back and something was established.

The very trim black and white parlourmaid came to remove the tea tray. Miss Rose said, "Clarke, Miss Draper is to have the Blue Room. Tell Stubbs to carry up her trunk. And she will be taking meals with me."

The Blue Room was very pleasant. Once again there was an absence of clutter; the dressing table had no petticoat, the bed no valance. There were blue curtains at the window and blue rugs on the floor. In this room Marion unpacked as though she were staying at Heatherton for an unspecified length of time.

She had a watch, not Papa's gift. It had belonged to Angela, a pretty trinket, the face surrounded by blue enamel, suspended from a true lover's knot. When, for a birthday, Angela's godmother had sent her a far more splendid one Angela had said, "Marion, I cannot wear two. You have this." Papa had been slightly displeased. "I intended," he said, "to give you a watch for Christmas. But since Angela has forestalled me, and you seem to be satisfied with her cast-off, I must think of something else, must I not?"

Now on the little watch the crucial moments ticked away. It was seven o'clock. In Alma Avenue Ellen would have spread the cloth, placed the cruet and the decanter . . . decanter . . . decanter . . . Take hold of yourself, do not weaken now. Within an hour you will all be free!

Miss Rose had said that she dined at seven-thirty and Marion, wearing a dress that had no happy or unhappy associations, went down to find the table set, somewhat elaborately in the pretty room. Miss Rose came in. She had abandoned the blue and white uniform and wore a curious garment, odd, yet attractive, high necked, full skirted, long sleeved, made of a green silk that matched the chair covers; it had cuffs and lapels of velvet. The lapels struck a masculine note.

"I have just made what I hope is my last round," Miss Rose said. "Do you drink sherry?"

"Oh yes. I like it very much." The decanter and the glasses stood on a silver tray on the desk that backed the window. Miss Rose poured two glasses. This was surely not, Marion reflected, the kind of treatment Papa had visualised when he said *"Heatherton."*

"It was the *house,"* Miss Rose said, towards the end of the meal. "My uncle left it to me. No money. A white elephant if ever there was one. I came down from London, actually to look over what could be sold, what I could do with it . . . It was June, early June, the cuckoo was still calling, but stuttering, and the first roses on that wall were in flower . . . and something came over me. I am very practical and I thought at the time, This is idiotic. And it was. But I made my decision there and then. This is my place, I thought; we'll sink or swim together. And so it happened," she said, telling Marion what she had never told anyone. Back in London, still staggered by the momentousness of her decision, and by the impact of an emotion of which she would have believed herself incapable, she had simply said, "It is a ramshackle old place, but I think it could be made into a paying concern."

At the end of the meal she made a most unusual concession.

"There is a comfortable chair in your room, Miss Draper, but if you prefer to sit here you will not disturb me. I have some correspondence to attend to."

A few people with relatives on the other, the idiot side, liked to receive regular reports. From time to time as Miss Rose composed one of these comforting documents she raised her head and looked across at Marion who seemed to be absorbed in the book she had chosen. With that hair colouring, and wearing a green dress, neither new nor fashionable, she fitted in with the chintz covers and the austere elegance of the room in a way that could only give pleasure to a discriminating eye. Miss Rose hoped that she would have such charming company for some time.

o   o   o

MR. DRAPER WAS A CREATURE OF HABIT. JUST AS HE ALWAYS went through the ritual of choosing his cigar, so he always studied his claret before pouring it. On this Monday evening the habit was justified. He lifted the decanter, scowled at it, shook it slightly and said, "Muddy!" No blame could be attached to anyone since he alone handled his wine. Ruffled, he drank water with his rump steak and when Betty came in with the pudding he vented his ill-humour on her. "Must you pant as though you had just climbed Mont Blanc?"

She gaped, realising that she was being rebuked but puzzled by the allusion. "Take this," he said, "and pour it away."

"Picking on me now Miss Marion's gone," Betty said when she was back in the kitchen. "I don't breathe to his liking. And he said throw this away."

Ada said, "He ourta try them stairs! Give me a look at that. You shook it up a bit, I reckon, but it'll settle."

At 10, Alma Avenue everybody ate well. It was not one of those households where orders to grocer, butcher, fishmonger went out in two halves, this for the family, that for the servants. Mr. Draper had his pride and held that if he could afford to employ servants he could afford to feed them. But naturally Ada and Betty never had wine and something rather more than half a decanterful of claret, the master's own drink, held promise of an unusual treat.

"Betty, you *sure* he said throw it away?"

"I may not breathe right but I can hear."

When the washing up was done and everything was tidied away, the pan of oatmeal porridge maturing away at the back of the cooling stove, Ada and Betty sat down to enjoy their wine. And very disappointing it was.

Ada said, "Well, I can't see what all the fuss is about. Sour old plum juice, I call it."

"Not a patch on my old granny's rhubarb," Betty agreed.

"Still there must be something," Ada said, remembering how carefully butlers, or gentlemen, handled wine. "Maybe you have to get a taste for it." She took another experimental sip and so did Betty. Then Betty said a sensible thing. "If it'd been fit to drink, he'd have drunk it, wouldn't he?"

"Tip it down the sink," Ada said. "Put a good handful of salt in the decanter and leave it to soak."

o   o   o

NOW IT WAS TUESDAY, ANOTHER LOVELY LATE SUMMER DAY, slightly misty to begin with. Marion expected a telegram. She was reasonably sure that faced with an unusual situation Mamma and Ellen would naturally turn to her. But she knew that she must not appear to be watchful or expectant.

Coming out of her bedroom at about half-past ten, having made her bed, she came face to face with Miss Rose, just closing a door, not quite, but almost opposite across the wide corridor. There was the faintest possible sickly smell.

"Miss Draper, you said last evening that if you could help . . . I have no wish to impose upon your good nature. But if you could just bear to look in and say good morning to Colonel Fraser, it would cheer him to see a fresh face, especially one so young and pretty. He is a *dear* old man, with little time to live, and no relatives who care."

It was not altogether a false speech. Miss Rose was capable of consideration even to men, men brought low, no longer aggressive; to them she could extend the chivalry once extended to prisoners of war by mediaeval knights.

"But of course," Marion said. She had swiftly reckoned that Colonel Fraser's room overlooked the front of the house; from his window she could watch for the arrival of the telegraph boy on his bicycle.

The wreck of what had been a fine handsome man lay on the bed. She thought how right Shakespeare had been about Falstaff, the nose sharp as a pen as one of the Merry Wives of Windsor had observed. But something of gallantry stirred in the aged bones; Colonel Fraser was delighted to be visited by someone whom he thought, and using an outdated word, called, "so bonny."

"If you could spare the time," he said, "to read to me a little. I take *The Times* but at the moment I find it a little difficult to manage, but I do like to keep up with the news and Miss Rose, good woman and kind as she is, cannot always spare time."

Marion sat down, near the window, and read, every now and then glancing out, waiting, watching.

It was just possible, she told herself, that Monday had been one of those rare evenings when Papa chose not to drink wine. There were such evenings. The decanter must always *be* in place but for some reason or another it could occasionally be ignored. Monday must have been such an occasion.

"It was extremely kind of you to read to him so long," Miss Rose said, over the luncheon table. "And now I am about to impose upon you again. I wonder whether you would cut the lavender for me. It is now at its best and I simply have no time. And I am a little afraid that you may find time heavy on your hands. You see, I was obliged to make this rule about nobody going out unaccompanied. A silly old man, overestimating his recovery, walked down alone to Sorley Post Office and dropped dead. If I make exceptions it is likely to be confusing to the staff."

"I have no wish to go out," Marion said. "And I shall enjoy cutting the lavender. And then I must write to my sister. You really need not think, Miss Rose, about time hanging heavy. I can most happily occupy myself." Until tomorrow. The summons to return home and take charge of things would surely come tomorrow.

On Wednesday, when Marion came to the breakfast table, Miss Rose was already in place, with quite a number of letters beside her.

"Is there no letter for me?" Marion asked.

Miss Rose went through the motions of resorting the envelopes and said, "No, but there is a later post." Actually there was a letter addressed to Marion, but it, like all but a few that came, would be perused by Miss Rose before being handed over. Much useful information could be gained and many upsets avoided by a little discreet censoring. Miss Rose had brought to a fine art the trick of steaming open an envelope and resealing it with the white of an egg. With outgoing mail she was even more arbitrary; who wanted to receive letters of complaint written by the deranged? One patient on the other side wrote continually, to friends, to distant relatives, to the police, to the Mayor of Bedford, always saying the same thing; she was not mad, she was perfectly sane, locked up in this horrible place and treated like a lunatic simply because she would not let her son play ducks and drakes with the business or her daughter-in-law to rule in what was, after all, her house. Such letters were destroyed immediately and the rescue for which Mrs. Selton waited never came.

Ellen's letter was, from Miss Rose's point of view, very uninformative.

My dearest, dearest Marion, the house seems so lonely and so empty without you and today has been particularly horrid because both Ada and Betty have been indisposed in a most unpleasant way. I will spare you the details and simply say, due to a surfeit of plums. I am actually writing this at the kitchen table, after preparing supper and I shall try to persuade Betty that a walk to the pillar box will do her good. I do miss you so much and think of you in that horrid place. Mrs. Taylor called this morning. She has had a letter from Angela, hinting that she is in an interesting condition! She was always hasty, was she not? I have no other news, except that that nice Mr. Horridge who was here on Friday offered Mamma his carriage, should she wish to visit you. It seems that he lives quite close to the horrid place. When Mamma mentioned his offer Papa said he would arrange a visit when he thought it advisable. Mamma said that she thought Mr. Horridge should be informed; so I will end now and write him a little note . . .

Mr. Horridge did live near, was in fact a next-door neighbour in the country sense, since Sorley Park adjoined Heatherton, a large spinney separating the properties. That was interesting, but not important. Resealing the letter which gave no clue to the puzzle as to why Miss Draper should be here, Miss Rose decided that in future any letter with the Bereham postmark and addressed in that girlish, back-sloping hand, could be handed to Marion immediately.

Marion read the letter with a slow draining away of hope. She did not connect the indisposition of Ada and Betty with the thing she had planned. Papa might have eschewed claret on Monday; he was hardly likely to have done so on Tuesday. It was now Wednesday midday. So she had failed; or rather Johnny had failed her. Fobbed her off with some harmless rubbish. So what now? An indefinite stay at Heatherton, which was in fact the very reverse of horrid. In fact Miss Rose had been much maligned.

Mr. Horridge had received Ellen's little note by first post and had brooded over it all day. He had been anxious to do things properly, in gentlemanly fashion and now the door had been slammed in his face. He also asked himself, what now? Being experienced in leaping over seemingly impassable barriers, or sidling round them, he was able to give himself an answer. One of his gardeners grew magnificent carnations. "A dozen red, a dozen white," Mr. Horridge said.

The days were drawing in, but at eight o'clock it was still light enough for Mr. Horridge to walk through his spinney and cross the little bridge over the stream between the two properties. At Heatherton he rang the bell and when it was not immediately answered, rang it again.

The cautious defensive way in which Stubbs eventually answered the ringing, the door narrowly opened, the Cockney voice saying, "Yes sir?" on a demanding, questioning note, somewhat confirmed Mr. Horridge's opinion of the place. He clutched his flowers in an aggressive manner and said, "I have come to call upon Miss Draper."

"If you will wait here," Stubbs said, admitting Mr. Horridge into the hall, "I will inform Madam. Miss Rose."

"I want to see *Miss Draper*."

"If you will wait here, sir." Stubbs vanished for a moment and then reappeared. "If you will come in, sir." Mr. Horridge went in, surprised by what he saw. The rumours about Heatherton had not been wasted upon him and the elegant beautiful room was vastly different from anything he had imagined. And so was the woman, turning away from a side table on which, spread on newspaper, lay masses of lavender. He had always thought of her as all starched collars and cuffs.

"Miss Rose?"

"Yes."

"My name is Horridge."

"Oh yes?"

"I thought . . . well, I dined with Mr. Draper and his family . . . on Friday . . . and they said . . . I was told . . . So I thought I'd bring her . . ." He held out the flowers in a singularly awkward manner, "And just ask how she was." Seldom in all his life had he felt so much at a loss.

"If you will take a chair," Miss Rose said. She rang the bell which was answered not by Clarke, that reliable girl, but by the younger, as yet untrained Sarah. Wednesday was Clarke's free afternoon and evening.

"Sarah," Miss Rose said, "will you find Miss Draper—I think she may be reading to Colonel Fraser—and tell her that Mr. Horridge is here. *If she wishes to see him.*"

She emphasised the last words, because her lively mind had taken a leap. This could well be the secret of why Mr. Draper had sent a perfectly healthy, perfectly sane girl to Heatherton. Propinquity. The man was too old, and he was ugly. She could well imagine that Marion had put up some resistance . . . and that Mr. Draper . . . Ellen's letter, twice saying that *horrid* place. In a horrid place a man carrying a great bunch of flowers might seem less old, less ugly than he actually was.

Very clever.

Clarke would have delivered the message verbatim; by the time Sarah had climbed the stairs, knocked, entered the sickly smelling room where the poor old man was dying, she had lost all but the gist of it. "There's a gentleman to see you, Miss."

Marion sprang up, dropping *The Times* on to the floor. Of course, Mr. Taylor! In an emergency Mamma and Ellen would think of *him;* and he would think about breaking news gently. He had come himself, to tell her, and to escort her home.

She said, "I am sorry to leave you so abruptly . . . I hope you sleep well . . ."

Going down the stairs she fitted herself into her role, surprise, grief.

The surprise at least called for no feigning.

"Mr. Horridge!"

"Being so near," he said, "I thought I should just step across . . . bring you a few flowers . . ." He pushed the carnations into her hands and she buried her face in them.

The red ones smelt of cloves. "How very kind of you, Mr. Horridge." Out of the depths of her disappointment she plucked a smile, and Miss Rose, watching, deduced that though the sight of Mr. Horridge was a surprise it was not an unpleasant one.

"Do sit down, Mr. Horridge," she said. They had been neighbours for some time but their paths had not crossed. Miss Rose seldom left Heatherton, had no social life at all and did not go to church. She bore him a slight grudge because he paid his servants—most of them related to hers—rather more than the customary wages, and that led to discontent. Now, seeing him at close quarters where he looked large in the elegant room, and shy and ill at ease, she found something disarming about him; she thought that he lacked the masculine self-assurance which she found so offensive and his infatuation with Marion was obvious. He simply could not take his eyes from her.

Miss Rose was not averse to marriage—for other people; for girls brought up to be useless it was practically a necessity. And of course Sorley Park was not to be sniffed at.

Thinking these things Miss Rose made two or three attempts at conversation which added to rather than diminished the awkwardness in the room, because each time she spoke Mr. Horridge had to turn to her with a visible effort and, having made the briefest possible replies, refixed his spaniel-like gaze on Marion.

"I still have several small things to attend to," Miss Rose said. One was to rebuke Sarah who obviously had not delivered that message in full. "I am afraid you will never make a *proper* parlourmaid, Sarah." Another was to organise *two* vases for the flowers. The combination of red and white—with no other colour—was a sure sign of death. A silly old superstition and it was ridiculous to take it seriously but Miss

Rose had had enough experience of sickrooms and hospitals to respect it.

When she had gone Mr. Horridge said, "I hope you didn't mind my coming so unexpectedly, Miss Draper. But I had a letter from Miss Ellen . . ."

"So did I. Telling me about your kind offer. It was most considerate of you, Mr. Horridge, and I am sure Mamma and Ellen were sorry not to avail themselves of it. I expect Papa did not wish to impose."

She smiled again. There she sat, lovelier even than his memory of her, and with her lap full of his flowers.

"And how are you finding things here?"

"Most comfortable. Indeed extremely pleasant. Miss Rose is so kind."

"I'm glad to hear that." A bit surprised, too. But then, who could be other than kind to her? A plan began to form in his mind. He was very far from being the diffident, awkward fellow which for a little time he had seemed.

"What do you find to do all day?"

"I read a good deal. As you see, Miss Rose has a number of books."

He had never in his life read a book for pleasure but his mind noted that she liked books and leaped forward to visualise himself presenting her with some, very large ones, bound in leather and tooled in gilt.

"I also read aloud to Colonel Fraser. He is very ill but he has retained a lively interest in the outside world. Especially anything of a military nature. Unfortunately the only thing in that connection today was a death. Still, he took it admirably. He said, 'So I've beaten old Fred at last. A live colonel is better than a dead brigadier.' I thought that so brave."

And who wouldn't be brave, or pretend to be, watched by those beautiful eyes?

"And today I cut the lavender." She indicated it with a movement that Mr. Horridge felt was the most graceful he had ever seen. "Later on I shall probably make lavender bags." For this was Wednesday; no news from home; her exile might be prolonged.

Mr. Horridge thought this sounded a dull programme.

"I wondered if you'd care for a drive. I don't use the carriage much so the horses stand about eating their heads off." A single man had actually little need for a carriage, but it and the matched pair of horses were what a gentleman should have; just as he must have a silver inkstand, though he did his writing with an indelible pencil, well-licked.

"I should like it more than anything, Mr. Horridge. But . . . Well, I am here as a patient. I should be obliged to ask Miss Rose's permission. And she has explained to me the rule against patients going out alone."

"But you wouldn't be alone. Not with me." However he was content to take one step at a time and to pay lip service to convention. "I'll ask her to come, too. Though to tell you the truth she makes me feel a bit uncomfortable. You may not have noticed but there's something a bit like a monkey . . ."

"I noticed it the moment I saw her. It is the eyes. As though they knew more, or were trying to communicate. There was an organ-grinder once, he had one and I never felt quite sure about *him*. So one day instead of giving the monkey twopence I gave it bananas and the man seemed angry. So to make it right I borrowed threepence from Ellen and that pacified him."

Tenderhearted, too! Where animals and children were concerned Mr. Horridge had a tender streak himself; with men, and some women, he could be ruthless in the extreme.

The talk about twopence and threepence sounded childish
so he said:

"That was when you were small." Like all people newly in
love he was anxious to know about, to share, the beloved's
past.

"No. I was grown up, about two years ago."

That struck an odd note. The daughter of a man who, if
not rich by Mr. Horridge's present standard, was comfort-
ably off, short of threepence. Kept short of spending money.
God, if only, if only. He began to think in lavish terms.

Mr. Horridge's attitude towards money was simple. It was
extremely important because without it you were nothing. But
its importance lay in what it could buy. He had known the
depths of poverty, he had been hungry, thirsty, hopeful, disappointed, despairing, bloody well near dead. Then in Africa,
in a hot hole called the de Kaap Valley, where this man's claim
to the gold-rich soil so nearly encroached upon the next that
mere walking was a hazard, he had one day struck it rich.
After that everything he touched had seemed to prosper,
but his fundamental attitude towards money had not changed.
It was something that you had to snatch out of an unwilling
world and having snatched it, you spent it. Had he chanced
to wake one morning to find himself ruined and penniless
he would not have cut his throat; he would have gone out
and tried to snatch some more of the spending stuff.

If only this beautiful, adorable creature would give him the
right to spend on her, how lavishly, how gladly he would do
it. Diamonds. Pearls. Sables.

Miss Rose refused the invitation to go driving.

"I am sorry, Mr. Horridge, I am too busy. The moment
I leave this house some crisis arises. Very occasionally in the
past I have escorted a convalescent patient to Norwich or

even to London. I always came back to disaster. Once Mrs. Selton had set fire to her bed. Another time there was that death in the Post Office—of which so much was made. That is why I made the rule about no patient going out unaccompanied. But of course, in Miss Draper's case . . . if she wishes to take a drive . . . and if you can find a chaperone . . ."

"My housekeeper, Mrs. Clarke, greatly enjoys an outing."

Mr. Horridge's Mrs. Clarke was an aunt to Miss Rose's parlourmaid; immensely respectable.

"Then I'll call tomorrow afternoon. At about three o'clock?"

"If Miss Draper then feels well enough," Miss Rose said, craftily leaving an escape route open.

"If you wish to encourage him," Miss Rose said. "And if you know how your father would feel about it."

"I know exactly how Papa feels," Marion said with an emphasis that was entirely misleading and which confirmed Miss Rose in her deductions.

"The poor man is plainly head-over-ears in love with you," Miss Rose said and though she spoke crisply the wistful, would-I-could-speak monkey look was foremost in her eyes, saying, Who would not be?

The cold, disillusioned creature who had been dredged up from the sea, a sort of hermit crab adjusting itself to its new carapace, knew that that statement was true. She had seen in Mr. Horridge's eyes the same doting look that she had once, across Mrs. Marriot's drawing room, across the church aisle, across the fruit cup directed at Johnny. Worthless. Always the one who kissed, or wished to kiss, and the one who accepted the kiss; always the loving heart and the heart that allowed itself to be loved.

It was sad knowledge, but it was true. And now, late on

Wednesday, Marion knew that she must accept it. In her effort to free them all, she had failed. But she saw that as the wife of a rich man she would not be without some power. Her ideas were vague; a piano—"Mamma, play as much as you like, as you like." Parties where Ellen might meet somebody as resolute as Mr. Horridge. And for herself absolute freedom.

Mrs. Clarke's liking for a drive was not much pandered to. She was fated to ride on that Thursday afternoon, down the lime avenue, to the door of Heatherton, where, the carriage having taken on its real passenger, turned around. Then she footed it back up the avenue, to prepare what Mr. Horridge had ordered: "A tea for a lady." Mr. Horridge knew about them, tiny triangular sandwiches, fragile slices of cake. Ladies, taking tea, removed only one glove so eating had to be made easy for them. Gentlemen fared worse, constantly jumping up, handing cups and silly little snippets. Mr. Horridge in his time had suffered. But his tea party was planned to be different. Just the two of them, a good solid table with everything within reach, and Marion wielding the tea pot.

He had fallen in love with her at first sight and everything that had happened after had confirmed his judgement. She had enjoyed the drive, and now she enjoyed her tea, taking off both gloves. She ate four of the little sandwiches and two slices of cake.

She was *real*.

After tea he showed her, with pride, over the garden, where there was a yew walk of great antiquity, and then over his stables in which he took great pride. Then, as he was about to order the carriage to take her back to Heatherton, she said, "Could we not walk?" So they took the path which he had beaten out on the previous evening. A few brambles, a few nettles had sprung back and he walked ahead, smoothing the path for her, in his mind quelling dragons. When they came to the stream, and the single-planked bridge, he said, "Steady now," and he walked through the sluggish water, reaching up to hold her elbow. When she was safely across she made no move to release herself.

Greatly encouraged, aware of something, magnetic, electrical that this close contact made, he said, "Would you like to drive with me again tomorrow, Miss Marion?"

Using her Christian name he had jumped at least six months of conventional courtship. But a man of his age could not spend six months and then say, "May I call you Miss Marion?"

"I should like it very much."

He had enjoyed sitting beside her in the carriage; but the man in the driver's seat was within earshot, and his own role passive.

"Then how about the gig?" he asked.

"I have never ridden in one. I always think they look rather dangerous."

"You'd be quite safe with me."

Safe with me, my pretty one. Safe and cherished as long as I live! He was aware of the difference in age and added to himself, Yes, and after I'm gone. But he need not think of that yet. He came of a long-lived family; his great-grandfather at the age of ninety had been capable of giving a boy a sound thrashing. Hard on fifty good years ahead and stupid to wish that he'd met her—or her like—earlier. The young wives of young poor men had a tough time and aged early.

"Then I shall look forward, very much, to a new experience."

"May I call for you at two o'clock? That cob of mine can cover the ground. Where would you like to go?"

"Anywhere. It is all new to me. Apart from going to school

in Asham and for holidays in Yarmouth I have not been out of Bereham."

I will show you the world, he thought. Not the humdrum, penny-pinching world which, apart from variations in climate, was much the same wherever one went, but the great wide glittering world. In Europe he had not been farther east than Marseilles; there was Venice; there was Vienna, Rome, Naples; and all in style, reserved first class compartments on trains, staterooms on ships.

"Would you like," he asked, "to run into Bereham tomorrow and make a surprise visit?"

She stopped dead. "Oh no, Mr. Horridge, that would never do. It would . . . It would unsettle Mamma and Ellen. And Papa would think I was not taking my convalescence seriously." Under his supporting hand her arm had gone rigid.

He had suggested Bereham because he wished, as soon as possible, to establish himself with her family, but he abandoned the idea without regret and said in a voice of real concern:

"I forgot that. You look so well . . . you seem so well. But of course . . . Maybe we'd better stick to the carriage."

"Oh no," she said again, but this time with that flashing smile, "the gig, *please.*"

The drive in the gig was uneventful. The easy, companionable relationship ripened so that it seemed that they had known each other for months. Mr. Horridge asked if she felt nervous. Was he going too fast? Was the sun in her eyes, because if so they would turn into a shadier road. Was she comfortable? Was she tired?

The drive had no destination and it was with surprise

that Marion noticed as they took a turn that they were on the outskirts of Asham and within sight of her old school.

"Could you slow down, Mr. Horridge? That is where I went to school." She thought what a lot had happened since that autumn afternoon, less than a year ago, when she had made her stolen visit to Miss Ruthven; the afternoon when in fact it had all started. Less than a year and it might have been a hundred years.

"Were you happy there?"

"I was indeed. To think," she said, giving him that smile again, "how many times I have walked on this road. And now here I am, in your beautiful gig. Life is strange, Mr. Horridge."

He said, "This thing about names is a bit lop-sided. Maybe I jumped the gun a bit, calling you Miss Marion . . . a kind of halfway house. But between Mr. Horridge and Edward there is no halfway house. Do you think you could ever bring yourself to call me Edward?"

She said, "Let me see. Edward. Quite painless. And the sky did not fall, did it? Edward is a very nice name. I shall use it. Edward . . ."

It was another stride forward. It emboldened him to ask whether he could take her for a drive on the Saturday morning; perhaps starting at eleven o'clock? And though she had willed herself to forget and had in a way forgotten her own period of infatuation, she understood. Move the clock backward, or forward, let time stand still . . .

"There is a letter for you," Miss Rose said, handing across the table the one from Ellen and reserving the other.

Dearest Marion, Ellen wrote, *it is almost a week and it seems like a year. Your letter sounded so brave but I cannot think that you are happy in that* horrid *place and we are not happy here. Ada and Betty have fully recovered. Mamma plays the piano more than usual the piano being now unlocked and whenever I mention you, or the possibility of visiting you, Papa snaps my head off. I keep thinking that you went away without a book. I have found one that you might like and there is a man who delivers groceries to Heatherton, perhaps he would bring it. Quicker and cheaper than post . . .*

"It is from my sister," Marion said, laying the letter aside.

"And you are going to take a morning drive?"

"If you have no objection, Miss Rose."

"Now," Mr. Horridge said, having tucked the light woollen rug about Marion's knees and taken up the reins, "how about going to Norwich?" That was his surprise for her. He knew the city pretty well. It had a cathedral into which he had never been and into which on his own volition, he would never have gone, but he thought she might like it. And in Norwich there would be a bookshop. That there was a good inn, he knew, having eaten there several times.

"We'll sightsee a bit and then have lunch at The Maid's Head," he said.

This, she realised, was the testing moment.

She said, "Mr. . . . Edward, that is not possible. If I lunched with you in a public place Papa would surely get to know. He has many acquaintances and business friends in Norwich. I should be seen and recognised. Someone would inform Papa, he would be horrified. And I should be in *such* disgrace . . . It is unthinkable."

"Well, maybe I have gone a bit too fast," Mr. Horridge said, knowing that he had gone much too fast. "And the

149

last thing I'd wish to do would be to offend your father. Look, we have to go through Bereham. We'll stop and ask his permission. How'd that be."

It was now Saturday and nothing would happen at 10, Alma Avenue which could make it essential to keep up the pretence that she and Papa were on good terms. So she could be frank.

"It would be quite fatal. He would forbid you ever to see me again."

"But *why*. My intentions are honourable . . . I mean, Marion . . . Look, I mean . . . I want to marry you, more than anything in the world I want to marry you. I know I'm a bit old and nothing to look at and it's all been a kind of hurry, but if you only would . . . I'd be the happiest, proudest man in the world."

"Papa would never agree. He has no intention of allowing Ellen or me to marry."

"But why not? Whoa, Stormer," Mr. Horridge said, halting the cob and turning to give Marion his full attention. He saw that everything with her was under control, except her hands; in their neat little gloves they were plucking away at the fringe of the rug. He put out one of his own big, blunt-fingered hands and took them both into a reassuring hold. Be still; trust me.

"Papa," Marion said stonily, "holds that daughters should stay at home and provide comfort for their fathers as they age. I am not at Heatherton because I am ill, or demented. I made a few incautious remarks and was sent to Heatherton to be tamed. Miss Rose has been kind; you have been more than kind; but if he knew, he would have a stroke."

"Well, I've heard some odd things in my time, but that's the oddest."

"But it is true. And if, Edward, you do indeed wish to marry me it must be done secretly."

The past echoed. But this time, at least, there would be no problem about money.

Masculine obstinacy remained.

"Oh no," Mr. Horridge said, lapsing as he occasionally did under stress, into the grammar of his youth. "We ain't going to have a hole-and-corner affair. We're going to have a real slap-up wedding! That is," he said with a half-quizzical look, "if *you* want to marry me. You haven't said so yet."

"I do. I do indeed. Edward, at this moment the one thing I wish in the world is to marry you."

Well, there he was. He'd proposed and been accepted. Life, as Marion had remarked, was strange. Joy had come to him as belatedly and as abruptly as wealth had done.

"Bless you," he said, shifting his hand and taking her into a bear hug. "You've made me the happiest man in the world." He gave her a kiss which, wavering between aiming reverentially at her forehead and heartily at her mouth, landed ludicrously on her nose. He tried again and did better and was pleasantly surprised by the way her lips responded.

"I should be happy too," she said plaintively, "if we could be married without Papa knowing."

"Oh no, sweetheart. We're going to be married in style; red carpet, bells, choir boys, lilies. You looking like an angel and your father saying 'I do' in the proper place."

"If you want that kind of wedding you must look for another bride, Edward. Papa would never, never in a thousand years . . ."

"How can you be so *sure?* Has anybody else ever asked for you?"

"No. But I know. I know Papa."

Mr. Horridge wanted to say, *Bugger Papa!* But he restrained himself. "We'll skip Norwich for today," he said, "and go straight in and ask him."

She said, "Edward, *please,*" just as she had said, "Johnny, please." It was hopeless. Men were all the same, set on their own way, intransigent. Papa's blood brothers. "I can tell you exactly what will happen. He will refuse permission. He will accuse me of encouraging you and make that the excuse for keeping me at Heatherton, perhaps forever. Perhaps on the other side of the house."

"He can't be that daft." Until that Friday evening Mr. Horridge had not met Mr. Draper socially, but he had had business dealings with him and regarded him as a sound, sensible fellow; on the Friday he had shown himself to be a genial, generous host. "I know I'm not half good enough for you, nobody could be that, but I worship the ground you walk on and I can't see what he could have against me. Anyway, let's go and see."

On this late August morning autumn had just breathed on summer freshening the air and bringing that sense of a season about to change, so exhilarating to those for whom the next season holds promise. On such a morning, with the girl he loved beside him, Mr. Horridge was full of *hubris;* he felt that he could move mountains.

Marion folded back the rug and prepared to get out of the gig. "I have no wish to be present at a scene. I have had enough of them to last my lifetime. And I should be infinitely obliged if you would not tell Papa that I have been driving with you, or took tea with you, or agreed to marry you."

He put out his arm and pulled her close.

"You're that scared of him?"

"I am afraid of what he would do. And not only to me.

When he is angry—about anything—it rebounds on Mamma and Ellen, even the servants. Last week, because he was angry with me he locked the piano, Mamma's one solace." Speaking bitterly and rapidly as the memories of petty persecutions flooded back she tried to explain Papa to Edward.

"I'll wring his bloody neck," Mr. Horridge said, forgetting himself entirely. It was not the cry of an untried novice; he had never wrung anyone's neck, but he had killed a man in a fist fight.

"If you could do that," Marion said with a peculiar smile, "and not be hanged, we might be married. Otherwise I see no hope. We may indeed never see one another again."

"That's daft, too," he said. He had already diagnosed Mr. Draper: a household tyrant, bullying helpless women. He'd act differently when faced with a man, a man such as Mr. Horridge felt himself to be this morning.

"I can walk back to Heatherton," Marion said.

"Give me a kiss for luck, then." It was a very different kiss, it was like kissing a statue.

The bay cob, corn-crammed, richly pastured, had found something in the roadside growth that was not only edible but delicious. Mr. Horridge jerked him away from it, and with green slime dripping, the cob headed for Bereham.

Marion walked the short distance back to Heatherton and to Miss Rose, who seemed to like her, seemed to be a woman of good sense, and who might, just possibly, side with her when Papa came storming down in his wrath. Not openly— that would simply inflame his rage. But perhaps, if Miss Rose were told everything—except, of course, about Johnny —she would pretend to lock her away on the other side and then let her out, to do humble jobs. To that had the high hopes for the future been reduced in the last twenty minutes.

"Back so soon?" Miss Rose asked, coming down the stairs.

"Yes. Mr. Horridge had some business in Bereham, and I thought the waiting would be tedious, so I decided not to accompany him. I shall be able to read to Colonel Fraser after all."

"He is past it, poor old dear. Deeply unconscious. I think he will just slip away."

In her eyes, as she looked at Marion, the monkey curiosity was foremost. For Miss Rose had just read the other letter addressed to Miss Draper; and that made interesting reading indeed.

Marion, my dearest, my darling. You said you would write. Now it is Friday and I have had no letter. Is it that shut up in that horrible place you cannot write? Is it that you have forgotten your Johnny? Ellen came into the shop this morning—Baxter's is closed for renovations—and as I served her I inquired as to your health. She said you were well and had written to her. So why not to me? Are only letters to the family permitted?

Chérie, without you life is now insupportable. You said you might be a week away. Shall you be home on Monday? If so I might, with difficulty, contain myself until then. But if not I will walk out to Sorley on Sunday and think it well worth while, even for a kiss, if you can get out and will tell me of some meeting place. Marion, having lived as one separation is not to be borne. Let me know by first post tomorrow if I am to come and where. If I hear nothing I shall live for Monday and the light in the window and your welcoming arms. With such uncertainty and loneliness, food has been disagreeable to me this week and my stomach has been unfriendly. Mr. Freeman lacks sympathy. Chérie, I miss you more than I can write.

Having read this effusion Miss Rose thought she knew all. The word "Chérie" and something about the phrasing informed her that the writer was not English; and he worked in a shop. It was likely that Miss Draper had been sent to Heatherton not in order to be near Mr. Horridge, but to be away from the man who signed himself *Your ever-loving Johnny*. Upon that thought Miss Rose found herself, surprisingly, in accord with Mr. Draper; her feminism did not override her class-consciousness and her nature, romantic under all the trappings of practicality, found something revolting in a love letter which included a mention of digestive disorder.

Many of the letters she intercepted were destroyed at once. This one she decided to keep thinking that should she have misinterpreted Mr. Draper's attitude to Mr. Horridge—and perhaps there she had taken a bit of a leap in the dark—she could produce this screed and say, Look what I saved her from!

Now, looking at Marion, she thought, how deep the still waters run! "Having lived as one." That was eloquent. One ardent and possibly accepted lover in Bereham, Mr. Horridge simply infatuated; and there the girl stood, saying:

"How sad. But perhaps there is something else I could do."

"Yes. You could cut the last of the red roses; to dry with lavender, for potpourri."

In the sunny garden Marion gathered red roses. Above stairs Colonel Fraser emerged from merciful coma and was glad that he had added the codicil to his will, "To Miss Eleanor Rose, a token of gratitude for her unfailing care and kindness the sum of £2,000 (Two thousand pounds)." He'd done that. It was very little but the best he could do. "Not enough," he said. "Never enough." He lay back and died.

Mr. Horridge swung his gig into the yard at the Maltings. A little boy ran out from some retreat and asked earnestly, "Sir, do you want your horse tethered or walked?" The answer might make all the difference between a penny and threepence.

"Walked," Mr. Horridge said, looking at the bay's steaming hide. He twisted the reins around the dashboard of the gig and jumped down, lithe as a boy. He knew his way to Mr. Draper's office, went to it and flung the door open. It hit the cupboard and Mr. Draper looked up, a rebuke on his tongue. Then he saw that the clumsy door opener was Mr. Horridge who owned a thousand acres of the best land in Norfolk and grew the best barley. He put on his affable manner.

All the way from Sorley to Bereham Mr. Horridge had been cherishing his own extremely eligible image. Not young, but sprightly, for his age very good. And rich. And yet, when Mr. Draper stood up behind the battered old table that served him as a desk and held out his hand and said, "Mr. Horridge, I hardly expected to see you on a Saturday morning. And how is your harvest going?" Mr. Horridge was suddenly reduced. He felt like an agent or a tenant farmer, reporting, and the report had better be good, or else . . .

"Very well," he said, "but that is not what I have come to see you about, Mr. Draper."

The battered old table was set at a slant in the window embrasure so that Mr. Draper could, by slightly turning his head, survey his yard. The visitor's chair was so placed that in order to look into the yard more movement was needed. Mr. Horridge made this effort and drew strength from the sight of his shining gig with the sun bouncing off the yellow spokes of its wheels, and his glossy, amber-coloured cob.

He said abruptly, "Mr. Draper, I've come to ask permission to marry your daughter."

Mr. Draper gave no sign of surprise or shock.

"I have two, Mr. Horridge," he said almost lightly.

"I mean Marion. Miss Marion."

"Having seen her once?" There was something of amusement, of mockery in his tone. It provoked Mr. Horridge into forgetting Marion's plea.

"Once would have been enough. But I've seen her since. I loved her the moment I saw her. Then I found we hit it off well together. So I asked her and she said, 'Yes,' so here I am."

"So I see. How very extraordinary," Mr. Draper said as though someone had just shown him a calf with two heads. "And how painful for you. Perhaps I am somewhat to blame. But a father could hardly make a public proclamation. Just over three weeks ago, Mr. Horridge, my daughter sustained a severe injury to her head. She is not now in a condition to make the simplest decision for herself."

"But that's not true. Marion is as sound in the head as you or me."

"Then why do you imagine I sent her to Heatherton? To facilitate your courtship?"

The sarcasm stung; but Mr. Horridge was not going to jeopardise his case by showing ill-humour.

"I knew, of course, that she had had an accident. But she's over it. I asked her to marry me and she said she would, subject to your consent."

"That at least was sensible."

"Then may I have it?"

"No."

"Why? What have you got against me?" Mr. Draper made no reply, but his silence and his glance implied, Everything! Mr. Horridge blundered on. "I'm a bit old, I realise that.

But she'd be all right—even when I'm gone. My affairs are in a sound way. You're welcome to investigate. Thorley's is my bank. I'd settle forty thousand on her. As a wedding present."

"I really wonder what I can possibly have done or said to convey the impression that my daughter was for auction."

Again Mr. Horridge kept his temper.

"I didn't mean it like that. I was trying to explain. I can understand a father wanting to see his daughter well provided for. Can you give me a reason for refusing me?"

"I can. I have never seen it as part of a man's duty to rear and cherish a female child in order to provide another man with a wife."

Mr. Horridge's eyes popped.

"Great God in Glory! Why, if every man thought like that where'd the human race be?"

"I was not laying down a rule for every man. I am explaining my position. I look to my daughters to provide company and comfort in my latter years."

Exactly what Marion, poor darling, had said! In Mr. Horridge the killing rage began to mount again.

"Is that your last word? You mean you don't want to see them married and cared for, with families of their own . . ."

"I seem to have made myself clear. And now, if you will excuse me, this is pay day." On the table before him lay a list of workmen's names, a bag of coins and some little piles already laid out. "Oh, there is one thing more, Mr. Horridge. My daughter is a patient in a Nursing Home. If you persist in forcing your attentions upon a girl who is not quite mentally sound you will draw upon yourself no small measure of opprobrium."

Mr. Horridge was not sure what opprobrium meant but he guessed something nasty.

He got up and put himself into a posture no gentleman

would ever have assumed. He placed his feet wide apart and hooked his thumbs into the top of his trousers. All the good humour had gone from his weathered face, leaving something primitive and dangerous.

He said, not loudly, "Now, look here. I wanted to do things properly, so I came and asked you. You say no. Man, nobody is coming between me and her! Get that into your thick head. When I want something like I want Marion I don't let nothing nor nobody stand in my way. You give me leave to marry her or I'll ruin you."

This was a possibility Mr. Draper had foreseen. He said, "I can buy barley elsewhere."

"I never even thought about such a piddling little thing. When I say ruin, I mean *ruin*. I'll go straight out and buy that old boat-building place. I'll start a Maltings. The men you give twelve shillings a week to I'll give fifteen, starting Monday. On every Corn Exchange, every farm within two hundred miles I'll offer five shillings over market price for barley. And what I sell I'll sell cheap, give it away if I have to. By Christmas all this'll be dead and done for. And whatever you do, wherever you go, I'll hound you down. If I get to work on you, Mr. Draper, sir, you won't want your daughters to comfort your old age, you'll want bread to put in your belly. You don't know what you're up against this time. I'll give my last penny."

In Mr. Draper's smooth cheeks the healthy colour disintegrated into little red islands in a sea of pallor; but he did not lose his dignity or self-control.

"Against such resources as you can command, I am powerless," he said. "I have my wife, my other daughter to consider. Very well, under compulsion, I give you leave to marry Marion."

Mr. Horridge wondered why, having gained his point, he should feel deflated and somehow in the wrong.

"Well," he said, "that's all I wanted. I don't want any hard feelings. What I said I only said because you drove me."

"Then we are both in the same boat," Mr. Draper observed. "But this, as I said, is pay day." He went to the window which was open and shouted, "Hardy." A man came running. "Hardy," Mr. Draper said, "something has cropped up that demands my attention. You pay out." With steady hands he passed out the piles already made, the bag, the list. "Mark off each as he's paid. Have you a pencil?"

"No sir."

"Then take this." He gave Hardy a pencil.

"Now," he said, resuming his seat, "we must discuss arrangements. I imagine that you would wish to be married as soon as possible."

"It can't be too soon for me."

Calmly Mr. Draper consulted the calendar.

"Then I would suggest the third Thursday in September. That would allow for the banns; and Thursday is a good day, many establishments observe early-closing and that gives the male members of the choir a chance to perform. I take it that you wish for a choir, and bell-ringers."

"I just want the best for Marion, from the start." Mr. Horridge then said something which was in fact prompted by some delicacy of feeling. "I know you're against it. I know you weren't prepared. It's sudden and it'll be expensive. I'll foot the bill gladly."

He had delivered himself into Papa's merciless hands.

"Mr. Horridge, if you would sit down and for a few minutes forget that you are a rich man while I am comparatively poor, we can pursue this discussion. Otherwise I would suggest written communication. For sheer vulgarity this interview must be unequalled."

Mr. Horridge sat down.

Mr. Draper said, "It is customary for the bride's family to arrange the wedding, doing their best, according to the circumstances. I shall give Marion the wedding, and the trousseau which I should have been prepared to provide had I ever wished her to marry. There will be no bill for you to foot."

Amongst other thoughts Mr. Horridge entertained one, What must Marion's life have been with this detestable man!

"Very well. As you wish."

"And I feel that there has been some flouting of convention," Mr. Draper said. "Presumably when you asked Marion to marry you you were alone with her."

"Yes. We were taking a drive."

"Indiscreet. We must make amends by being very careful now. Marion must return home tomorrow and for the next three weeks you must be content to see her only when she is properly chaperoned. Hasty marriages cause talk and we must be careful not to give the wrong impression. If it is indeed wrong."

"God damn you! I never laid a finger on her until this morning when I asked her to marry me and she said she would. Then I kissed her."

"I will, as soon as possible, arrange a party to celebrate this engagement. Perhaps you could provide some good reason for haste. Business?"

"Pleasure. I want to take her to Paris for the honeymoon. All those chestnut trees and the entertainments starting up." One of his first jobs had taken him to Paris, a menial attendant to a couple of race horses. He had been there since, as a rich man, a little dismayed to find that the shops were less entrancing when you could walk in and buy what you wanted than they had been when you could only stand outside and stare. And the lights had seemed more garish, the entertainments less entertaining. But with Marion beside him all would be new.

"That sounds good enough," Mr. Draper said. "And of course, the very rich are allowed their whims." That was an acidulous remark. The next was worse. "In the circumstances, Mr. Horridge, you can hardly expect me to wish you well. In fact I hope she will make you thoroughly unhappy. She is capable of it."

Less than a mile out of Bereham Mr. Horridge had forgotten everything except that he had won. He thought of Marion getting out of the gig with the remark that they might not meet again. "Pick your feet up, Stormer," he said. "Get along, boy. Move!"

At Heatherton he rang the bell violently and Miss Rose said, "I will go, Stubbs," in a voice that boded no good for the ringer of that bell.

When she saw him she thought, Drunk!

"Where is she? I've got something to tell her."

"Miss Draper is washing her hands before lunch."

He made for the stairs, calling, "Marion!" Miss Rose took him by the arm; one of her master holds. It sent pain running down to the tips of his fingers and up as far as his ear.

"There has been a death in the house," she said. "If you will go into my room, I will call Miss Draper."

Marion had heard his cry and was on her way down.

"Darling, my dearest, sweetest girl. It's all right. He said yes. We're engaged!"

One of her dizzy spells hit her. She seemed to totter. Mr.

Horridge picked her up, hugged her, and put her on one of the sofas.

"I'm a clumsy brute."

"It was such a surprise. I cannot really believe it. What happened? What did he *say?*"

"It took a bit of persuasion," Mr. Horridge said. He had won. He could afford to show a victor's magnanimity.

"I never before knew Papa to yield a point."

"He never before had me to deal with. Darling, the third Thursday in September. I swear you shall never regret it. The one thing from now on, to see you're safe and happy. We'll have such times . . ."

He was suddenly aware that Miss Rose stood in the doorway.

"Here," he said, "you be the first to congratulate the luckiest man in the world. I'm sorry about the old fellow, but it can't be helped and we mustn't let it spoil this day. We're going to be *married!*" He was behaving like an overgrown boy but again Miss Rose found this disarming. She shot a glance at Marion who looked pleased, or rather as though she would look pleased once she had recovered from amazement. "I'm sure I do congratulate you, very heartily, Mr. Horridge. And Miss Draper, I wish you every happiness in the world. I think this calls for champagne."

She kept a modest stock. Sometimes it was ordered medicinally, usual in conjunction with oysters. Sometimes gentlemen on the way to recovery would demand it. And Miss Rose herself, at the end of any particularly tiring and trying day, found it a useful pick-me-up.

She rang the bell and gave the order. While waiting for the wine to come Mr. Horridge gave details of the plans for the immediate future which included Mr. Draper's order that Marion was to go home on the next day, Sunday, and not driven by Mr. Horridge. The cab would be sent for her.

"I shall be genuinely sorry to leave Heatherton," Marion said to Miss Rose. "You have been so kind. I hope that you will come to our wedding." Saying that made it seem suddenly real. "And afterwards we shall be neighbours."

The champagne came, a better brand, Mr. Horridge observed, than he would have given the old girl—or indeed any woman—credit for choosing.

"Many, many happy years," said Miss Rose, raising her glass. She was about to sip when Stubbs came in and muttered into her ear.

"Nothing," Miss Rose said, "has happened in this house during the last three years without Mrs. Selton trying to divert attention to herself." She put down her glass and went quickly away.

"Well now, I'll wish you many, many happy years, sweetheart. And if they ain't happy it shan't be my fault."

"I wish you happy, too," she said, giving her charming smile. She did not love him; she had known love and its aftermath of disillusion; but she liked him and would always be grateful to him because he had set her free. She would be amiable, companionable and faithful. "I am not all you think me, Edward, but I will try to make you a good wife."

"All you have to do," Mr. Horridge said, coming as near poetic expression as was possible to him, "is go on breathing. You just breathe and leave the trying to me."

Very faintly, from behind the padded door that divided one side of the house from the other, there came a sound of a scream. And another.

Mr. Horridge said, "A Dean is a sort of parson. Am I right?"

"A Dean is a church dignitary."

"I wondered if you'd like one at the wedding. This one at Asham they keep on at me about. He's no kin to me, though his name is Horridge. But if he's got a church he's got a roof that needs propping up . . . I could get him, if you'd like that, if I set about it the right way."

He wanted to give her the moon and the stars. He would give her a Dean.

"You see, I never even thought of that kind of wedding. I never dreamed that Papa would ever give his consent."

And you were dead right. Nobody but me could have pulled it off.

"Then there's the ring. I'd have liked you to choose it. But I don't see your father letting you come to London with me. So I'll have to do it alone. What do you fancy? Sapphire? Emerald? Diamond? I do *know* a bit about diamonds." That was a modest statement. His interests in Africa had expanded and now included the gem stones which in the raw state looked anything but precious.

"Whatever you choose will please me," Marion said.

"Then I'll do the best I can in London. Given a bit more time I'd have had one made up specially. But your father said something about announcing the engagement, so we must have a ring. There'll be time, after. And we're going to Paris for our honeymoon—that is if that's agreeable to you. There're some pretty good shops there, too." A whole new world had opened to him. He had provided himself with everything that a gentleman could need; now he could buy pretty, expensive things for a lady. For Marion. For his love.

Miss Rose came back. The palm of her right hand was scarlet and stinging.

"Mrs. Selton," she said lightly, "has taken a sudden dislike to curry, she emptied her plate over Mrs. Awkwright's head. Not that that mattered, Mrs. Awkwright is as near a vegetable as a vertebrate can be; but it made a great deal of clearing up for those who, goodness knows, have enough to do. And unless checked she might next time choose a more sensitive target." The glass was cool against the palm that had done the checking. What she called the idiot side could be very trying, but it was the paying side. People would pay twice as much to have a demented relative kept out of sight and given a modicum of attention, as they would for the nursing care, the good food, the pampering on *this* side. And medical patients either recovered or died; idiots lived on and on . . .

o   o   o

AFTER ELLEN HAD VENTURED A FEW REMARKS, MET WITH monosyllabic answers, it was obvious that Papa had returned home in a bad mood. Something to do with business?

Then, halfway through supper, Papa said:

"Marion has disgraced herself." That was the line which he had decided to take, within the family: and he was convinced that he was right. He had always known that there was more than met the eye in the de Brissac affair, and it was all too plain that no young woman who behaved properly could have brought a man to the point of proposal within eight days.

Mamma put down her spoon very quietly and said nothing. Ellen dropped hers with a clatter. Papa deliberately allowed the moment of suspense to prolong itself. Marion, by sheer chance, had slipped from his control. Those who were left must be the more subdued. And there they sat, waiting upon his word. He emptied his mouth and spoke.

"She has been playing fast and loose in such a manner that only marriage can retrieve her reputation."

166

"Marriage!" Mamma knew her husband's views upon that subject.

"Who to?" Ellen asked.

"A man of whom I thoroughly disapprove."

Not Johnny Brisket! Yet whom else did Marion know?

"A cad of the first water," Papa said. "One of the most ill-bred fellows I have ever met. A purse-proud vulgarian."

Johnny could not be called purse-proud.

"He was here yesterday week. A man named Horridge. In the six days since Marion left home she has so misconducted herself that he was encouraged to propose to her. And she, without a word to me, accepted him. He called upon me this morning and described a state of affairs which left me no choice but to give my consent. The wedding will take place four weeks on Thursday."

Mamma dared not, at this stage, say anything; so she sat and exonerated herself; she had done her best to bring up both her daughters properly; whatever had occurred during the past week had not even occurred under her roof.

Ellen thought, unselfishly, how wonderful for Marion! And then, selfishly, of how much she would miss her.

"I have ordered the cab to bring Marion home tomorrow afternoon. From now on I want everything to be as seemly as possible. In public we must pretend that the match is welcome and that the brevity of the engagement is due to Mr. Horridge's desire to catch a certain season in Paris. They will honeymoon there." He changed his tone slightly. "What I want both of you to understand is that Marion has shamed us all; you are not to behave to her as though she had come home in a blaze of glory. She has," he said, "broken my heart."

Mamma now felt that she could venture a remark if she made it sound like a complaint.

"It allows very little time."

"Very little. And I shall expect it done as though we had had six months at least. We must give a dinner party—I think on Wednesday—to announce and to celebrate the engagement."

"Shall I be a bridesmaid?"

"Naturally. I said everything was to be done properly."

"We shall need others." Ellen was now preparing to make the most of the occasion and to ignore the gloomy future. "Has Mr. Horridge any suitable female relatives?" She meant of the right age and size. His sisters would be too old, but he might have nieces.

"No relative of his would be suitable, except to serve in a low tavern. But of course you must ask . . ."

Having thus injected misery into what might for the two women have been a joyous occasion he felt slightly better.

o   o   o

IT SHOULD HAVE BEEN BETTY'S FREE SUNDAY AFTERNOON, but Mr. Draper cancelled it without apology. "Miss Marion will be returning. There will be her trunk to deal with, and if she needs help with her unpacking you must see to it." The sullen look with which Betty served the meal did not surprise him, but he resented it and used it as a platform from which to attack Ada, and through Ada, Mamma. "If we had two servants instead of one and a half," he said sourly, "we should not be driven to these shifts."

"Papa, I could have . . ." Ellen began.

"I spoke once before on that subject, my dear. Nothing that has happened since has changed my feeling. And I hope that you will remember what I said last evening. Marion has not come home in a blaze of glory. Also, you have enough to do helping your Mamma with the invitations for Wednes-

168

day." He had made the list of guests; he had made a draft of the letter which Mamma was to copy. Ellen was to address and stamp the envelopes.

Betty said, "It'll slide, Miss," and the trunk did so, easily down the stairs. Not so easily across the stretch of floor to the bedroom. Marion lent a hand.

"I dunno," Betty said apologetically, "I can remember when I could have managed. The truth is I never rightly got over that turn. Can't seem to get my strength back."

"My sister wrote to me that you had been unwell."

"Me and Ada both. And they can say what they like, it wasn't *plums*. Nobody never nearly died eating plums and as a matter of fact I never ate a plum all Monday. Ada, I grant you, did, and she's off plums for the rest of her life. But I know different." Betty looked round furtively. "I wouldn't say this to anybody but you, Miss. It was the wine. The master told me to chuck it out but Ada and me thought we'd try it. And he was right. It wasn't fit to drink and it nearly killed us."

Being able to make this confidence brought home to Betty the fact that Marion was the one human being above stairs who ever regarded *her* as human.

"I am glad to see you back, Miss. And better. The house didn't seem the same somehow."

"I shall not be here long. Betty, you must not say a word until it is made public. Promise?"

"Swear across my heart."

"I am going to be married, quite soon."

"Coooo," Betty said. "Who to?"

"Mr. Horridge. He dined here, last Friday week."

That old man, was Betty's first thought. Her second was a by-word, "Better an old man's darling than a young man's

169

slave." But she thought immediately that this was one of Mr. Draper's arrangements and as such must be accepted and made the best of. "I do hope you'll be very happy, Miss. I thought he was nice . . ." That was true, she'd thought him nice, but a bit old, as were all the gentlemen at all the parties at 10, Alma Avenue. "And, Miss," Betty said practically, "when you are married and have a place of your own, find a place for me. Please. With you gone, and Ada, Monday shook her up more than anybody realised, this'll be a dead house."

Marion stood there and realised that Johnny had not failed her; she had, in fact, almost killed two innocent people. But she thought that once she was married, safe and away, she could shelter them all, not only Betty and Ada but Mamma and Ellen, too.

She had not yet, as an engaged, about-to-be-married woman, come face to face with Papa. A bit like God from Sinai he had issued his orders, and made his will known from a distance.

"Good evening, Papa."

"Good evening, Marion." He did not look at her; neither then nor throughout the meal. She had been the cause of the most complete humiliation he had ever known in his life. His hatred of her was second only to the hatred he felt for Mr. Horridge who, on this Sunday evening, was licking his indelible pencil and composing a letter, presently to be written, more painfully, in ink, on the best paper.

A profound and terrible gloom loomed over the table.

Ellen said, "The Harvest Festival is early this year, on account of the good weather. The Sunday after next."

"Mr. Walker's pumpkins may not have attained full size," Papa said.

"But they will be ripe, I trust," Mamma said. "I always buy one of his pumpkins, for Ada's special pie."

That subject died in silence.

Marion had had warning how it would be. Mamma had snatched her moment, administered a kiss of quite surprising quality and said, "I hope you will be happy. It is all very sudden, but I think he is kind . . ." Ellen had snatched her moment. "Darling, how wonderful. I am so happy for you, but what I shall do now . . . And Papa is enraged. All those letters saying how *pleased* he is . . . and I'm hardly supposed to speak to you. It is confusing."

"Not for long, dearest. He can hardly refuse to allow you to visit Sorley. We'll have such parties . . . As for the interval, we can bear anything for such a short time."

Such a short time, thought the sixteen people whom Mr. Draper regarded as his friends, when, on Monday morning, they opened their letters and found themselves bidden to a party on Wednesday evening to celebrate the engagement about which he was so pleased. It was not the brevity of Marion's acquaintance with Mr. Horridge which made them exclaim, for about that they did not know, and Mr. Horridge could well have been an acquaintance of some long standing. It was the shortness of the engagement period which was startling. It was a period of prolonged engagements in circles where convention was observed and here was an engagement just long enough for banns to be read and no more. Goodness knew, Angela Taylor's had been a hurried-on wedding; this was even more so. Poor Mrs. Draper, how could she possibly have things ready in time?

Opinion about the match varied. The man was quite a catch, of course, and more presentable than his slightly mysterious background warranted. Rather old? But then dear Marion had always seemed older than she actually was, the contrast was not so sharp as it might have been, and Mr. Horridge might even be younger than he appeared; Africa might have aged as well as enriched him. On the whole it was regarded as satisfactory.

Mrs. Draper was managing very well. Once she emerged from her protective shell she showed herself capable of organisation. First thing on Monday morning she had a long interview with Ada who on Wednesday would again have the opportunity to prove her sterling worth.

Then she revealed to her daughters the results of her ponderings as to how so short a time could best be employed.

"I asked Papa to bespeak Jarvey's carriage for half-past ten. We will go first to Proctor's and select material. Proctor's dressmaker is good enough, but not as good as Miss Bussey. Miss Bussey must make the wedding dress, and mine. Ellen is easier to fit; Proctor's woman can make her dress and that of the other bridesmaids. Your street costume Baker can make as usual. You will need at least two other dresses and to get them done in time I think we must try Ransome's. Then there are the underclothes. I think Nanny would be pleased to be asked to do a little plain sewing—the night-gowns, perhaps. For the rest there is that little woman in Fargate, I forget her name, but I can find the house."

Mamma was loquacious, brisk, happy. To hear her one would imagine that this was an ordinary, long-hoped-for marriage and that her own married life had been such a time of unclouded happiness that she wished nothing better for her daughter.

"I do not need, or wish for, a lot of new clothes, Mamma," Marion said. "A wedding dress, yes, that I must have. For the rest what I already own will do, until I am married and can have new ones."

"But Papa said everything must be done properly, and no expense spared."

Papa had said a number of other things, too. Last evening. To Marion, the last person in the world to sympathise, he had exposed his near-mortal wound—look what you, my daughter, have done to me! He gave her a word for word account of that interview with Mr. Horridge. "A purse-proud vulgarian, shamelessly using his money as a bludgeon." The thought that in a lesser way he had behaved exactly the same in the Freeman-Baxter business never once occurred to him, and if it had he would have brushed it aside. Rules were made for other people. "I quite understand that he has found it difficult to find any decently brought-up young woman to marry him. To him you must seem like a godsend, apparently well-reared, member of a decent family, so weak, so yielding, so lost to grace. Small wonder he priced you so high! Had I been a man with no family," Mr. Draper said, being for once a little illogical, "I should have sent him about his business. As it was, I had no choice. So you must marry your guttersnipe, who, once married, will show himself for what he is."

She would have liked to say that Edward had been un-vulgar enough as to conceal the more sordid side of that interview from her. But the next three weeks would be trying enough, without adding to Papa's rage, for which there was, for once, she could see, good reason.

But now, faced with the prospect of spending Papa's money on a wedding, the thought of which was so hateful to him, she was stubborn, insisting that at least she needed no new underclothes. She visualised others, not sewn by Nanny or Mamma's little women. She thought in terms of silk.

Mamma was willing to concede on that point, knowing that Papa was concerned mainly with appearance.

So they went to Proctor's and to Ransome's and to Miss Bussey's, and all was well; everywhere obsequious promises. Then Mamma said to the hired driver, "To Corder's Domestic Agency."

It sounded as though the moment for Ada's replacement had come. The reverse was true. Mamma wished to hire a good strong woman who, on Wednesday, would help Ada and Betty. She was a little shocked to find that casual help was, by comparison with the other sort, expensive. Two shillings for one day. But it was all part of doing the thing properly, of sparing no expense. On the whole it was a very satisfactory day: out of Papa's presence Mamma and Ellen found it easy to forget that Marion was in disgrace and to remember only that she was about to be a bride, the centre of all this exciting busy-ness. Their mood was infectious and Marion could see that she had been profoundly fortunate. She could also see a kind of pattern, one thing leading to another in an inexorable way to this happy culmination.

The past, however, was not to be so easily shuffled off. On neat, rather too-expensively-shod feet it came padding along, down Honey Lane, into Alma Avenue and it tapped with a well-cared-for hand upon her window.

She realised that she had been very foolish not to have written him a final, dismissing letter as soon as she was in Heatherton, safe behind the barrier of Miss Rose. But there had been so much else to think of; she had in fact forgotten him. She let him in in the usual way, avoided his lips, slipped out of his embrace, found the hair tonic bottle that held the pilfered brandy and poured him a good measure. While he drank he would not be kissing or fondling her, and brandy was good for shock.

He began by reproaching her for not writing to him.

"I had no time. So much has happened in a week."

"I made time to write to you. I was prepared to *walk* to Sorley to see you yesterday."

"Papa ordered me home yesterday."

Here again the past served; Johnny had met Papa and been overborne by him, so he would understand. The forceful and dreaded figure that had loomed over and darkened her whole life, was now a rock of refuge.

"Papa," she said, "has arranged for me to be married. Next month."

The glass slipped through his fingers and shattered with what seemed, in the sleeping house, a loud noise.

"Mon Dieu! C'est impossible!" He dragged in a noisy breath. "And you agreed? How could he? How could you? You belong to me. You are my wife in all but name. Here in this room. How can you sit there and say . . ."

"Quiet," she said. "You will rouse the house."

"I will rouse the house. Let him come down and find me here. I'll tell him . . ."

"He'd kick you out. Unless you lower your voice, Johnny, that is what will happen."

Less loudly, but more bitterly, he said, "And you agreed to this iniquity?"

"You know very well that where Papa is concerned my wishes count for nothing. What else could I do?"

"You could have made a stand. You never did." He was back with his old grudge. Back with his fantasy. "If from the first you had faced him, taken me by the hand and said, Here is the man I wish to marry and nothing will change my mind, things would have been different."

"As different as it would have been if at Yarmouth you had said you wanted, not a new suit, but my hand in marriage. Papa is, and you must know it, not a man to be faced up to."

"Who is the man?"

"Mr. Horridge."

"Ah. I know. Very rich . . ." Rich beyond reckoning, some people said he was a millionaire. And to his possessions was to be added this attractive, passionate girl with whom, up to a minute or two ago, Johnny had believed himself to be in love, and the five thousand pounds due to her when she became of age. "And old," he said, "with a face like an old boot. You wish to marry him?"

Better be firm and definite. "Yes, having no choice."

"Then you must be saved from yourself and from your father. Tomorrow I will see Mr. Horridge and ask how he feels about robbing me of one who was in all but name my wife, who almost bore my child."

For a second everything went black. Behind the nicely healed scar, the healthy new growth of hair, the scar began to throb. It was like going down into the water again, and finding it hard. But she forced herself to the surface. The words, *Please Johnny,* formed in her mind, almost on her tongue, but it was useless to implore. How many times had she not started a sentence with those useless words.

"Mr. Horridge would not believe you. He would not wish to believe you. He has a high opinion of me. And naturally I should deny everything."

The little room had seen many changes in their relationship, now, for the first time a definite hostility was present.

"He will believe me," Johnny said. "And so will your Papa. You see, I have your letters."

The letters had hardly seemed to have any physical existence once they had been smuggled out of the house and into the postbox. Written in the white heat of passion, often begun before Johnny had reached Honey Lane, they had been communications between soul and soul until they became frenzied appeals for marriage. And he had promised to destroy them as soon as they were read. She had exacted that promise before she had written many when he spoke laughingly one evening about how thoroughly Mrs. Fenner cleaned his room, moving everything and putting nothing back in its former place. Then, for an agonised moment, she had seen her letters as tangible things. "They are in a safe place," Johnny assured her, "but if you wish I will destroy them—though it will be like tearing out my heart. And in the future I will carry each letter about me, all day, reading it from time to time, kissing it often. And then into the stove . . ."

Now, seeing how she had been deceived and with what complete disaster she was threatened, she was filled with a vast cold anger, not unlike her father's in kind but so much greater that beside it his was mere peevishness. But years of control came to her aid.

"I thought you burnt them," she said, almost casually, "but if you have preserved them, it alters everything."

"I could never bring myself to do it. They are so beautiful."

"Papa and Mr. Horridge will think otherwise. Papa, indeed, will regard them as final proof that I am insane. Before you could blink I should be back at Heatherton—*and on the other side!*"

"But I shall not use them unless I am compelled. In order to save you. I cannot stand by and see you forced into marriage with another man. Sweetheart, forget the letters; forget that I mentioned them. Let us go back to our other plan. We cannot now wait until you have your legacy; we must escape at once, run away to London. Tomorrow."

"I would sooner go to Heatherton and live with lunatics than go to London to live with a man who does not love me."

"But I do, Marion. I do. How can you say that?"

"Because you threatened to shame and expose me as no woman was ever shamed before. The other side of Heatherton is not pleasant, but provided one behaves, not intolerable. Run along, Johnny, do your worst. I have done with it all."

Against this he was helpless. For a moment at a loss for words.

"And why I bother to warn you," Marion said, "I cannot understand. But I will. Mr. Horridge is quite likely to do you some physical damage. I will let you out now."

She stood up. Accepting the worst she was impregnable. He flung himself, in a theatrical gesture, on to his knees and clutched her midway between knee and waist. She said, "Let go of me, Johnny, or I shall call Papa."

He began to whine and whimper. He had meant no harm. He wished only to save her from a loveless marriage. He loved her. Had not meant what he said. What could he do to prove his good faith? He would go home and burn the letters.

"You said that before. I trusted you then. Why should I trust you now? Even if we married, Johnny, I should always feel that in those letters you had a weapon to use against me. In them I showed you my inmost heart and you could always show it to the world."

"But if I brought the letters, burned them in your presence. Would that convince you?"

"It might." It was the point to which she had been working, as Mr. Draper would work towards a price for the barely he bought, the malt he sold, and bargains were not things about which one displayed any emotion.

"And then you will consider coming away with me? At once?"

"I might. But, Johnny, I need more than that . . ." She must confound him, lead him to think that the letters were not of prime importance. "I should need your assurance that after we were married you would never remember, or mention, even to me, that I had been indiscreet and given myself to you outside marriage. With that forgotten and the letters burnt, it might be possible to make a fresh start."

"On Wednesday?"

"No. Thursday. For a very simple reason, Johnny. On Wednesday evening Mr. Horridge will present me with a very valuable ring. He is buying it today. And he knows about diamonds. It could be useful to tide over the lean times we may have."

"Tomorrow then. I will bring the letters and we will plan for Thursday."

"Yes, we will plan for Thursday."

She let him out. The moon, so rightly called the Harvest Moon, for by its chill and eerie light men were still scything and stacking on Mr. Horridge's fields, and on others, anxious to earn the stipulated harvest money in the shortest possible time—by the kitchen door of 10, Alma Avenue where nothing was sown and nothing reaped, the moon made a world sharply black and white. The area was a well of darkness; Johnny climbing the steps, emerging into whiteness, suddenly looked colossal, raising one hand in salute.

Halfway along Honey Lane Jean de Brissac's Gallic common sense caught up with him.

179

On Tuesday morning Mamma opened envelope after envelope and finally reported, with complacency, that all invitations had been accepted and that everyone was *delighted* to hear the splendid news.

On Tuesday, Ada said, "I reckon this'll be my last, Betty. I'm bloody near done for, but let's give Miss Marion a good send off." She hammered violently upon the eggshells which would clear the consommé and make it sparkle. One of her secrets. Nine out of ten people thought it sufficient to drop a few eggshells into the brew of beef and bones and vegetables; they were wrong; the shells must be thoroughly smashed.

"When you go, I go," Betty said.

Ada thought that this would be hard on Mrs. Draper, whom she still thought of with a lingering sentimentality as Miss Emily, but she could see which way the wind was blowing, the hiring of a stranger to help on Wednesday showed all too clearly how things were shaping.

"I could've trained you to take my place," Ada said, "but there was never any time, you being so busy. I said, twenty years back, this was an awkward house, needing three to run it and room only for two. And I was right. How could you learn how to make gravy when you're up there setting the table. Stands to reason. Not that it matters," Ada said, shuffling off her feeling of responsibility to Miss Emily. "These days you just go along to Corder's and hire what you need. Not that it's the same. Not by a long chalk."

For Marion, Tuesday was a curious day. The party on Wednesday was occupying Mamma's attention and Ellen's; a kind of hurdle to be taken before the smooth, unimpeded run to the wedding day. With something so much more vital, literally a matter of life and death awaiting her at the end of the day, she listened to their chatter, gladioli in the drawing room, dahlias on the dining table, or vice versa? And the ever present question of what to wear.

Johnny arrived and was admitted. He appeared to be emptyhanded, but she refrained from mentioning the letters. In a pocket, perhaps. But he was slim and his clothes fitted so well that the bulge would have been perceptible.

"On my way home this evening," he said, "I went to the station to assure myself about trains. The London train was just in, and your Mr. Horridge was being met by his man. I thought of what he had in his pocket. I thought of the surprise in store for him. I almost laughed aloud."

"There is a comic side to it all, I suppose," she said. *Where are those letters?*

She bore the kissing and the embracing with a scarcely curbed impatience. Then, before he sat down, he did what all gentlemen careful of their appearance did, arranged his coattails to avoid creasing.

"Oh yes," he said, and produced from the coattail pocket a bundle of letters tied with blue ribbon. So much useless agitation; she should have remembered the rear pocket, a favourite repository of men vain of their figures. Holding the bundle in his hand he said, "I dared not reread them for fear I should weaken. This will be truly a burnt offering to love." He seemed to have forgotten how, twenty-four hours earlier, he had been threatening to use the outpourings.

Even this mean little room had been furnished with a grate and she had prepared it; the white paper fan removed, the box of matches on the meagre ledge of a mantelpiece. Johnny dropped in the bundle.

"Shall I light the pyre?"

"Yes." The sooner the better. Let me be done with this.

"Now," she said, "you must try this brandy. I filched it today; it is Papa's very best, because of the party tomorrow."

"It will settle my stomach which is suffering from Mrs. Fenner's beef pudding."

In the grate the closely tied letters burnt very slowly and smoulderingly.

"You should have taken off the ribbon," she said and took up the poker. Under its prod the ribbon flamed and broke, the bundle fell apart and began to burn briskly. A single page reared up, writhing like a living thing. It said, "I love you, I love you, my darling, my dear one," and then it turned brown and collapsed.

She felt sorry for the girl, young, innocent and loving, who had written those words.

"On Thursday I shall take the first train to Norwich," Johnny said, happily sipping and planning. "We should not be seen to leave together. You must catch the one at eleven o'clock. At Norwich you will get into a Ladies Only and I shall get into the next carriage. At Liverpool Street I shall run ahead and engage a cab and wait for you. Now, you must give me your baggage; I will take it with my own. If I take one valise tonight and one tomorrow, you need carry nothing on Thursday. All you need to do is walk out."

"That is thoughtful, Johnny. But not necessary. I also have made plans. I propose to pretend that I wish Miss Bussey to copy some of my favourite old dresses. That gives me a good excuse for taking all I need, openly. In a cab, too. Let me fill your glass. It will be the last time you drink at Papa's expense." That was a slip. "I mean, tomorrow—it will be a big party and it may go on and on, and we shall be late. And if you intend to catch the early train . . ."

182

It sounded reasonable. He accepted the second drink, remarking that Englishmen did not understand brandy, or indeed any wines, being too much inclined to reckon everything by its cost. Mr. Draper's special brandy was definitely inferior to his everyday one.

In the grate the last detached flicker of flame over a heap of blackened flakes, expired.

"I think you should go now, Johnny. I must sleep if I am to give a good performance tomorrow."

"Yes. I can bear this parting . . ." He stood up. Despite the brandy Mrs. Fenner's suet crust still lay heavily but his head was clear, his hopes high. "Because we shall meet again so soon . . ."

"Yes, indeed." In some murky outpost of Hell, those who betrayed, those who had been betrayed, those who had lied, those who had believed the lies, would meet, recognise one another, share a common condemnation; for to be stupid was as culpable as being wicked, being wicked as excusable as being stupid.

"And you will catch that train? And remember, always, that I saved you."

"I shall remember everything."

"Then I will say good night and au revoir, darling. Until Thursday, at Liverpool Street."

"Yes." An impulse of pity—for he could no more help what he was than she could help what she had become, she took his face between her hands and kissed him. "Goodbye, Johnny. Goodbye."

She used the screwdriver. Moving stealthily she brushed every flake of burnt paper into a dustpan and conveyed it to the kitchen stove and replaced the white paper fan.

"I CAME EARLY," MR. HORRIDGE SAID, "BECAUSE I RECKONED
Marion should have the ring on her finger. And I wanted to
show you this. I know you said the bride's family made all
the arrangements. But this may be worth a look."

It would, in any other circumstances, have been worth two
or three. In response to Mr. Horridge's simple, honest letter,
claiming no kinship, merely stating that he got himself
engaged to the most wonderful girl in the world and wanted
her to have the most wonderful wedding and if the Dean could
spare time . . . Dean Horridge of Asham had written a most
enthusiastic letter. He was, in fact, an unworldly old man
who had spent a good deal of his spare time in tracing his
ancestry back to a Joshua Horridge, martyred in Bloody
Mary's reign; not only a martyr but a hero, "He it was who
by his courage and determination, encouraged the weaker
sort." "At the stake Joshua Horridge cried, 'God save the
Queen and England from Popery.'" Little crumbs of information such as this had fired Dean Horridge's imagination
and started him on his harmless hobby, making him search
parish registers and country graveyards, many in the neigh-
bourhood, some farther afield. But it was only a hobby and
he only an amateur genealogist and he ran into several blind
alleys. One was confusing because in the early eighteenth
century an Eliza Horridge married a man called Crook, and
gave her eldest son Horridge as a Christian name. In later
years, when he became a wine merchant he prudently
dropped *Crook* and used his Christian name as his surname.
Of his two sons one had carried on the business and prospered,
and become a baronet. The other son had vanished without
trace. So now the Dean wrote, "Throughout there is a strong
tendency—see enclosed—to choose Edward and Joshua as

names for boys. Your name is Edward; if your father or grandfather bore the name of Joshua it is very probable that you are a member of what I always call the lost tribe and that you are not only distantly related to me, which is small distinction, but to Joshua Horridge who was both a hero and a martyr." He had been so excited by this possibility that he momentarily forgot why this Edward Horridge had approached him in the first place and the remark that he would be delighted and honoured to help to officiate at the wedding had to be added as a postscript. The enclosure was a copy of the relevant corner of the family tree. The whole now spread over several sheets of cartridge paper, carefully pasted together.

Mr. Horridge could make neither head nor tail of the family tree and his limited imagination did not take fire at the thought of possible descent from a martyr; he had, however, hoped that Mr. Draper would be impressed. So he was, but in the wrong fashion.

"Upon reading this you promptly re-Christened your father, I have no doubt."

"There was no need. His name was Joshua. He was always called Young Josh because my great-grandfather was still alive, he was Old Josh. My grandfather was Edward."

"The Dean is to be congratulated. Asham Deanery is falling down and the bells of the church cannot be rung lest the tower should collapse."

Mr. Horridge ignored this jibe. "Can I see Marion?" Mr. Draper rang the bell, giving Betty one more trip up and downstairs.

When she came Mr. Draper stayed just long enough to note that her hair was dressed in the fringe again and that she wore the same shabby old green dress. Mr. Horridge's

185

tastes were obviously thoroughly perverse for he said she looked beautiful and kissed her in an indecently hearty manner.

"I do hope you like it and that it fits," Mr. Horridge said, "I should have taken a piece of string." He displayed his offering. It was not quite the largest diamond to be found in London, but it was sizeable and of the best quality. Eight smaller ones were set around it so that the whole formed the shape of a shield.

"It is beautiful," Marion said, looking at it as it glittered against its bed of dark blue velvet. "But far too grand."

"Nothing is grand enough for you. Let's try it on."

He had been lucky, or clever; it was a perfect fit.

"And you're sure you like it? It can be changed. I must say I like it better now than I did before. Your hand sets it off." He kissed the hand. Other guests could be heard arriving.

This was altogether a more animated party; only the eldest ladies could be seated. Mr. Draper, putting a good face on it, delegated the pouring of the Madeira to his future son-in-law. Everybody congratulated that fortunate fellow, everybody wished Marion great happiness. The ring was inspected and admired—not always sincerely; it was, most ladies thought, vulgarly ostentatious; any one of the stones set by itself would have been quite adequate. Mrs. Draper received congratulations too. "How I envy you, having Marion so near," Mrs. Taylor said. Her Angela was far away in the West Country and her last letter had hinted that she was pregnant; it was a time when Mrs. Taylor would have liked to be near enough to keep an eye on her and indulge in cosy feminine talk. Mrs. Marriot envied Mrs. Draper for another reason; her beloved daughter had made a love-match with a poor curate, had three children, an unwieldy old vicarage in Stepney and great difficulty in making ends meet. When there were Jumble Sales and people contributed children's clothes in fair condition Mrs. Marriot was glad to price them low and then buy them for her grandchildren. How different would be Marion Draper's lot.

Apart from the fact that the hired woman did not know from which side to hand vegetables and had to be instructed in a hissing whisper the meal went well; and before it was over the news that Mr. Horridge was not, after all, without connections had spread about the table. Mr. Draper had started it on its course in the most normal fashion, asking Mr. Marriot, whose church it was, whether he would mind sharing the ceremony with the Dean. "It turns out that he's a kind of distant cousin."

As this news spread the ring on Marion's finger lost much of its vulgarity.

The meal was excellent; Ada, making the last enormous effort of her career, had superseded herself. Several ladies remarked, with wry smiles, that though they had wheedled a recipe out of her at various times, the dish was never *quite* the same. Answering one such remark, Ellen said, "Ada has her secrets."

Then, into one of those lulls to which the most animated dinner table may be subject, Mr. Marriot dropped a discordant note.

"How sad about that young de Brissac."

Who was he? And what was sad?

The sudden death of a chemist's assistant, and a foreigner at that, would not be likely to cast much gloom over a celebratory dinner party in Alma Avenue, but both the Marriots were inclined to elaborate; Mrs. Marriot spoke of his beautiful manners and regular attendance both at the Musical Society and the Literary Salon. Mr. Marriot spoke of his regular attendance at church and his talent: "I shall always remember the talk he gave us about French novelists."

"It sounds incredible," Lady Mingay said in her loud masterful way. "I was myself in the shop only yesterday morning. He was then perfectly well. What ailed him?"

"Some digestive trouble, I understand," Mr. Marriot said delicately. "I could not get much from his landlady, Mrs. Fenner, who came to see me about . . . hmm hmm. She was very upset, poor soul."

Talk with one's neighbour was resumed.

Mrs. Fenner had been upset indeed.

"Well, you see, Doctor, he'd had such turns on and off and always got better. He was French, you see, and English food didn't seem to suit him. He'd eat, but he'd say, laughing like, 'Now I take my life on my fork.' Last night was beef steak pudding, suet crust often upset him. Mind when it was a joint I did favour him a bit and give him most lean, but with a pudding you have to treat them all alike. He didn't eat all his crust . . ."

She'd had dozens of lodgers, all men, mostly nice enough, but she'd never had one she liked so much as Mr. de Brissac and as she remembered his nice manners, his jokes, she shed a few difficult tears.

"Did anyone else suffer from eating this pudding?"

"No. They all ate it. I ate it myself. And last night when I heard him moving about, I just thought—bilious again! And I never knew anybody to die of being bilious. Then I heard him moaning and groaning so I went. If I'd known this time was different I'd have sent for you then. And if I'd known he'd be dead when you got here I'd have waited and let you get your breakfast."

"At what time was he taken ill, Mrs. Fenner?"

"I don't know. I never looked. I just heard him and went and you never see—well maybe you did, being a doctor, but I never did . . . I wrapped him up warm and got him a hot water jar and I said, 'Use your chamber pot, Mr. de Brissac, what's a chamber pot for?'"

"The chamber pot is handy?"

It was, but it was empty, scoured clean. With the doctor sent for and Mr. de Brissac lying quietly at last, Mrs. Fenner had cleaned up in readiness for the doctor's arrival.

"Did you happen to notice if there was blood in the vomit?"

She had not. There'd been no time; she was singlehanded; the other four men in the house all slept like pigs. And, more fastidious than she looked, her main thought had been to get rid of it. But she realised that she had been unwise to mention the pudding and was now offered a chance to give it an alibi. So she said, "Yes."

"And he was subject to such attacks?"

"Yes. Always a very delicate stomach."

A stomach ulcer, of some long standing, ignored, suddenly perforated. Thinking of the death certificate, Dr. Barlow asked, "Do you know how old he was?"

"No, I never heard him say. Twenty-six, at a guess . . ." As she said this she realised that there were a number of other things which she did not know about her favourite lodger— who would pay for his funeral, for instance.

The parish would have given him a pauper's funeral; but that would have involved a visit from Mr. Stubbs, the Relieving Officer, and much of Mrs. Fenner's time and energy had been devoted to keeping Mr. Stubbs away from her door; when the children were small, when Bill was out of a job, when Bill was ill, when Bill died, always somehow she had managed to keep clear of the parish and the stigma that parish relief implied. She wished now not to be involved with it, even by association. So she sent for the cheaper of the two undertakers in the town and explained that what was needed was the plainest possible box; no black plumes on the horses, just the least, the most essential service. How much? He said five pounds, five shillings discount for prompt payment. She could, as she said, put her hand on that amount, because both rent and rates were due at the end of September and she had been saving towards them, and for the coal— so much cheaper by the ton.

To this outlay of four pounds fifteen shillings she hoped that Mr. Freeman might contribute. She called at the shop in the late afternoon. To break dramatic news, however horrible, conveys a certain importance and Mr. Freeman's shock was relished by Mrs. Fenner. "I was just about to send Bobby round to inquire. Dead you say? I thought he was malingering again. Dead? What of?"

"Something wrong with his stomach. It burst. The point is, Mr. Freeman, he's dead and he's got to be buried. I wondered if you . . ."

"No!" Mr. Freeman said almost violently. "He worked for me; I liked him well enough. But I paid him wages regularly. I really see no reason why . . . No, I cannot assume that responsibility. With things as they are . . ." Baxter's, closed for alterations, likely to reopen in a burst of splendour; trade might make one of its sudden shifts. Mr. Freeman had been seriously considering whether he could afford to employ an assistant.

"When is the interment?"

"I thought Saturday. The room is wanted, you see. I'm going along now to fix up with the parson."

Trudging along on her painful feet—in the house she wore

slippers and could walk and stand, cook and clean, hours on
end without much discomfort, but the combination of shoes
and pavement lamed her—she went along to the Rectory,
cuddling the hope that Mr. Marriot might help. Mr. de Brissac had been a churchgoer and he'd gone to all sorts of
meetings and things, connected with the church. And there
was no question about it, Mr. Marriot was more upset than
Mr. Freeman had been. "What a tragedy! So young and so
gifted!" he said.

"The nicest lodger I ever had. And I couldn't let him be
buried by the parish, could I?"

"No, no, of course not." Mr. Marriot was not so sharp in
catching her meaning as Mr. Freeman had been. He was
nicer, saying things about not grieving and the life everlasting
and Saturday being all right, leave everything to him.

The fine harvest weather broke and it was raining on Saturday when Jean de Brissac was laid to rest. There were three
wreaths; one large and lavish, "From all at 18, Brewster
Street." Johnny's la-di-da airs and ways had not endeared
him to his fellow lodgers, but there had been a tolerance, a
recognition of difference; the suddenness of his death had
sparked off sentimentality, and some feeling of superiority;
they were alive and he was dead, they'd drink a little
less in the coming week, but they could afford lilies.

The other wreaths were modest. One from Mr. and Mrs.
Freeman—it would look bad not to send. A circle of box,
dotted with scabius. And from the Rectory came the result of
a long-standing order—for every church member, except in
particular cases. Years ago it had been arranged; whatever
was in season and therefore reasonably priced. This time
dahlias.

At the moment of the interment Marion was having the first fitting of her wedding dress.

Mrs. Fenner went home on that Saturday afternoon, kicked off the hurtful shoes and put on her easy slippers, hung up her decent black, and donned her working garb. The room must be made ready for the new lodger, a friend of one of her present ones, who was anxious to move in on Sunday afternoon. Her rooms were seldom vacant for long, she was known to keep a decent house and to set a good table.

She had, immediately after the death, taken a thorough look round, searching for something which would inform her who should be told, who should be consulted about the funeral. She had found nothing of any use. In fact no papers of any kind. His clothes hung in the cupboard; his boots, all on trees, stood lined up on the floor below, together with a box of boot-cleaning materials. The wash-hand-stand bore his toilet preparations; and on the top of the chest of drawers lay the door key which she had given him and about twelve shillings in loose change. The drawers themselves were neat as could be; clean socks, handkerchiefs, shirts, underwear. Apart from three books, all in what she took to be French, and not one inscribed, that was all the room held. There was no clue at all as to where he came from, whether he had a relative, a friend. Baulked in her purpose, Mrs. Fenner had not entered the room again until now, and she did it with reluctance.

She had told the old woman who acted as layer out to pay herself from the money on the chest; she had taken it all and that was understandable. The key lay there alone and she put it in her pocket; the new man must prove himself sober and reliable before he attained to a key.

Mr. de Brissac had arrived with one valise; but he had bought several clothes in his eighteen months at Bereham; so, when she had filled the valise, Mrs. Fenner fetched her wicker washing basket. As she emptied the cupboard and the drawers her mind was busy with the old business of ways and means. It was a pity that the clothes were, in the main, so fashionable and gentlemanly; it meant that their secondhand value was almost nothing. Gentlemen did not buy their clothes from old-clothes' dealers and the people who did buy second-hand clothes did not want cut-away coats, lawn shirts, narrow boots of black patent leather with grey suede tops, or gloves, grey or lemon coloured. It was not a very nice thing to *think,* but there it was, one of the facts to be faced, any one of her other lodgers, dying in similar circumstances and being buried at her expense, would have been less of a dead loss. Charlie-the-carpenter's overalls were worth more than Mr. de Brissac's top hat which reposed in a box specially shaped to enclose it.

It was to Charlie that she called, when, her melancholy task completed, she needed a hand with the removal of her favourite lodger's effects.

"Anything any of you can use," she said, "you can have. Not for nothing. After all, I had to pay for the funeral. But they'll be cheap and it wouldn't hurt any of you to have a few extra socks and collars and handkerchiefs, would it?"

After Saturday tea, boiled beef, carrots, onions and dumplings there was a macabre little auction, not competitive. It netted her ten shillings. "Put the rest into the shed, Charlie, there's a good chap. Give him a hand, Tom," she said. Nobody, not even Mrs. Fenner, noticed that the hatbox remained, pushed away at the corner of the dresser.

Mrs. Fenner noticed it on Monday afternoon when at about three o'clock she sat down to repair, by drinking strong hot tea, the ravages of wash day. The man who bought discarded clothing, not to resell as garments, but by weight, was due to call in the morning, his rounds were regular, his mournful cry part of the regular pattern of life in the shabbier streets. And even a top hat weighed something. Mrs. Fenner, with her cup of tea in one hand, leaned down and pulled the hat case towards her, prepared to add the hat to the pile of stuff in the shed and to use the case as fuel on the stove.

And there, inside the hat, which smelt faintly of the oil which Mr. de Brissac had put on his hair, were the papers for which she had searched, the papers which linked him with somebody else . . .

On the kitchen table the tea cooled; on the stove the pigs' trotters simmered almost to disastrous dryness as Mrs. Fenner's eyes took in and conveyed to her worried mind that Mr. de Brissac had a wife. *"Your ever loving, ever faithful wife, Marion."*

Johnny had retained only the most damning of the letters, and the envelopes, to give bulk, should Marion take notice, had all been included in the blue-ribboned parcel. Marion had dated nothing except by such inexact words as *"Monday, and you have just left me,"* but the story was plain and Mrs. Fenner pieced it together. Mr. de Brissac had got this Marion in the family way and married her. Secretly.

As Mrs. Fenner read, the image of the ideal lodger, the perfect gentleman, receded and that made the sum which she had expended on his funeral loom larger. If the rubbish in the shed fetched two shillings she would still be more than four pounds to the bad. And surely, if anybody buried dead men it should be their wives. She'd buried Bill. In the last letter—they were not arranged in any order—the answer came. *"Darling, be a little late this evening. I write in haste to tell you that Papa has gone to one of his Maltsters' meetings and will come home on the late train. I live for the moment when I can let you in—and Darling I do not mean only into the house."*

There was only one Maltster in Bereham. Mrs. Fenner knew him and hated him. Her husband had once been in his employ, overworked, underpaid, treated like a dog. Once, not long after they were married, Bill, lifting sacks, had ricked his back, come home all bent over, and despite her ministrations—a good rub with horse liniment and an old-fashioned remedy, a relic of an old grandmother's lore, bashed-about larkspur leaves and stems—in the morning he could not move. So she had gone down to the Maltings to explain to the foreman and she had encountered Mr. Draper himself. He had said, "Ah, yes. Fenner. One of the few who chose not to take advantage of my medical scheme . . ." And it was true. Bill had not paid his twopence a week, because though it sounded so small, twopence mattered with four children to keep. Twopence bought a large loaf, or a pound of beef pieces, or a pound and a half of sugar. But Mr. Draper had managed to make Bill and her seem feckless and undeserving of sympathy. "You may tell him that I will keep his job open, until the end of the week . . ."

Her other brush with this horrible man had come years later. Bill was dying and, suffering from a heavy cold herself, she had run down to Baxter's for the pills which were the only relief for his pain. She had handed in the prescription and Mr. Baxter had it in his hand when the bell jangled and Mr. Draper stalked in. "Ha, Baxter, I want a large bottle of eau de cologne."

It was years since Bill had worked at the Maltings; she had always paid on the nail for anything she had bought from Baxter's and when she saw the chemist put down her prescription and turn to the shelf where such useless things as scent were stocked, rage and blood rushed to her head.

195

"Here," she said, "I was first," and with that she had begun to cough. Over her head Mr. Draper said, "Never mind about the wrapping. I have no wish to catch a cold."

Then she had hated him even more. When such of her acquaintances as frequented the Church Bazaar spoke of him as a generous, jolly gentleman, Mrs. Fenner retorted with one of her eloquent sniffs.

Now, here on her own kitchen table she had what would shock and humble him. One of his stuck-up daughters married to a shop assistant! Married secretly, lest the child should be a bastard. Mrs. Fenner's mind checked there with a jolt. A birth could not be kept secret, could it? So perhaps that proud, harsh man already knew and would not be surprised at her disclosure. Perhaps—her mind leaped forward again— he had been paying Mr. de Brissac to say nothing. That would account for the clothes! But, even if he knew, it would give him a pretty jolt to know that she knew; she looked forward to seeing his face. And certainly now the funeral expenses would be paid, the whole five pounds, no need to tell him about the discount and the sale of oddments.

And why stop there?

Why stop there? She was now in possession of a secret. People paid well for their secrets to be kept. How about fifty pounds? Even had there been no mention of secret marriage, no mention of a baby, the letters in themselves were things any respectable man would pay not to have shown or talked of; the girl was plainly a hussy, writing things enough to make a decent woman blush. The more Mrs. Fenner thought about it the more the fifty pounds seemed as good as hers. And actually Mr. Draper owed her and the wife of every other man who had worked for him for any length of time, at least that much; he'd always underpaid.

She took the washing in from the line, went in slippers and

overall round the corner to the butcher's and bought the material for what was a most popular dish with lodgers, sausages and streaky bacon. She boiled and mashed a huge mound of potatoes. When, having served the meal, she sat down and attempted to eat she found that she had no appetite; her stomach was already tumbling and churning as though she had eaten some indigestible dish. She drank two cups of strong sweet tea, and then rose. "I have to go out," she said. "You can put the things in the kitchen." It was rarely that she deserted her post, but on such occasions she expected to find upon her return, not a sinkful of dirty crockery, but everything clean and back on the dresser, all in the wrong places. If this should not be so tonight it would be a long time before this lot had sausages again.

She put on her decent black, the remains of her widow's garb; she forced her feet into the hurtful shoes, put the letters into her reticule of plush worn threadbare.

Mr. Draper had finished his meal and was selecting his cigar when the bell rang. Betty ceased clearing the table and went to the door and came back, saying, with nice social sense:

"There is a person to see you, sir. She says it's important." A person meant someone unrecognised by Betty, and of a lower class.

"A person without a name?"

Mr. Draper's question was a reproof. Betty said, "I'm sorry, sir. Shall I go and ask?"

"No. Show her into the study and light the lamp on my desk. I'll come along."

He had a pretty good idea who the woman was—the wife of a man he had sacked on Saturday. And if she thought that she would do herself, or her husband, any good by coming here, to his home, and disturbing his evening, she was in grave error.

"We could hardly be served worse," he said, lighting his cigar with care. "A cook who cannot walk and a maid who cannot remember. There will be changes here."

He had a retentive, orderly memory and he recognised Mrs. Fenner, despite the years. Husband dead; several children of an age now to be seeking employment. She had been sent, poor old widowed woman, to solicit a job for a son or a son-in-law.

"Mrs. Fenner, is it not?" He passed her and took his seat at the desk, the freshly lit lamp on his left. He did not ask her to sit down. "If it has anything to do with business," he began, ready to administer a stinging rebuke.

"It's private. Very private. Nothing to do with business. More of a family matter." Her stomach rolled audibly and her feet hurt.

"Your family, I take it."

"Yours. You got a daughter named Marion."

"Miss Marion Draper is my daughter." He resented the woman's familiarity and the fact she had not once called him "sir." He remembered that she had once been what he called uppity in Baxter's.

"It's about some letters. Letters I found in poor Mr. de Brissac's room. He lodged with me."

Her way of life for the last few years had given her much experience in dealing with men—sheepishly explaining that they were not drunk, they'd just stubbed their toes on the stairs; that they couldn't pay their rent until next pay day because they'd had to send money home. Her keen eye now saw that Mr. Draper did *not* know. He recognised the name, probably from reading in Friday's *Bereham Free Press* the paragraph headed, "Sudden Death of Chemist's Assistant."

198

Well, all the more shock to him, she thought vindictively. "They were married," she said.

That, he knew with certainty, could not be true. Marion was mad enough and bad enough, but she had never been unsupervised for long enough to commit such an act of folly. Granted, he had never been completely satisfied about that cheeky young man and it was quite possible that he had suffered delusions, not unlike those which made people claim to have done a murder.

"That is utter nonsense," he said firmly. "I should be interested to hear what led you to jump to such a conclusion. Some rubbish your lodger wrote?"

"What your daughter wrote." Mrs. Fenner's fingers, encased in wrinkled black gloves, moved on the threadbare reticule. "She's Mrs. de Brissac, all right. And she had a baby."

How that could have been managed without Mr. Draper's knowledge was a mystery, but to the rich all things were possible. Perhaps the girl's mother was in the know.

"You must be out of your mind," Mr. Draper said. "For the last three years, ever since she left school, my daughter has breakfasted and dined with me, lunched with her mother and sister. Except for last week she has never spent a night under a roof where I was not. What can possibly be your object in coming here with this fantastic tale I fail to see."

Mrs. Fenner was a little confused; she was also angered. Ever since Bill died and she had begun to take lodgers, she had been within her humble sphere, a power. Treated with respect. Being told that she was out of her mind and that her tale was fantastic made her angry.

"See what you make of them then," she said with spite. She took the letters and almost flung them at him.

One glance showed him Marion's unmistakable hand.

"It will take a little time," he said. "Perhaps you had better sit down, Mrs. Fenner." The only other chair in the room stood by the wall, a little distance from the desk. She wanted to see his face as he read, and would have edged the chair forward; but it was heavy and the thick pile of the carpet was an impediment. So far as she could see, however, he seemed not to flinch or blench. It struck her that he was not taking the letters seriously; he flipped the pages over and said, almost petulantly, "They all seem to say the same thing. Must I read the lot? Yes, the term *wife* is certainly used. But there must have been some ceremony. Where and when performed? If I read on, shall I learn?"

He took the dead cigar from his mouth and put it neatly in the ash tray. Mrs. Fenner's experience did not include familiarity with cigar smokers, so she missed the significance of that action.

"No," she said, answering his question. "I read the lot and there's no mention of a wedding, or what happened to the baby."

"And you missed nothing? No other letters which might be more informative."

"No. That's the lot."

"But there must be," he said. "In some pocket. At the back of a drawer. Tucked inside a book." Now he was criticising the thoroughness of her turn out between lodgers.

"I stripped the room. I looked everywhere. There's nothing else. But that's enough, isn't it?"

"Quite enough," he said. He began to put the pages together. And then, with the quickest move she had ever seen anyone make, he held them, corner down, over the lamp and they burst into flame. Smoke and the smell of burning paper filled the room. Mrs. Fenner heaved herself out of the chair and plunged forward. "No," she cried. "You can't do that!"

200

But it was done. Holding the flaring torch in his hand Mr. Draper turned in his chair and dropped it into the grate behind him. The pleated fan of white paper caught light and added to the brief blaze.

"You shouldn't have done that. They wasn't yours to burn."

"But I have burnt them—as you would have done, had you had a shred of decency and not beeen bent on blackmail, Mrs. Fenner."

Shaken and reduced she said, "It wasn't that. I just wanted the funeral paid for."

"You must try elsewhere. In and around Bereham there are a number of young women who share a name with my daughter." Before she could speak he said, in a different voice, "I believe that Mr. Andrews is your landlord."

The fermentation in her stomach settled into solid lead. I was a fool. I might have known. Mr. Draper rang the bell and when Betty came panting up he said, "Show Mrs. Fenner out."

He heard the front door thud. He sat there behind his desk and experienced one of his rare moments of indecision. His immediate impulse was to go to Marion and pound her into dust. Mrs. Fenner had been wrong in thinking that his reading of the letters had been cursory. Every word was branded on his brain. Incredible, indecent words, written in this house. Fornication committed under this family roof; deceit and lies, and a pregnancy, how ended? Opposed to this impulse to attack and denounce was his genuine wish to protect those who accepted protection. At the moment when he rose to choose his cigar and Betty came in to clear the table, Ellen had taken up some samples of material and said, "Between these two pinks I cannot decide. Both are pretty." And the woman who long ago lost her identity and became Mamma had said, "I have almost decided on the Parma violet. It would be a change." They must be protected.

Presently, when he could trust himself, he turned down the lamp and went into the dining room. Mamma and Marion and Ellen were still at it, with samples of material and pages torn from fashion books all over the table. Mr. Draper looked at his elder daughter and thought coarsely, A bitch, perpetually in heat. Any stray dog; a chemist's assistant, a millionaire, all one to her; horrible, disgusting, beastly, and yet what he had always sensed, always in a way suspected. Dirty, lascivious-minded little slut.

Presently Ellen yawned and yawning being catching, so did Mamma. She yawned and said, "I think I will say good night," and did one of her swift vanishing tricks. Ellen lingered. "I cannot decide beside the bunch up and the bow. They give the same effect. But bows could be removed if fashion changed and we must bear in mind that Constance, anyway, will be wearing her bridesmaid's dress for the next two years. Yes, I think this one, with bows." She yawned again and Marion said, "You are sleepy, too. Go to bed. I'll clear all this away."

"Good night, Papa."

"Good night, my dear. Sleep well."

"Good night, Marion."

"Good night, Ellen. I think you chose well."

She busied herself by putting the samples of stuff, the pages torn from magazines and fashion supplements neatly in order. To her they mattered little. Edward had decided upon Paris for the honeymoon and that decision had done much to explain the brevity of the engagement. In the last week of September and the first weeks of October Paris was beautiful . . . and she would go shopping in Paris.

Mr. Draper watched. Then he said, "Come here," and when she had obeyed and stood on the hearthrug between his chair and Mamma's he said, with infinite venom, "Good evening, Mrs. de Brissac!"

Again that black dizziness and the desperate effort to fight it down. The letters were burned, Johnny was dead. All she could think was that he had babbled on his deathbed. That must be it. The person must have been his landlady. Her word against mine. Stout denial my only hope. Her lips, indeed the whole of her face felt so stiff and taut that she was surprised to hear herself speaking more or less as usual.

"Why do you say that?"

"It is your name, is it not?"

"I do not know what you are talking about."

"I will tell you," he said, with slow relish. "I am talking about a girl, respectably born, gently reared, given every advantage, who became a trollop. Who turned her father's house into a brothel. Who was obliged to beg a shop assistant to marry her. Who wrote stuff which, had it been printed, would have been banned as filthy pornography. You are that girl and I have the misfortune to be your father."

She still did not guess at the trick Johnny had played. She thought that he must have left the letters in some accessible place and the old woman had read them. That was shaming enough; but still word against word.

"Whoever said such things of me is a liar. I was never married to Jean de Brissac."

"No? Yet you wrote, *'Darling, I am now in very truth your wife, your ever loving, ever loyal wife.'* Together with other things which I will not soil my tongue by repeating. Expressions so lewd and indecent that used by the lowest prostitute they would be shocking." An ignorant old woman could not have read and remembered and quoted so exactly. Johnny

203

had played her false, to the end. "There were six letters, in your hand, signed by your name. So we will have done with lies. What happened to the baby? Did you go to some back street abortionist? Or did you use a non-existent pregnancy to force a chemist's assistant to marry you?"

In the whirling chaos she clung to the fingerhold of truth. "We were never married," she said.

Somewhere, deep inside Mr. Draper, something exploded, blowing into shreds the self-control, the cold equanimity which had served him even in the moment of humiliation at Mr. Horridge's hands. He jumped up and took her by the shoulders. "You dare stand there . . . You lying bitch. Foul-minded slut . . ." He shook her, more and more roughly. Her head lolled as though her neck had snapped. And then suddenly he was shaking nothing. She slipped from under his hands so that he almost lost his balance and only saved himself from falling by taking two short steps and catching at the back of a chair.

Marion lay where she had fallen.

o o o

MRS. FENNER MADE HER WAY HOME. HER BUNIONS WERE screaming, but her sense of having been fooled, ill-used, cheated, hurt more. She had formed—from being so much alone in her house—the habit of muttering to herself and she muttered now. She was not given to the use of bad language and never allowed it in her house, but now some kind of barrier had broken and she muttered words which she hardly knew she knew. Not only about Mr. Draper and his daughter; Jean de Brissac too was obscenely abused, the seeming gentleman whom she had favoured whenever possible and who was really as bad as the rest; dying like that and taking the rate

204

money to bury him. And she was just as bad; she might have known; dogged by ill luck from the day she was born . . .

She hobbled and mumbled; two passers-by thought she was drunk.

In the kitchen at 18, Brewster Street, where all the cups and plates had been washed, and the gas lighted, her nearest neighbour and closest friend, Mrs. Clara Foster, sat waiting, tea things to her left on the table, a pile of old newspapers to her right. On the stove the kettle steamed. Mrs. Fenner, pulling herself together, remembered that it was bum paper night. Lodgers used a lot of it and every Monday Mrs. Foster brought what paper she had saved or cadged, and Mrs. Fenner added hers, and they sat, chatting, drinking tea and folding and cutting and pushing skewers through the corners of the oblongs and threading string, so that the paper could be hung on hooks in the privy. A custom of long standing.

"Make the tea, dear," Mrs. Fenner said. "I'll just take my things off. There's a currant cake . . ."

"Couldn't think what'd happened to you."

"I had to go out. Bit of business. Shan't be a minute."

At the foot of the stairs she removed her shoes and the relief was sufficient to improve her mood. She'd manage. She always had. Never any luck, but count your blessings and a good cup of tea would be welcome. Only one corner of her mind nursed its grudge.

Mrs. Foster earned her pittance by taking in washing, so to her weather was of prime importance. A good drying day, she said, enjoying the tea and the currant cake of a quality she could not afford to make or buy and only encountered at Mrs. Fenner's.

"Pity it rained for the funeral. I'd have come to show friendly, but I was starching. Hard at it all day." Mrs. Fenner knew, without resentment, that had Mr. de Brissac's funeral been a prelude to a feast of ham, salt beef and sausage rolls, it would have been better attended. So she answered obliquely.

"I did the best I could."

"And more than most would."

They folded and slit and stacked and pierced. Presently Mrs. Foster said, "Look. This is marked." It was. Mrs. Fenner had marked it herself, meaning to cut it and the paragraph on an earlier page, out to keep. What were irreverently called Matches, Hatches and Dispatches were in the *Bereham Free Press* gathered together on the back page. Clara had already folded and sliced before noticing the pencilled cross. There was a dividing line on the quarter page. Death having priority "Suddenly, at 18, Brewster Street," Jean de Brissac's death took precedence over Mr. and Mrs. Draper's pleasure in announcing the engagement between their daughter Marion and Mr. Edward Horridge of Sorley Park.

"Yes," Mrs. Fenner said, "I'll keep that. Thank you, Clara. Have another slice of cake."

There was a man, once one of her boys, married and gone away, and looking the worse for it, who drove a grocer's delivery van. On Tuesday, unless his route had altered, he drove in a circle which included the lunatic place, Sorley Park, some other big houses and several village shops. He'd give her a lift. I might put a spoke in his wheel, yet, she thought, thinking of Mr. Draper.

o   o   o

MR. HORRIDGE SAID, QUITE AMIABLY, "YOU KNOW YOU should be in clink. And that's where you'll end if you ain't careful." Oddly enough, they had been at home with one another from the first moment. He knew her, he'd met her before in many places. Old women, in shabby black, the badge of decency, with worn faces and anxious eyes and glib tongues and sore feet; they cropped up everywhere, ready to do, to say, to sell or procure anything, even their own granddaughters—in order to turn a dishonest penny.

"You can't say that," Mrs. Fenner said. She had met him before, in a number of different guises. "All I've done is come and told you the truth. Something you oughta know, if only to make your wedding legal. A word wrong on the marriage lines and it wouldn't be, would it? Not if it said spinster where it should say widow."

His disbelief was absolute.

"D'you make your living this way?"

"I told you how I make my living. I let lodgings. Mr. de Brissac lodged with me."

"And now he's dead and can't contradict you when you say what you found in his hat!" Her choice of a mythical hiding place amused him, and he grinned.

"Laugh away," Mrs. Fenner said sourly. "You think I'd come all this way, wasting my time to tell you a pack of lies?"

"No. Not for that." He leaned back in his chair and looked her over again. Down to the bunions that misshaped her shoes she was familiar to him; but her game was new. Maybe because he had spent so much time in circles where there were no reputations to be tarnished. He could just see, however, what dreadful damage such a wicked story could do, say to a girl with a more credulous father, a less certain suitor.

"Well, I don't believe a word. Not one bloody word." She had used worse words on her walk home, but she bristled at being sworn at and Mr. Horridge noted that fact with amusement; he'd bet that sooner or later she'd say, I'd have you know I'm a respectable woman! They all did. "What I am interested in is what made you pick on Miss Draper."

"What d'you mean, *pick?* There was the letters, signed with her name, mentioning who her father was. She's the one wrote the letters. She's the one married Mr. de Brissac."

"But you see I don't believe there ever were any letters."

"Ask her Pa then. Ask him why he was in such a hurry to burn them and threaten me with my landlord. Ask the girl what she took out of the grate this morning. Better still, ask *her.*"

"You bet your life, I will." But now he thought of two things. The old woman had described Mr. Draper's swift, destructive action. "He held them over the lamp and they flamed up." Wouldn't a liar, with a completely invented tale, have said, He set fire to them in the grate. Also, why in a hat? In a drawer, in a pocket, in a cupboard. This old liar was out of the ordinary and all the more dangerous for that.

"What were you hoping to make out of this?"

"Well, to begin with, I looked to get the funeral money back. I had to bury him and it took my rate money. And that didn't seem right, not with his wife alive. I buried my husband, others should do the same. I shall get a bill from the doctor too, I just remembered. Then I thought things over and I reckoned this was something they wouldn't want talked about. Marriage to a shop assistant on the sly. I thought, if I let him have the letters and promised to keep my mouth shut it'd be worth fifty pounds."

"Blackmail!" Just as he had suspected.

"I don't see it that way. Blackmail you do over and over. He went for me; said I hadn't got a shred of decency about me. But I thought I had acted decently. Not a word to anybody. There's a lot of women would gone rushing about saying, Look what I found. But no, I went straight to him and all I got was rudeness."

"So then you came to me?"

"Yes, so I did . . ." Something beside her fundamental honesty was now involved. She had arrived just as Mr. Horridge, who did not as a rule bother with tea, was pouring himself the first whisky of the day. He had imagined that she had come to ask for employment, either for herself or some relative; and because she looked poor, part of the world he had so long inhabited, he'd told her to sit down and offered a drink. She chose as he knew she would. Gin.

Mrs. Fenner liked gin, but she drank it seldom, holding that those who drank what they could not afford were simply asking for trouble. At a wedding or a funeral or at Christmas. She was not hardened to spirit-drinking and Mr. Horridge had poured generously. So now the gin said:

"I reckoned you oughta know. And I wanted to get even with *him*. Grinding everybody down. Riding roughshod over everybody. Treating everybody like dirt. My Bill worked for him, years till he could get a better job. Proper old slave-driver. So I thought . . . But then you don't believe me either and with the letters gone . . . I never did have any luck, anyway. Just got the children off my hands and Bill took and died. Just got the lodgings going and up went the rent, and the rates and the coal. And Mr. de Brissac wasn't the gentleman I took him for. If I'd known last week what I know now, I'd have let the parish bury him."

She began to pull the shabby gloves over her knuckled, work-ruined hands. She was a wicked old woman, a would-be blackmailer, a liar, and now very slightly tight. But there were things in his own past which would not have borne close scrutiny and she was of his kind.

Still innocent girls must be protected.

"Wait a bit," Mr. Horridge said. He leaned over and unlocked the bottom left-hand drawer of the handsome writing table which he had bought because of its wealth of ornamentation. He took ten five-pound notes from the drawer and laid them on the table top.

"Can you write, Mrs. Fenner?"

"I should hope so. I went to school for a year."

From another drawer he took a sheet of his best paper, and because the table was wide, moved nearer to her the silver inktray in which cut-glass bottles, lidded with silver, were socketted and a dip in the surface held an assortment of pens.

"The money's yours," he said, "if you'll write what I tell you—in your own words. What's your name?"

"Fenner. Martha Fenner."

"Then start off, I Martha Fenner. Then put that what you've said about Miss Draper is a lie and you promise never to play this game on anybody else."

There lay the fifty pounds, infinitely desirable; just what she needed, and as the price of silence, acceptable. As payment for what she was asked to write, unthinkable. All the tensions and worries and efforts of the last few days combined with the gin and this last, most deadly insult, to spark off a temper never noticeably placid.

"Make me out a liar, would you?" she said. She took up one of the cut-glass bottles and aimed it straight and true. A quarter of a pint of the best blue-black ink hit Mr. Horridge on the head and from that water shed showered down, splashing everything on the table, including the crisp white paper which represented money.

"You old vixen," Mr. Horridge said, blinking his eyes and fumbling for his handkerchief. He said several other things, too, things which Mrs. Fenner knew must be "language" of a very extraordinary kind. But she had made her point. As he mopped and swore he thought, Not a liar. But utterly, utterly mistaken!

Having vented her temper, Mrs. Fenner knew a swift descent of mood. She'd done herself no good and she had damaged Mr. Horridge's property; in a way that could be assessed. Property-owner herself and ruthless about compensation—"That cup will cost you twopence, Mr. Smith"—she saw where she stood. But she knew that with men to apologise was to put yourself in the wrong.

"You've only got yourself to thank for that mess," she said sternly. "Whatever you may think of me, I'm a respectable woman!"

And what was there about that to make him throw back his ink-streaked face and laugh, a bit like a dog barking.

"You're wrong," he said, "and I'll prove it." She knew that it was not her claim to respectability that was in question. "Take that," he said, pointing to the money. "In a way you earned it."

He flung out of the room and she could hear him yelling for hot water, and for his gig to be hitched up.

She looked at the notes and thought, Well, in a way, that is true. I never run blabbing about. I didn't say a word, even to Clara. She dried the notes with a tender care—but wondering whether she had not been fooled again. Would the ink blotches render them useless? It was not a currency with which she was familiar—maybe the slightest thing wrong . . . Nevertheless, having blotted them she folded them and tucked them into her old reticule.

Tom, the ex-lodger, who had given her the lift had taken her right up to Mr. Horridge's house because he had groceries to deliver there. But he had arranged to meet her near the Park gates, "You wait for me, or I'll wait for you, Ma." The horse he drove was getting a bit old and must be spared unnecessary exertions. So Mrs. Fenner's bunions suffered all the way down the avenue, and she was glad to sit down on the bank by the gateway. Mr. Horridge, washed and reclad, smashing by in his gig, did not see her. He stared straight ahead, his blunt, ugly profile like something hewn from stone.

Tom said, "You know, Ma, I always thought, we all thought, you made a good thing out of us, but I know different now. Give Elsie fifteen bob and what's to show for it? She ain't a clever shopper and she can't cook worth a spit. Mind you, she's a nice girl," he said loyally. "But there's times when I think what you did with fifteen bob, Ma, rent rates, washing and food—them beef puds and always a joint on Sunday. Then I reckon you're a bloody marvel."

"Language, Tom!"

"Sorry, Ma."

She was contemplating the test to which her windfall must be subjected. Not in a shop, she decided; the rejection of an ink-spattered five-pound note might be witnessed—and people always thought the worst. Somewhere more private.

"Tom, do me one more favour. Stop at the station. I won't keep you more than a minute." Her coal merchant, like others, had his coal store there, and a little shed that served as office.

He took the most stained note without hesitation; indeed with alacrity; he promised delivery of a ton of the best coal first thing in the morning and he gave her change in *real* money. Out of the brimming handful of gold and silver she selected a half sovereign. "You have this, Tom, and lots of thanks as well."

"Well, I don't really like . . ." he said; but ten bob extra, ten bob Elsie didn't know about, looked like a small fortune.

That's done Tom a bit of good, Mrs. Fenner thought. And I've done myself more than a bit, after all. Don't things turn out funny?

o   o   o

MR. HORRIDGE DREW UP OUTSIDE NUMBER 10 AND COMmitted the antisocial act of tethering his sweating horse to the railings in such a way that the footpath was completely impassable and the gig occupied half the roadway. He plucked at the bell and Betty opened the door.

She looked a bit more distraught than usual; she looked as though she had been crying.

"Oh, sir. Come in. I'll call Miss Ellen."

"Is Miss Marion not at home?"

"Oh yes. But she's . . . Miss Ellen will tell you, sir."

In the dining room, the table reduced now to its normal size, he waited with a sense of foreboding; the few minutes before Ellen appeared seemed like a year and when she came she brought no reassurance. In her white face her nose and eyes looked as though they had been boiled.

"Mr. Horridge, something so awful has happened."

"What? What Ellen?"

"Last night," she said, beginning to cry again. "Last night . . ."

Last night Papa, steadying himself against the chair, had looked down and seen, not without relief, that Marion was not hurt. She had fallen near the corner of the fender which was decorated with a kind of cone, or pineapple, and she must have hit it because the tongs, the shovel and the poker were displaced. But she was not hurt. There was no blood and she was not stunned. He took her by the arm and dragged her, roughly, to her feet. "Pull yourself together," he said. He was the more angry because, collapsing as she had, she had almost made him fall. He withdrew his hand and she still stood without support, but looking oddly like the dummies which, in the cheaper tailor's windows, served to display suits.

"Pull yourself together," he said again; and then sharply, "Marion. Do you hear me? We'll leave it. Get along. Go to bed."

She just stood, her eyes, her face blank.

"Come along," he said. "Stop pretending. You can't get out of things by assuming a daft expression, so don't think that you can. But I have had enough for one evening. Go to bed."

She stood.

"Stop acting the fool," he said. "Get along to bed." He took her—touching the tainted flesh again—by the elbow. She moved easily, like a piece of furniture on well-oiled casters, but as soon as he ceased to propel her, in order to open the door, she stopped. It dawned upon Mr. Draper that something was wrong. So he rang the bell. All his life— for even in his relatively humble beginnings there had been pauper slaveys—bells had been rung and answered.

By a complicated system of wires the bell he rang was connected to another in the servants' bedroom now occupied by Ellen. But Betty, though not in direct communication, heard it too and said, "Oh, blast. What now," as she helped Ada into bed.

The two girls arrived in the dining room at the same moment. Mr. Draper addressed himself to his daughter. "Marion swooned and fell," he said. "I think she may have hit her head on the fender. She is stunned. Help her to bed."

"It is so awful," Ellen said. "She doesn't know me. She doesn't know anybody. She won't talk, or look at you. It's so different from last time . . . only a tiny bruise and not that kind of long sleep. This is worse, and all my fault. I alone am to blame. I left her to clear up. I didn't think that she had a tiring day and was not yet fully recovered. She was always so brave; she never complained and Mamma and I always leaned . . . So we . . ." Ellen relapsed into weeping incoherence.

"You've had the doctor? Ellen, howling does no good!" The uncivil word steadied her.

"Oh yes. This morning."

"And what did he say?"

"That she did hit her head, though there is so little to be seen. And that the blow fell on exactly the same place, where her skull was weakened already. She may have injured her brain . . ."

"He's only a country doctor," Mr. Horridge said staunchly. "And old. We'll get a man from London. The best. May I see her?"

"Of course. But it isn't Marion. I knew last night . . . It was like putting a doll to bed. She makes no attempt to feed herself or, or anything." She ate, if the food was put to her lips, and pushed through the kitchen, steered into the area privy seemed to know what was required of her.

Ellen led the way down, not up and, as the basement smell, cooking and washing up and old floor-cloths met his nose, Mr. Horridge thought with disgust, Servants' accommodation! Mamma rose from the chair beside the bed and said, "Oh, Mr. Horridge! What a calamity! Just when we were all so happy for her."

"We'll get a specialist," Mr. Horridge said. "They work

wonders these days." He spoke to Mamma, but he looked at the bed.

Marion lay high on the three pillows advised by Dr. Barlow. Ellen had plaited her hair and one plait lay on each shoulder. He saw for the first time, the scar of the former accident. Her expression was serene and completely blank.

He said, "Marion," and she did not even look towards him. Her hands lay limp on the folded sheet and his ring shone on her finger.

It was bad enough, but worsened for him because he, like Ellen, felt an irrational remorse. He knew now that he should not have listened to the old bitch's talk, leave alone have examined it so critically. Been so tolerant. He lifted the hand on which the ring was and kissed it, as near tears as he had been for thirty years. Marion, my dear one, my darling, we will get you well and I will have no thought except to make up to you for that moment's disloyalty.

"Doctors know about specialists," he said. "I'll go and see Barlow now." He was prepared to move Heaven and earth.

"I think," said Mamma out of infinite experience, "that it might be best to consult with Mr. Draper first."

She was right, of course. "I'll wait." But upstairs, not here, with that mute reproach under his eyes.

"He will be home at any minute," Mamma said.

In fact Mr. Draper was home. He had entered the house three minutes earlier. No one to greet him. No Ellen to pour his sherry. It was not a house centring around a sick room, for nobody was sick. But it had drawn itself together and concentrated its attention elsewhere than upon the master and the dining room that was his province.

Mr. Draper poured his own sherry and took his usual chair, seeing again that vile, depraved creature, standing, prone, raised, and then being embraced by the innocent Ellen. Now tended, fed, by Ellen. Against this discomforting thought, needing some stir, some diversion, some acknowledgement of his presence, he was about to ring the bell and order that the fire should be lighted. The evening was cool enough to justify that act. Then the door opened and Mr. Horridge, looking his full age, and more, and very pallid, came in.

"Ha!" Mr. Draper said. "May I offer you a glass of sherry?"

"No, I want a real drink," Mr. Horridge said uncouthly. "Whisky if it's handy. This is a terrible thing, Mr. Draper. But we'll get the best brain specialist in London . . . Thank you." He had asked for whisky; he needed it; but he had been drinking whisky when Mrs. Fenner told her tale and now it tasted of her, of dingy black, sweated into and hoarded, of shifts to make ends meet and bunions and lies. Yes, lies, clever enough and brassy enough to kindle doubt. After one sip he put down the glass, knowing that it would be some time before he could drink whisky again.

"We must be guided by Dr. Barlow. When he suggests asking a second opinion it will be obtained."

"But he's old. Old-fashioned. We mustn't waste time waiting for him to admit that this is a bit more than he can deal with."

"Dr. Barlow has been my physician for over thirty years. I trust him completely. He diagnosed a cranial haemorrhage. If he is correct—I think he is—time alone will effect a cure."

"Well, you may be content with that. I ain't," Mr. Horridge said, jumping up. "For Marion I want the best and I want it now."

"I am not opposing you. I am in no position to oppose you. Call in whom you wish. If you could do so without insulting Dr. Barlow, I should be grateful."

"I'll go along now."

"Yes. It would be as well for your conveyance to be removed. We shall be having complaints."

Mr. Horridge let himself out without aid from Betty. But Mr. Draper rang the bell and when Betty came he said, "Perhaps Ada could watch by the bedside for an hour. Will you tell your mistress and Miss Ellen that supper is about to be served?"

"There's no change, sir."

"It was not expected."

He was annoyed with his wife and daughter because they were melancholy, disinclined to eat. He thought, If you only knew what I know about her . . . But he sat there, a solid barrier between them and anything squalid or unpleasant. And he did not intend that their future should be devoted to the care of a living doll.

Mr. Horridge's first specialist, named by Dr. Barlow, summoned by telegram, played straight into Mr. Draper's hands. He used some long words; cerebrospinal fluid, localisation of function, neurological disturbance; but it all amounted to what old Dr. Barlow had said. No justification for surgical interference; let time do its work. However, looking at Ellen, very lachrymose and at Mamma whose manner inspired no confidence, he felt bound to offer a word of advice. Relatives were perhaps not ideal nurses in such a case; not that actual nursing was needed, but constant attention was and the patient would be better with someone not emotionally involved. "Or if space is a consideration," he said, and it must be, otherwise the daughter of the house would not be in this claustrophobic, semi-basement room, "I would suggest a good Nursing Home."

He seemed to remember hearing something about a most

efficient matron of one of the London hospitals he knew, setting up in a place of her own in Norfolk. He could not immediately recall her name, but he was accustomed to little lapses of memory and dealt with them by a process of word association. The name he now wanted had some connection with gardens. Gardener? Green? Hedge?

"There is a very excellent Nursing Home in this area," Mr. Draper said. "A place called Heatherton. My daughter stayed there after her former accident and Miss Rose . . ."

"That's it. Rose. Miss Rose. An excellent woman. Your daughter could not possibly be in better hands."

Mr. Horridge said with unusual diffidence that he would esteem it a privilege to be allowed to pay for this consultation and Mr. Draper retorted that when he needed Mr. Horridge's help in meeting his family obligations he would not fail to let him know.

o   o   o

"BUT WHAT ON EARTH?" MISS ROSE EXCLAIMED, APPALLED. This time she had received no warning. Mr. Draper was so anxious to get Marion out of the home she had disgraced that he had not wasted time on an exchange of letters. While Ellen, weeping, had packed Marion's clothes, he had gone round to the livery stable and come back with the cab. If, when they reached Heatherton, Miss Rose should say that she had no accommodation, he was prepared to argue that she must have some corner somewhere. Did it matter where this thing slept?

With an ungentle hand he propelled Marion into Miss Rose's room and as soon as they were within, let go his grasp and Marion stood still, not looking about her, seeming not to recognise the place, nor Miss Rose.

"My daughter has suffered another unfortunate fall," Mr. Draper said. "A Dr. Fawcett, a specialist from London, advised her immediate return to your care."

Miss Rose walked forward until she was within hand-shaking distance of Marion, smiled and held out her hand. "Good afternoon, Miss Draper," she said in the voice she reserved for those she liked. Marion did not stir. Some form of concussion? Amnesia?

"Come and sit down, Miss Draper," Miss Rose said, and taking Marion gently, but firmly by the arm, steered her into one of the chintz-covered chairs. There was, she noticed in that few seconds, no impairment of function; the girl walked normally, with her usual grace and sat down in the ordinary way, not dropping into the chair all in one piece as people who had lost muscular control did. But, once seated she remained remote, looking straight ahead.

"What happened exactly?" asked Miss Rose, turning her attention to Mr. Draper, looking at him and speaking to him as though to some underling nurse who had failed in her duty.

"It may be that she stumbled against the edge of the hearth-rug," Mr. Draper said. "She fell and hit her head against the fender. There is, this time, no visible injury, but she is as you see."

"Were you there when it happened?"

"I was present." He resented the catechising tone. "I hope you have room for her."

"Oh yes," Miss Rose said. She looked back at Marion and remembered how companionable she had been, so appreciative of little things, so ready to help, cutting the lavender, arranging the flowers, reading to old Colonel Fraser. "She can have the same room. And I am reasonably certain that she will make a full recovery. She has youth on her side." This hopeful statement appeared to rouse something in Mr. Draper;

he seemed to wince. A very curious idea occurred to Miss Rose; she wondered if something had gone wrong again between them and that he had struck Marion, perhaps knocked her down, and so was not anxious for her to regain her memory. "We'll do our very best for her, anyway," she said briskly, dismissing him.

When he had gone Miss Rose went and stood in front of Marion and said, quietly, but insistently, "Miss Draper." Marion remained immobile, staring not at, but through Miss Rose. Using the same voice Miss Rose said, "Marion. Look at me!" When that brought no response she put her hand under Marion's chin and tilted her face up so that she could look into her eyes. Just as beautiful as ever, but blank as a doll's. And yet Miss Rose had another strange thought —that just behind the blankness there was something, a whole personality, gone into hiding. She addressed it. She said, "I don't know what happened, but whatever it was it is over. You're back at Heatherton, with me. You are quite safe. With me."

It seemed to be a failure, but one never knew. Miss Rose rang the bell to indicate that she was ready for tea and was pleased to see that Clarke had shown what she called initiative and had prepared the tray for two.

"That was thoughtful of you, Clarke," she said. She believed in giving praise where praise was due.

"Stubbs said, ma'am, that Miss Draper was back." Clarke looked towards Marion as she spoke; looked and then stared. Stared.

"Thank you," Miss Rose said trenchantly. Clarke went out quickly and Miss Rose poured two cups of tea and placed one within easy reach of Marion who took no notice at all. This was something new in Miss Rose's experience, the craziest person on "the other side" responded to food, usually in a very gluttonous manner. Patiently Miss Rose put one of the dainty little sandwiches and a slice of cherry cake on a plate and put that within reach, too. Then she drank her own tea, looking thoughtfully at Marion all the time. Just occasionally a very old person, not crazy but ill, would refuse food, and really in such cases it was kinder not to insist, to allow them just to fade away. But here was someone not ill at all, the gloss on the hair, the clearness of the whites of the eyes refuted the idea of ill health.

Finally Miss Rose got up, went round to Marion's side of the table, lifted the cup and held it to her lips. Marion drank; not sloppily, not greedily but exactly as she would have drunk had she lifted the cup herself. And when Miss Rose held the little sandwich and then the slice of cake to her mouth, she ate as she had drunk, neatly and normally.

To whatever it was that lurked, aware and lively behind that blank façade, Miss Rose said, "You're pretending, aren't you? You have no need to pretend with *me*. Whatever it is *I am on your side.*"

Another failure.

Presently Miss Rose, being a practical woman, thought that after the ride out from Bereham and two cups of tea, Marion might have another need. And thinking of that and all it implied she knew that if Marion could not manage *that* then she must go over to the other side where people who could not manage were managed. It would be terrible for someone so young and so pretty . . . But steered across the hall to the downstairs water closet, Marion managed very well. So well that Miss Rose's suspicion of pretence were confirmed and she was encouraged to try another mode of communication. Back in the sitting room she took a book from the shelf, carried it over to the chair into which Marion had been steered and said, "You always liked reading, didn't you? Look a nice *new* book."

Offering a stone to a stone. Marion did not even look at it.

Safe to leave her while she made her rounds, got into her easy evening clothes? It seemed to be so. But before going out of the room Miss Rose once more addressed whatever it was in hiding. She said, "Stay here and be good. I shall not be long."

When she came back Marion was sitting as she had left her, the book in her lap, her eyes blank, a look of absolute peace on her face.

Dinner was served. Oxtail soup and chicken in cream sauce.

Miss Rose said to what remained of Miss Draper, "Very well, you will eat when you are hungry. Do you understand me? If you want to eat you must rouse up and make an effort."

And what remained of Marion Draper slid about behind those beautiful blank eyes, evading, escaping. Miss Rose gave in and spooned the cooling soup and then the tender chicken into the mouth which had preserved its function after the mind had detached itself . . . Miss Rose had never had this exact situation to deal with and she was feeling her way. And for once, when the door bell rang and Mr. Horridge was admitted, she was almost glad to see a man. Mr. Horridge could at least explain what happened.

"Thank God," Mr. Horridge said, "she's here with you, Miss Rose. Now we can get a proper man. Somebody Barlow never heard of."

Miss Rose said, "Sshh; shush. I am not so sure that she is as far away . . . Senses vary. The dying, Mr. Horridge, *hear* long after they can see or speak. Miss Draper is in my room and I would advise you to say nothing that you would not have said in her presence a week ago."

Mr. Horridge said, "Marion," and various other things, such as "Look at me, darling," and "Listen." And he had no luck. Miss Rose said, "I think bed. Sleep is a good doctor. I may be a quarter of an hour . . ." She took the doll and it moved, easily, willingly up the stairs, into the upstairs water closet, out again, and it stood while Miss Rose undressed it and put on its nightgown. It lay in the bed, supine, undemanding. Miss Rose closed the door and went down.

"Can *you* tell me what *happened,* Mr. Horridge?"

"She had another fall. I wasn't there. I . . . I drove in to visit her and learned what had happened. It was a great shock to me."

He did indeed look broken, a very different creature from the man who had so exuberantly announced his engagement. But Miss Rose had a feeling that he was being evasive, too. It was as though he and Mr. Draper both knew something more than they cared to divulge.

Well, liquor often loosened men's tongues. It was with this in mind that she asked:

"Have you dined?" Upon his answer would depend what she would offer him to drink.

"No. I didn't bother. To tell you the truth I'm a bit off my grub these days."

"Your missing meals does nobody any good," she said bracingly. "May I offer you a drink?"

"Thank you. Whisk—no. Anything except whisky."

"I have none. I always have brandy in the house."

"Thank you," he said with humble gratitude. "You're very kind. That's another reason why I'm glad she's here. Her father is anything but kind, you know."

"Indeed," said Miss Rose, feigning a surprise she did not feel.

"He's a detestable man. I've knocked about a bit, you know, and met some nasty characters. I never met his match." Mr. Horridge drank his brandy and brooded and seemed to be upon the verge of some revealing confidence. But when he spoke again he only said, "He wouldn't even have called in a specialist, but I insisted. And then, of course, he chose a man named by old Dr. Barlow. But we can do better now, can't we?"

"I hope so."

"Do you know a likely man?"

"I know several. The very best, in my opinion, is a man named Hellmutt; he was trained in Vienna."

"A foreigner?" Mr. Horridge said rather dubiously. Long sojourns in foreign places had not overcome his prejudice that to be of the best a thing must be British. "Myself, I'd thought about Edinburgh."

"If it were a question of an amputation, certainly. But this is different. For a case like this Dr. Hellmutt is far and away the best man, probably the best man in the world."

"Then he's the one I want. What do *you* make of her?"

"I've had very little time to observe. I very much doubt if there is any permanent injury—in the physical sense. She walks normally, once she is set in motion; she eats normally if she is fed. This would hardly be the case if the fall had injured her brain."

"Fawcett said much the same. He said time would heal."

Heal *what?* Miss Rose asked herself.

"How do you spell this name? And where does he live?" Mr. Horridge asked. "I'll send a telegram first thing in the morning. I'll meet his train; if he wants to stay overnight, I'll put him up."

He was obviously anxious to do all in his power and once again Miss Rose found herself approving of him as much as she could of any man.

Dr. Hellmutt arrived two days later on the last train, was met at the station by Mr. Horridge himself and driven straight to Sorley Park. Small, sallow, and bespectacled, he was not impressive; and Mr. Horridge's lavish hospitality was wasted upon him, he was a vegetarian, an abstainer, a non-smoker. He did, however, seem dedicated to his work and spent the after-dinner hours in asking questions, some very probing. He led off by asking if Miss Draper had any family. Then why had it been Mr. Horridge who sent for him?

Under this kind of inquisition Mr. Horridge kept his head and slanted his answers in a manner that would have sur-prised those who looked upon him as a bluff, rather blunder-ing fellow. Marion's father, he explained, was a very old-fashioned kind of man, placing all his faith in the ancient family doctor, and taking the word of the specialist rec-ommended by that doctor as final. "I reckoned he was dis-couraged too easily," he said. He did not mention his dislike of Mr. Draper or the lengths to which he had been obliged to go in order to get engaged to Marion at all. He managed to make everything sound very normal. Now and again Dr. Hellmutt made a scribble in a little book.

"And the young lady, you say, is eighteen?" Dr. Hellmutt looked thoughtfully at his host. Over forty and obviously very well-to-do; more likely to be a parents' choice rather than the girl's own. Then, in the course of his censored version, Mr. Horridge happened to say a significant thing. "I put the ring on her finger only last Wednesday." It was easy for Dr. Hellmutt's lively and somewhat freakish imagination to visual-ise a girl, giving way under pressure, accepting well-meant advice, being compliant up to the moment when the ring was on her finger and it was too late to withdraw by any means short of complete withdrawal from life. He said:

"You must forgive me, Mr. Horridge; female preferences, as we all know, are unpredictable. This engagement was in full accord with the young lady's own wishes?"

"Marion wanted to marry me as much as I wanted to marry her. I'm not the man to force myself on a girl."

"Naturally not."

"We'd planned to go to Paris for the honeymoon. I was going to give her *everything*. She hadn't had much of a life."

"Why do you say that?"

"Well, she'd never been anywhere or done anything. As I said, Mr. Draper is old-fashioned."

"Domineering, would you say?"

"Yes. You could say that."

"And what are his circumstances?"

"Comfortable. Modest. He owns a Maltings."

The pattern seemed to emerge; not necessarily sinister; a father anxious that his daughter should make what was known as a good match; paternal preference going to an older man, established in life. One must not pre-judge, of course, but all this was helpful and would give Dr. Hellmutt something to think about in the night. He seldom slept more than four hours. The thought *paternal preference* set him off on another tack.

"Had the young lady other suitors?"

"No," said Mr. Horridge. It was not an intentional lie. He had set himself to disbelieve Mrs. Fenner's story and now did disbelieve it. But he remembered it; he also remembered the words, *How sad about that young de Brissac,* spoken across a dining table. Marion had neither winced nor fainted nor shown any sign of distress. Once again he blamed himself for giving that old hag one second's credence.

o   o   o

AT TEN O'CLOCK THE NEXT MORNING MR. HORRIDGE DROVE Dr. Hellmutt to Heatherton. He would have liked to stay, to be at least on the premises while the examination, for which he was paying, after all, was made. But Dr. Hellmutt managed to make it clear that this was not desirable.

"How long will it take?"

"I cannot possibly tell."

"I'm anxious, you know."

"That is understandable."

"How shall I know when to pick you up?"

"I can walk back. It is no distance."

"What about lunch?"

"I seldom bother with it. Look, Mr. Horridge, I am here to do what I can for this young lady—and for you. As soon as I have anything to tell you, I will return to your house."

Miss Rose received Dr. Hellmutt in the hall and they exchanged the remarks usual with people meeting after a lapse of years; how long since they met and you do not look a day older. Then, adopting her professional nursing manner, Miss Rose led the way upstairs and into the bedroom where a pretty—no, a beautiful—doll lay on the bed. In the course of the overnight talks Mr. Horridge had said that Marion was the most beautiful girl in the world and Dr. Hellmutt had made allowance for a lover's preference. Marion was not the most beautiful girl Dr. Hellmutt had ever seen, but even now, blank and expressionless, she was very good-looking indeed and of course, animated, her face would have a charm it lacked at this moment.

He proceeded to make a most careful physical examination;

228

his long delicate fingers investigated the old scar and then the rest of her skull. He tested all her reflexes. To a bright light—there was no gas here, so he used the best oil lamp, stripped of its globe—her eyes reacted normally, the pupils contracting and the lids lowering protectively. He asked Miss Rose to sit her on the edge of the bed and to cross one leg over the other. A sharp chop with the side of his hand just under the kneecap of the hanging leg provoked the desirable response, a good jerk. Both legs responded in the same way. He could not apply the usual test to the hands because Marion took no notice when he lifted one of hers and said, "Grip my hand as hard as you can." He had, however, another test and he made it ruthlessly, striking a match and bringing it nearer and nearer until the hand he was exposing to the heat pulled away. In the end he was satisfied that her brain and her nervous system, of which the brain was the centre, were completely normal. The fault lay in the mind, in the will, an area as yet uncharted.

Now and then, in the course of this investigation, he asked questions of Miss Rose who answered them as truthfully and concisely as she could. He missed little and he noticed that Miss Rose would lower her voice and throw cautious sidelong glances at the patient as though she realised that Marion, deliberately wishing not to hear, actually did. He noticed, as Miss Rose had done, all the signs of physical health, even down to the smooth, strong finger nails. And he noticed something else, a thing which, being a woman Miss Rose would probably not have observed, the distinct parallel creases, halfway down the white throat; Nature's own accolade, a sure sign of vigorous sexuality. Also, of great significance, was the fact that this seemingly complete retreat had actually stopped short of the ultimate humiliation which accompanied genuine mindlessness.

"See for yourself," Miss Rose said. She took Marion by the elbow and walked her along to the water closet.

"Leave the door open," Dr. Hellmutt whispered. The doll closed the door and managed what with extremely mentally afflicted cases had to be managed by others. But the doll did not open the door; that was left to Miss Rose.

"I propose now," Dr. Hellmutt said, when they were back in the pretty bedroom, "to make a little experiment which may strike you as absurd. Put her in that chair."

He pulled up another so that he was sitting knee to knee and face to face with Marion.

He said, "You do not have to marry Mr. Horridge, Miss Draper. I think you can hear me, though you will not listen. Listen! The engagement is broken. You are free. It is all over and done with . . ." He went on, expending himself, exercising *his* will upon this singularly obstinate one until the sweat ran down his face. She would not listen, she would not hear. But he remembered that she could *feel;* so finally he lifted her hand and pulled off the ostentatious ring. "All over," he said. "Done with. Look, look." He threw the ring away and then moved the ringless hand to and fro before the blank eyes.

That was not the secret. What was?

"I was in error," Dr. Hellmutt said, downstairs in the pretty room. Miss Rose had remembered that he did not drink sherry and had provided some excellent coffee. "For such a condition one must seek a reason and I imagined that an unwelcome betrothal might be to blame. Too little is yet known about the mind . . . I was remembering a man, in Vienna. He was a minor government official; one evening he *walked* from his office to his home which was up one flight of stairs. At the foot of the stairs he became paralysed—and that paralysis was genuine, for tickling the soles of his feet, sticking a pin into his calves or thighs, made no impression at all. He had, you see, that afternoon, been told that he had been passed over in the matter of an expected promotion; and if he walked up those stairs he would be obliged to tell his wife. His mind so much repudiated that prospect that he became paralysed. And so remained. Everybody laughed at me when I suggested that a possible cure would be to give him the promotion. But then, they laughed at Columbus. Yet America was *there*." He sipped his coffee and brooded. "I must confess I expected some response when I removed the ring. I cannot bring myself to think that she has retreated beyond recall."

"I am always aware of her being there, Dr. Hellmutt. As though, if one could just break through . . ."

"How well did you know her, Miss Rose?"

"Fairly well, considering how short a time she was with me. She was then my only mobile patient and took her meals with me. To be honest I became very fond of her and, though I know one should remain detached, to see her as she is now distresses me very much."

"Conflict. Shock. Guilt," Dr. Hellmutt said as though testing each word. "And somehow hinging upon that engagement. I suppose she never confided in you . . . I was thinking in terms of another man. Something that would make her engagement to Mr. Horridge acceptable to her conscious mind but completely unacceptable to her very nature."

As she had done when she decided to give up her steady job and take a gamble on Heatherton, Miss Rose took a risk.

"There *was* another man. Quite ineligible. A shop assistant. French."

All the spirit and confidence that had seeped out of Dr.

Helmutt, while he sweated to draw Marion's attention to the fact that she need not marry Mr. Horridge, flooded back.

"Ah! I should have considered that earlier. She talked to you about him?"

"No." Miss Rose took her ring of keys from her pocket and opened the lowest drawer of her writing table and after a second's search produced Johnny's letter. "On her former stay with me Miss Draper borrowed several of my books. She left this in one of them as a marker. I read it in order to discover whether to throw it away or take the trouble of sending it on to her. Before I got around to doing so, she was back."

Dr. Hellmutt read the letter.

"Did she ever keep this rendezvous?"

"Certainly not from this house; she never left it except accompanied by Mr. Horridge. Besides you will see that it was planned for Sunday. By that time she was back at home —and engaged to Mr. Horridge."

Conflict! Dr. Hellmutt brooded for a minute or two.

"The information that she need not marry Mr. Horridge was *negative*," he said, as though thinking aloud. "It evoked no response. How would she react, I wonder, to the news that this Johnny was here, wished to see her. You see, it is as you say, if one could just break through, then reasoning and persuasion could be used . . . Johnny may well be the Open Sesame."

Outside the sealed cave into which Marion had retreated, he spoke what he hoped would be the magic word; saying it again and again, quoting phrases from the letter. No door flew open, no voice answered, no expression, however fleeting, came into the empty eyes.

It dawned upon Dr. Hellmutt that he still had to report to Mr. Horridge.

He began as hopefully as he could, no physical damage, even the original blow on the head a mere surface wound, of no more importance than a broken finger nail; he spoke of excellent health and of the single sign that Marion's withdrawal was not complete. Mr. Horridge listened attentively but with growing impatience.

"Well," he said, "and what are you going to do about it?"

"Seek the cause," Dr. Hellmutt said. "I think it would be as well if I went and talked to her family."

"They'll tell you what they told me. That she fell and hit her head on the fender."

"The fall had nothing to do with it. Miss Draper's state is due to her mind, her emotions. Something must have happened. Something that gave her a profound emotional shock. I *think*—one can never be sure in such matters—that it must have been a sudden shock. I have tested the theory of breakdown under prolonged strain and . . . and another possibility and now I am driven back to the idea that it could be shock. Something that happened on Monday."

Mr. Horridge knew what had happened on Monday. Mrs. Fenner had called at Alma Avenue—or so she had said; here he was, believing her again! But if Marion had overheard, or that old ogre of a father . . .

He said violently, "It's all a pack of bloody lies. Some damned old woman trying to blackmail . . ." He had, as he had told Miss Rose, lost his appetite since the catastrophe and he had increased his drinking, not of whisky to which he was so hardened and accustomed as to be almost insusceptible but of brandy, far more insidious. He had spent some hours waiting; he had been sure that Dr. Hellmutt, the best man money could buy, would have had something practical like an operation to suggest. Now he broke down.

"All a pack of bloody lies," he said again, drunkenly bellicose; "and if you want to go and listen to that blasted beastly man telling lies about his own daughter, you can bloody well walk. Go on walk and talk, talk, talk. You're a fraud. My good God! I've seen a man with his head bashed in, as good as dead, cured by a drunken old man, drummed out of doctoring, with nothing but a penknife. Marion hit her head on the fender and I'll find somebody who can cure her. I don't believe a single bloody lie and if her father *did*, and he *would*, he'd believe the worst of anybody . . . all right, she'd be upset, but she wouldn't go daft. Mind you, I nearly did, just for a minute and being clouted on the head with an inkbottle didn't help. But *she* knew. And if only I could have talked to her . . . If I could have asked her, if she could have told me . . ." He broke off, put his hands to his face and made the harsh, hurtful choking noise that Dr. Hellmutt recognised as a man sobbing. It was a distressful sound and Dr. Hellmutt thought, Poor fellow! with a sympathy that was genuine, if limited. It must, of necessity, be limited, because a man could tackle only one job at a time and the job that had brought him from London to Norfolk was concerned with Marion Draper. He could be sorry for Mr. Horridge and at the same time take advantage of his state now that his guard was down, so he said, kindly, but with an edge to his voice:

"Mr. Horridge, you would help Miss Draper—and me —if you would tell me *all* that you know. What, for instance, was the lie which you refuse to believe?"

Mr. Horridge did not reply.

"You need not mind telling me," Dr. Hellmutt said. "I am

a doctor. It would only be the equivalent of telling me a physical symptom which would aid in a correct diagnosis."

Mr. Horridge brushed his hand across his face.

"More talk," he said. "Jabber, jabber. What's the use? There's been too much already. I wanted something *done* and all I've got is talk." He made that painful noise again. "Anyway, I told you all I knew last night."

"Not quite, Mr. Horridge. You did not mention lies or blackmail or a blow struck with an inkbottle last evening."

"And I ain't mentioning them now. They're nothing to do with her." He glared at Dr. Hellmutt. "You go and jabber to somebody else. Listen to lies if you like. Strikes me that's your trade."

Exploring in the dark, Dr. Hellmutt said patiently:

"Did the lie by any chance concern someone named Johnny?"

Accustomed as he was to surprising and violent reactions, Dr. Hellmutt was a little taken aback by what happened to Mr. Horridge at the mention of that name. His face bleached and seemed to shrivel as though the bony death's-head moved forward through the living flesh.

"Who said that? I'll kill the bleeder. Who *said* it? You going to tell me or must I choke it out of you?" He was on his feet, his big hands menacing, eyes, nostrils, mouth dark as burnt holes in a paper white mask. Recognisedly mental cases were sometimes violent, but then one was prepared, seldom alone.

"Nobody," Dr. Hellmutt said, a little breathlessly, *"said* anything."* He remembered with a sense of overwhelming relief that after quoting sentences from the letter in an attempt to reach Miss Draper, he had stuffed it into his pocket. Defying, beating off Mr. Horridge with what he hoped was a level, steady stare, he now pulled it out and said, "Read for yourself."

Mr. Horridge took the letter as a savage dog might take a peace-offering. It stopped him in his tracks, holding it he retreated, sat down again in his chair; but he did not read it. Dr. Hellmutt could tell that by the movement of his eyes.

"That bloody old bitch said he'd burnt the lot. And I gave her fifty pounds to stop telling lies. So what's this?"

"A letter. Found by Miss Rose in a book which Miss Draper borrowed during her former stay. I did hope that it might be the key, but it was not. At least not directly. It would be very helpful, Mr. Horridge, if you could tell me what you know about this man."

Mr. Horridge's eyes, seeming even to the expert observer unfocussed, had snatched up the words "darling," "your Johnny," "a kiss," "light in the window."

So it was true. The thing which he had once almost believed, and then blamed himself fiercely for believing, *hated* himself for believing even for a minute. It was true and it was horrible. But now, accepting the horrible truth, Mr. Horridge fell back onto the real rock bottom of whatever it was that had made him a survivor in a rough and cruel world.

"He's dead," he said, with as much satisfaction as though he had killed him. *"Dead and buried."*

"Suicide?" Dr. Hellmutt asked, thinking, Ah, here is the clue! Guilt. Guilt against which she must shut her eyes, her ears, her mind, her consciousness.

"In a manner of speaking," Mr. Horridge said. "He dug his grave with his teeth. The old bitch he lodged with dished up a lot of muck he couldn't digest. He had a weak stomach, or so they say. Not that you can believe a word . . . I didn't; but not more than a minute anyway. And for me it's over. Done with."

"No," Dr. Hellmutt said, "we are now only beginning. Death. Remorse . . . It could explain . . ."

"Explain!" Mr. Horridge brought out the word like an expectoration. "How'd you like your fee? Cash or cheque?"

"But, Mr. Horridge, I have done nothing."

"You've done quite enough. You've put me out of my misery. There's a decent train in an hour's time. I'll order the gig." He opened his money drawer and took out his chequebook and twenty-one gleaming sovereigns. "Which?"

"I cannot take money I have not earned. Nor can I abandon a case just at the moment when there is some hope of a breakthrough. Mr. Horridge, I am well aware that whatever lies behind all this rouses the most painful emotions in you, but if you could ignore them and tell me everything . . . Come, Mr. Horridge," Dr. Helmutt spoke coaxingly, "you wish to see Miss Draper restored, do you not?"

"I don't give a tinker's damn what happens to her," Mr. Horridge said.

Mr. Draper said much the same thing though he put it differently. He said, "I have resigned myself to this misfortune."

"But that is what we must not do, Mr. Draper. She is young; not yet beyond recall; and there is always the danger in such cases that with the passing of time the—one might say—vegetable state will encroach."

Since Dr. Hellmutt had said no more about visiting Marion's family, the gig had been at his disposal and on the outskirts of Bercham he had asked to be driven to the Maltings instead of the station. Having ascertained that Mr. Draper was in his office, he dismissed the gig, saying that he could walk to the station. He had already decided that if his inter-

237

view with the girl's father turned up anything useful he would stay in Bereham and return to Heatherton next day.

Mr. Draper, however, was far less vulnerable than Mr. Horridge. Very dignified, blandly polite, and, as he said, resigned. To the name of Johnny he did not react in any betraying way; he said simply, "I never heard of him. I think it most unlikely that my daughter should have engaged in a clandestine love affair and to be honest I resent the suggestion."

"But you will agree that it is a love letter," said Dr. Hellmutt who had prudently retrieved the document from the table on to which Mr. Horridge had thrown it.

"I agree," Mr. Draper said, eyeing it with a distant distaste. "But apart from the use of a fairly common Christian name I see nothing to connect this effusion with my daughter. Was there no envelope?"

There had been but Dr. Hellmutt had never handled it, Miss Rose had slipped the letter out and passed it to him.

"Let us assume, Mr. Draper, that this letter was addressed to your daughter, that she was, or had been, attached to the writer of it. I understand from Mr. Horridge that the man is dead. That in itself might be a grief which she could sustain; but her subsequent engagement to another man may well have aroused other feelings, possibly conflicting, from which she could only retreat."

"Dr. Hellmutt, you must forgive me. I know that in our several ways we must all earn our livings; but to me what you are saying sounds like clap-trap. My daughter—and may I say that she was most carefully guarded, I think that until her first stay at Heatherton she never left the house except in the company of her mother or her sister—met with an accident while on holiday; she appeared to have recovered from that blow on the head; she then had the misfortune to fall and strike her head again in the same place. Her brain was injured, her mind deranged; and to that, as I have said, I am resigned. She is well cared for; she is not unhappy. All this"—he tapped the letter as though fearing infection from the contact—"is quite irrelevant. No, worse! An invention to fit a theory . . . I will not go so far as to say that Miss Rose connived with you, but I will say that you—on the slender evidence of a letter found in a book—have jumped to a conclusion which any reasonable man must repudiate."

"But you are wrong. You are so wrong," Dr. Hellmutt said. "I assure you, physically there is nothing wrong with her. It is emotional; it is concerned with this man, with his death. If only you would help me, Mr. Draper, I could help her."

Mr. Draper shifted his ground. Smoothly he moved from the defensive to the offensive. He said, "Mr. Horridge engaged your services?"

"Yes."

"He had no right. Marion is my daughter; she is eighteen years old. When she had her accident I called in our family doctor who called in a specialist in whom he had faith and who advised a Nursing Home. Dr. Hellmutt, I do not think that there is a father in the country who would not consider that I had done all that could be done for my daughter, or who would disagree with what I am now about to say. I do not wish Marion to be bothered, inspected, looked over, treated as though she were an animal in a laboratory. Had I realised how wilfully misguided Mr. Horridge was I should have issued an order for her protection. I shall write to Miss Rose this evening. If Marion ails Miss Rose may call in Dr. Barlow or any other doctor who is near at hand. Otherwise nobody is to be admitted."

"Mr. Draper, you are condemning your daughter to a living death."

"In your opinion. To my mind I am protecting her from the activities of charlatans. And now, may I wish you a good day?"

Miss Rose said "Really, Dr. Hellmutt. I am extremely sorry, but Mr. Draper's letter was specific. If I disregard it he is capable of removing her from my care; and you know, as well as I do, where she is likely to end."

"I know. I know. But yesterday I thought it was a simple jilting. Now I know that the man is dead. I could try a different approach. Allow me five minutes, I beg you."

"I am extremely sorry. I dare not. I cannot risk the danger of her being removed."

"Then, Miss Rose, you must try. You have begun well by understanding that her mind has only retreated. Appeal to it; constantly. Talk of this Johnny and assure her that she is in no way responsible for his death. There, I now think, may lie the root of the trouble."

"You may depend upon me to do my best," Miss Rose said.

"If ever she should respond," he said humbly, "I should be grateful if you would let me know. There are mysteries here."

o   o   o

THE YEAR SLID DOWNHILL INTO AUTUMN. MR. HORRIDGE left his staff on board wages and went off to Africa, telling himself that certain concerns with which he had retained a connection, though doing well, could be prodded into better performance. Eventually he found himself able to drink whisky again.

Mr. Draper was less fortunate. First, there was Ellen's quite excessive grief and senseless remorse. She kept saying, "If only I had not let her overtire herself; if only I had not been so selfish," until Papa was compelled to point out that her present behaviour was very selfish indeed and that if she had any affection for her parents she would try to be less mopish. He planned little treats, most of which were spoiled by Ellen saying innocently, "Oh, how much poor Marion would have enjoyed this." When Mr. Marriot, indefatigable, started an amateur dramatic society Papa said that if Ellen wished to join, he would join too. Ellen said, "Papa, I would prefer not to. It would only remind me."

Then Ada gave notice, saying that she was sorry to add to Miss Emily's troubles but she really was at the end of her tether and must go to the Poor House where she could sit. Betty held to her decision to leave when Ada left and Mr. Draper was free to instal the active cook, the less hard-breathing maid of whom he had so often spoken. Betty was easily replaced by a girl named Daisy; a substitute for Ada was harder to find. The Domestic Agency sent, in rapid succession, a woman who could not cook at all, a spoiler of good food; a woman who could cook but drank; a sober, fairly competent cook who was caught red-handed giving a basket of stores to a ragged little boy at the back door; a sober, honest, good cook who had a quite alarming epileptic fit.

What in the world had happened to all the splendid women, honest, sober, with a light hand for pastry and not prone to fits who had been so plentiful while Mr. Draper was cumbered with Ada. He blamed the new clothing factory where stupid women crouched over long seams and ruined their eyes making buttonholes.

In the interregnum periods Ellen cooked. At first she made

simple dishes and Papa encouraged her modest achievements by exaggerated praise and admiration. At least while she was cooking she was not crying; indeed when 10, Alma Avenue was without a cook Ellen seemed quite cheerful. Her performance rapidly improved; she had a flair; she had always been practical and clever with her hands and she discovered that making things to be eaten and enjoyed was far more rewarding than bead work or making shell boxes.

Ada had left her recipe book in the dresser drawer and though, as Ellen had once said, the secrets were not written down in its almost indecipherable pages, one could always invent and experiment. Many of Papa's favourite dishes reappeared. Very nice indeed; but . . .

But when Mr. Draper had said that he looked forward to receiving comfort from his daughters in his latter days he had certainly never visualised one of them in the basement kitchen. He hated to think of Ellen doing things that hirelings should do. He was also uneasily aware of a change in Ellen's manner into which something crisp and brisk and self-assertive had crept.

"Yes, Papa; the Agency did send another woman. I looked at her and decided that I should not care to eat anything she had handled. I gave her short shrift."

"Yes, Papa; a woman did call in answer to your advertisement." To such extremes had Mr. Draper been driven; exposing his need to the world. "I took the precaution of asking her a few simple questions. She did not know the difference between sirloin and topside and seemed never to have heard of curry."

Such women threatened Ellen's new status and were summarily dealt with. But occasionally Papa was at home when an applicant called and then, uncritical, asking no questions, thinking only of freeing Ellen from the kitchen, he would hire her. None of his candidates lasted more than a week. Ellen was a ruthless and cunning saboteur, not above putting salt in the baking powder and mustard in the ground ginger and so contriving that Papa's breakfast egg was not fresh from the farm but out of the preserving bucket, good enough for buns and cakes but useless for frying. Papa whose complaints had been so ready and so loud now showed fortitude, but Ellen was extreme to mark what was done amiss. "I am sorry, it is uneatable. The woman simply cannot cook. She must go."

"But my dear Ellen, I cannot have you back in the kitchen."

"The kitchen," Ellen said, "would be quite a pleasant place if it had a new range—one of those pretty tiled ones. And if the window could be made to open. And truly that old soft-stone sink is impossible to keep clean. There are new ones now, a kind of porcelain in a very pleasant shade of yellow."

Mr. Draper had never denied his family any material thing within his means. The women who came and went and Ellen, who was always there, operated in a kitchen transformed and beautified.

One evening, shortly before Christmas, Mr. Draper came home with a brace of pheasants, a present from a farmer. Daisy was setting the dining-room table and he held the birds out to her.

"Hang these in the outside safe," he said. She acted as though he had offered her a deadly snake.

"Oh, sir, I couldn't. I never could touch a dead bird. Never. Not even when our little old canary died."

Silly bitch! He stamped down the stairs and there in the kitchen was Ellen, wearing a big white apron with a bib. He had momentarily lost track of the current kitchen situation and the sight of Ellen gave him a slight shock.

"Surely, my dear, this is carrying things to extremes. If you must wear an apron . . . Something pretty."

"Papa, I am frying chicken for supper. Muslin, even *with* frills, would not offer sufficient protection." She pulled the frying pan aside. "What beautiful birds. Young or old?" She examined their legs with care, with knowledge. "This one will roast. The other . . . Yes, I will try my hand at a game pie."

But who would pluck and disembowel them?

He hung the birds in the outdoor meat safe that served as a game larder and then, coming back, answered his own question.

"When they are sufficiently hung—they were shot yesterday—I will take them to the poulterer's and have them dressed."

"Oh no," Ellen said. "One can never be certain of getting back one's own birds. I have never dressed a pheasant or seen it done, but I am sure I can manage."

Over the excellent fried chicken Mr. Draper made what was, apart from his submission to Mr. Horridge, the major concession of his life.

"There is no help for it," he said. "Ada must come back. If necessary I will buy her a wheel chair."

Mamma shot a glance, unnoticed across the table; it was infinitely malicious and triumphant.

Ellen said, "She would not come, Papa. Ada is the one completely happy person in the Poor House. You see, they divide women from men and that makes lots of them unhappy, especially married couples, but Ada has never known men's company, so that does not affect her. And though most people grumble about the food Ada enjoys it. She says let the porridge be watery or lumpy, so long as somebody else cooks it she does not mind."

"You speak," Papa said and halted. "Ellen, am I right in thinking that you have visited Ada in the Poor House?"

"Of course," Ellen said placidly. "I always knew that the recipes she gave people were not complete. She had secrets; things not in her book. I went to pick her brains—and to take her a blanket. Those in the Poor House are heavy, but not very warm."

In Mr. Draper's mouth the crisp and tender chicken turned to sawdust. Once he had owned three pretty dolls. One he had broken; she sat there waiting to escape to her piano or her knitting. Another had broken itself, whore, slut, trollop, living out an idiot life at Heatherton. And the third, the meekest, the prettiest, calmly sat here, a visit to the Poor House behind her, the dressing of a brace of pheasants before her. She, too, was lost to him.

"I must say, my dear, that had you consulted me about a visit to the Poor House I should have advised against it. There was typhoid there only a few months ago."

Ellen noted the change in his manner, in his speech. Advise against, not forbid.

"I suffered no harm, Papa. And please, do eat your chicken. I took such great pains with it."

"And it is excellent, my dear. Superb." Mr. Draper munched his sawdust. Ellen waited and chose her moment. The excellent, the superb chicken disposed of, Daisy brought in the damson cheese. Damsons were going out of fashion, unprofitable things with little flesh between their dark skins and their stones; but if they could be obtained and treated properly they made a most delicious sweet.

"Papa," Ellen said, "I truly do think that with Christmas so near, one of us, or all of us, should go to see Marion."

Mr. Draper put down his spoon and turned his withering stare upon his daughter.

"Perhaps you could tell me what would be the purpose of a visit to someone who would not recognise us."

Undeterred, Ellen said, "There are two reasons, Papa. One is that not to go conveys the false impression that since her affliction we have ceased to love her. The other is that I should like to see for myself that she is being properly treated."

"We know that she is well treated. Miss Rose reports to me most regularly, as you know."

"I know. What worries me a little is that Miss Rose does the treating *and* the reporting. She is hardly likely to give herself an unfavourable report."

On the verge of his mind Mr. Draper again acknowledged the change in Ellen, once not very fluent and always softly spoken. He had always used words as a weapon himself and he recognised the touch.

"If I am satisfied that should be sufficient. There is no cause for you to fret."

"But I do. Also I am tired of meeting people like Mrs. Andrews who invariably asks have I seen my sister. It embarrasses me."

"I would suggest that in future you refer such inquiries to me." He also was subject to questions prompted by sympathy or curiosity and he had his own way of dealing with them, answering with such massive dignity and deep grief that the inquirer felt rebuked for ever mentioning the matter at all. "I certainly have no intention of allowing you to make a visit which would simply result in fresh tears."

"Very well, Papa." Ellen returned to eating her damson cheese in a manner that convinced Mr. Draper that she had not taken this refusal to heart. In fact he congratulated himself on the line he had taken, for presently Ellen said, reverting to her old coaxing way:

"Papa, can you let me have a little money? I have not yet bought a single Christmas present. And this year I must buy, having been too busy to make any."

"I will try, my dear. How much do you need?"

"I have no idea," Ellen said with great truth. "Perhaps even as much as thirty shillings."

The little case ejected two sovereigns and Mr. Draper made his joke. "You may keep the change," he said.

"Papa, how very generous! Thank you indeed."

In the past months Ellen had become accustomed to going out alone. There had been a little tussle about that with Papa suggesting that Mamma or Betty should accompany her to do such shopping as could not be ordered and delivered. But Mamma's slight stores of vitality seemed to have exhausted themselves on the preparation for the wedding and once in Baxter's she had had to be given sal volatile. And after the household was disrupted by Ada's going it was palpably impossible for the house to be left in the sole charge of an untried maid.

"I do not like it," Mr. Draper said. "A young lady should not go wandering about in the town alone."

"Papa, believe me, I do not wander. I do my errands as quickly as possible. And it is quite customary now for girls to go out by themselves." She named a few. And Mr. Draper reflected sourly that Marion had always been accompanied everywhere—and look what she had done! So he had given in and there was nothing extraordinary in Ellen, at ten o'clock in the morning, coming down, dressed for the street, her basket, a small, decorative thing, more a toy than an article of utility on her arm.

"Mamma, if I should be a trifle late for lunch, do not wait. I half promised Mrs. Marriot that I would lend a hand with the preparation of the stalls for the Church Bazaar. Having had no time to make anything this year, I felt that was the least I could do." Actually she had dodged the making of objects for the Bazaar because the very thought of it brought up unbearable memories of Marion, of former years when they had worked together and made their little jokes. To make things for the Bazaar would have been as hurtful as the cooking was helpful. Busy over the stove, engaged in an activity that Marion had never shared, she could for quite long stretches of time, forget.

On this December morning—not very cold, in fact a luminous, pearly day, winter but winter with a promise of spring—as soon as she was out in Alma Avenue, Ellen knew a regression of confidence. She was about to do something that she had never done before—Papa always saw to such things. Moreover she was blatantly defying Papa and if he ever got to hear of it his wrath would be fearsome. However, she had made up her mind and was prepared to ignore the quivering of her calves, the weakness of her knees.

"It is Miss Draper to see Miss Draper," Stubbs said.

"Show Miss Draper in," Miss Rose said. Surprise visits by relatives were rare, but not unknown. Sometimes they caused a little confusion because some patients on the other side, unable or unwilling to dress themselves, were not in a state to be visited. Old Mrs. Selton, momentarily expecting to be released, every day washed and dressed, hooked her earrings into her ears, but she was the exception; most of them slopped about in loose robes over night clothes and slippers. But Marion, now Miss Rose's doll, was fully prepared to face even this unexpected visit.

"Good morning, Miss Draper," Miss Rose said, extending her hand. Taking it and returning the greeting, Ellen looked past Miss Rose and saw Marion seated in a low chair near the fire. Her hair was beautifully arranged in the style which

248

Ellen herself had devised, the lace at throat and wrist gleamed white against the dark green of her dress, she looked so absolutely like herself, so ordinary that Ellen who was not quite certain what she had expected to find was astonished, and, for a second, hopeful.

"Your sister has come to see you, Marion," Miss Rose said.

Ellen went forward, dropped to her knees and embraced Marion. "Marion, darling. It's me. It's Ellen."

Nothing had changed. No recognition in the eyes; no response at all. Ellen sat back on her heels and, as Papa had foreseen, burst into tears. One of the buttons on her jacket had caught in a strand of Marion's hair and pulled it loose. She freed it gently and then fumbled for her handkerchief.

Miss Rose took her by the elbow and assisted her to her feet. "You must just look at the garden," she said. "We have such beautiful winter-flowering shrubs." Ellen, sobbing and bewildered, momentarily as will-less as Marion, was taken to the French window and out on to the little paved terrace. There Miss Rose said, "It is *essential* to behave normally, Miss Draper. Marion may appear not to notice, but we must not assume too much. She is not far away, you know."

Ellen knuckled her hand and pressed it against her chin. "Of course. You are right. But when I saw her, looking so well and you spoke . . . in such an ordinary way . . . I did hope for a moment and then . . . to see no change at all."

"Had there been," Miss Rose said, "I should naturally have informed the family at once."

"Of course," Ellen said again. She used her handkerchief, gulped, mastered her emotion and was able to say, "Yes, indeed, your shrubs are beautiful."

Back in the room, so beautiful in its own uncluttered way, a bowl of one of the flowering shrub's twigs scenting the air and another bowl, jonquils, forced and almost in flower, Ellen

249

stood, a little at a loss. Miss Rose walked over to Marion and lifted the loose strand of hair and tucked it back into place. It was a gesture ordinary enough—a thing that Ellen herself should have done, probably would have done, given time, but there was something; lingering; fondling, possessive, like women with pet dogs . . .

The pretty little basket sat where Ellen had dropped it when she embraced Marion.

"I brought a few little things," Ellen said, picking it up and displaying its contents—a bottle of eau de cologne, six fine lawn handkerchiefs. She had not dared spend too much for she had no idea what the cost of Jarvey's horse and cab would be. "And these, I made them myself. She never liked sweet things." Ellen opened the shrouding paper and showed the work of her hands, slender cheese straws like bundles of faggots, encircled by rings made from the same pastry.

"How delicious they look," Miss Rose said, lifting the paper and holding the offering under Marion's blank eyes. "We shall enjoy them, shall we not? With our coffee. And here it is."

Here it was, brought in by Clarke who had again shown initiative and brought three cups.

"Do sit down, Miss Draper. You will take coffee?"

Ellen took it, but she did not drink it. She watched while Miss Rose performed for Marion the service which she herself had performed in that short, terrible interval between the second fall and the return to Heatherton. The only difference was that Ellen had cried all the time and Miss Rose talked.

"Now isn't that delicious?" she said, when the touch of a cheese straw against her mouth did evoke some response from Marion who bit off a piece and chewed it. "Your sister made these for you, dear. Is she not kind, and clever?"

Once, at one of Mr. Marriot's fund-raising entertainments,

Ellen had seen a ventriloquist and his dummy. She now had the half-hysterical thought that at any minute Miss Rose might answer herself, mimicking Marion's voice. Between that idea, in which Marion, had she been Marion still, would have seen the humour, and the necessity not to cry any more, Ellen found the strain upon her self-control becoming intolerable. She must get away. She was doing no good here. She might not have been in the room. She wished she had not come. She put her untasted cup of coffee behind the bowl of jonquils and stood up.

"I am afraid I must go now. I must not keep the cab waiting."

Miss Rose turned to her, wearing something of the air of a priestess, disturbed from the performance of some elaborate ritual.

"One second," she said, "then I will see you to the door."

This time it was the coffee that she held to Marion's mouth.

"Now dear, your sister must say goodbye." Ellen repeated the embrace and the kiss.

"I shall be gone only a minute," Miss Rose told Marion.

In the hall Ellen gave way and cried again. With a sudden change in manner Miss Rose said, "Really, you know, Miss Draper, there is no reason for such distress. Your sister is in good health, well cared for."

"I know. I know. I can see that you take the best of care of her. I am so glad about that. And so grateful to you. But it all seems so sad. So sad."

"Not for *her*. In fact I think one would be safe in saying that Marion is *happy*."

"Yes," Ellen gulped. "I suppose that is how one should look . . . She certainly looks peaceful. Goodbye, Miss Rose. And thank you for all you are doing for her."

"I take pleasure in it," Miss Rose said. "I am very fond of

251

Marion." Ellen was too innocent to recognise this for the understatement that it was.

In the cab Ellen realised that she must stop crying. Even Mamma might notice and wonder what had happened in the Guildhall. So she told herself sternly that crying did no good at all; that if Marion were no better she was certainly no worse; that she seemed serene, and was certainly being superbly well cared for.

So why am I left with the feeling of something horribly wrong? Ellen asked herself as the hired horse plodded along back to Bereham.

She wished she had somebody to whom she could talk about it; to whom she could confess that about the pretty, fragrant room, about Miss Rose's voice and manner, the loving, lingering touch with which she had replaced the strand of hair, and most of all, about the pretence that *Marion was still there,* there was something sinister; something not as it should be.

There was no one to whom these things could be said, and even had there been she knew that she could never have brought herself to say anything so entirely ridiculous.

Back at Heatherton old Mrs. Selton who had heard the cab arrive and imagined that her last letter of appeal—addressed to Queen Victoria—had been successful, heard it drive away again and fell into one of her rages. Miss Rose dealt with her even more roughly than usual for she had been obliged to exercise considerable self-control during Ellen's visit, confining herself to the non-committal "my dear." When they were alone together she addressed Marion in other terms, saying "My pretty one," saying "Darling," saying "My love."